Published by Penfold Books
87 Hallgarth Street
Durham DH1 3AS
England

Author's website:
mileshudson.com

ISBN: 978-1-7395577-0-6

Cover Photo: Graeme Hall

Acknowledgements:

Many thanks are due to:
Joan Deitch; Chris Donald; Graeme Hall;
Jane Hamilton; Carol Hudson;
Tim James; Andy McDaid;

About the Author

Miles Hudson loves words and ideas.

He's a physics teacher, surfer, author, hockey player, inventor, backpacker and idler.

Miles was born in Minneapolis but has lived in Durham in northern England for more than thirty years.

By the same author
Penfold Detective Series

The Cricketer's Corpse

The Kidney Killer

By Miles M Hudson

Audiopt Surveillance Series

2089

The Mind's Eye

The Times of Malthus

To Bob!

Penfold and DS Milburn
investigate The Case of the

Burns
Night
Burns

M M Hudson

Ⓑ PENFOLD BOOKS

One

Melville Armstrong stood tall on the small dais and looked out at the seated members of the Durham Friendship Society, all dressed up for the annual Burns Night Supper. Waiting until all eyes were on him, he raised the ceremonial dagger, which glinted in the candlelight, then plunged it down hard into the haggis, which had been doused in whisky and set alight for the prelude of the evening.

The haggis yielded to the knife with a hiss. Jets of clear liquid sprayed either side of the blade and ignited in a bright blue *whoosh* of flames. For a brief moment, Durham Castle's function room was bathed in a flash of blinding light.

The two men, Armstrong and his colleague Joel Hedley, who stood a little distance away from the table, reeled and began smacking themselves in a frantic attempt to put out flames. Hedley then fell screaming to the floor, rolling back and forth in agony, his cheap dinner suit melting onto his skin. No sooner had the fireball exploded than it vanished again, but the men continued to flail and thrash at themselves as if they were still alight.

Armstrong staggered backwards against a huge wall hanging, and where it touched his burning kilt the frayed cloth edging ignited, smoky yellow-orange flames licking upwards. The plush red velvet caught fire rapidly. As the fabric burned, it changed from scarlet to black, whilst glowing ashes fizzed and floated away.

Hedley and Armstrong lay, writhing, on either side of the presentation table, thin blue flames hovering a few inches above their bodies. Bizarrely, they themselves barely appeared even to be on fire.

Nobody else had yet moved. The white cloth on the presentation table was aflame in front of the fire-spitting tapestry, like a bonfire in the middle of a Guy Fawkes celebration. The guests stared, mesmerised. Even the head chef, who had been bagpiped into the large hall, proudly bearing the haggis, remained frozen not ten feet away, gripped by shock. Sounds of crackling, as furnishings caught fire, were drowned out by the howls of the two men. Time stopped.

Some diners had videoed the entry procession, followed by Joel Hedley's careful rendition of Robert Burns' poem *Address to a Haggis*. Many continued recording, not through any morbid malice, but because they had forgotten they were even doing it. Hands holding up phones went unnoticed by their owners. Without knowing what they were doing, these filmmakers were creating vital police evidence and high-value news footage.

Jaws hung open, and when they'd regained the power of speech, guests questioned their neighbours at the round tables, asking if this was part of the evening's entertainment. 'What are they doing?' . . . 'Is this a joke?' . . . 'Was that some sort of stunt? An indoor firework?' . . . 'I've never seen this at a Burns Supper before. What's going on?'

Detective Inspector Godolphin Barnes sat in a distant corner. The tall policeman was a longstanding member of the Durham Friendship Society and always attended their Burns Night Supper. As with the rest of the crowd, Barnes was initially nonplussed by the action, hints of a smile even playing at the corners of his normally grim mouth as he watched the 'entertainment'.

Melville Armstrong and Joel Hedley led the Friendship Society, as President and Honorary Secretary respectively. Armstrong, a corpulent man, was close to being spherical. His lifelong business partner and colleague, Hedley, stood as the physical antithesis: Joel Hedley ran marathons and fell races across their native Northumberland. Whilst their little and large statures could have put Hedley and Armstrong in line to be a comedy double act, slapstick would be the last activity on earth that the pair would have engaged in together.

BURNS NIGHT BURNS

Melville Armstrong considered himself something of an after-dinner raconteur, while Joel Hedley, sporting round, wire-framed glasses, struck most people as a cerebral introvert, with the ideal appearance for a straight man. The audience confusion stemmed from the fact that a theatrical stunt to open the Burns Night proceedings was the opposite of what the Society's membership would expect from their executive officers. Constituted after the model of Freemasonry, the Durham Friendship Society observed formal traditions at all events.

Only a few seconds after the burning whisky on the haggis turned into a raging fireball, the smell of burnt hair and flesh hit the nostrils of the stunned diners and broke the spell. Joel Hedley's face contorted in a final rictus and was visibly blackened. People gasped, or screamed, an elderly woman fainted, and several individuals vomited. The phone videos became chaotic views of the vermilion carpet or the grandly chamfered wooden ceiling, as guests instinctively moved a hand to cover their noses or clutch the edge of the table.

After the initial fireball from the haggis, Joel Hedley and Melville Armstrong continued to writhe and scream in terrible pain, as if they were still on fire, but the lack of visible flames baffled all who had witnessed it.

First to come to his senses was the event's head chef, Randall White, who stood closest to the dais that held the two men up for the audience to view.

'Get another fire extinguisher!' he shouted to a stunned waiter by the next table, and gestured urgently with his left hand towards the end of the Fellows' Meeting Room. This action exposed his maimed little finger. From knuckle to tip was completely missing, the stump long since healed. The young waiter ran to obey him, his floppy blond fringe bouncing like the flames. Then, aware that he was responsible for having brought in the source of combustion – one ceremonial flambéing haggis – the chef grabbed up the nearby fire extinguisher and belatedly sprayed foam over the prone Joel Hedley.

Although the tablecloth continued to smoulder slowly, the wall hanging danced in flames, as if it were the second performer in the unexpected entertainment. Suddenly, an unspoken panic arose; fearful that the fire would spread and engulf them, people tried to flee the conflagration. The room was a matrix of tables and chairs, bedecked in the finery of a fancy black-tie dinner. Fast movement proved difficult, exacerbated by some pushing chairs out of their own way into the paths of others.

A different waiter charged back up the central aisle, from the direction the blond one had taken. The new man had a South Asian appearance with dark, close-shaved hair. He screamed as he charged towards the dais, a fire extinguisher held in front as he ran, spraying in arcs left and right. Continuing in his course, he ran right past the two stricken men, and carried on all the way to the exit at the far end. There he cast aside the red cylinder and continued out of the doorway and down the stairs immediately beyond.

The centuries-old stone space was well protected in case of fire, and the thick smoke rising from the velvet hanging kicked the sprinklers into action. Water sprayed, and those present or trying to escape were dealt a new shock from the chill of the indoor rain. The system was well-designed and effective. Before the chaos of the fleeing Burns Night diners could turn into a crowd crush disaster, the fires were out and people stood still again, shivering and dripping wet.

In life, and at work, Godolphin Barnes generally observed, took things in and considered carefully before pushing himself into action. In a movie about Durham Police, this DI would not be the policeman chasing a suspect through back gardens and leaping over fences. He would be the one who walked casually in the opposite direction, before appearing in just the right place to smugly trip the suspect as he rounded a corner.

4

BURNS NIGHT BURNS

Alongside the confusion as to what was actually happening, and his position stuck in a far corner of the room, this approach to life meant that Barnes had not run forward to lend a hand putting out the fire. Nor had he whipped the cloth from a nearby table to wrap around one of the victims and extinguish the flames. So far, he had done nothing but observe while the annual Burns Night Supper came to a mystifying and terrible end.

Two

Saturday, 8.19 p.m.

Lanky Detective Inspector Barnes had finally moved, placing himself next to the head chef, and the two stood looking down at the disfigured bodies at their feet. Randall White was as tall as Barnes, but more athletic. Bony Barnes gave the impression of a skeleton on the Day of the Dead, all decked out in his best dinner suit. A large, pointed nose stuck out from the policeman's face, which was so pale it added to the sense that he had attended the dinner as the representative for the undead.

In contrast to the pasty Barnes, Randall White was from one of the few black families in the West End of Newcastle. He had risen through the restaurant kitchens of Newcastle's Quayside to become head chef at Desanti's restaurant in the heart of Durham City. It was this position that had given him the opportunity to guest in the Durham Castle kitchens as chef for the Friendship Society's Burns Night Supper. White stared wretchedly at the scene, his right hand nagging at the stump of his left little finger. His audition for the Society was not going well.

Melville Armstrong's kilt and tweed waistcoat had taken longer to burn than his shirt and jacket. This had protected him a little, but his exposed fleshy face was covered in red and blackened welts, and he lay unmoving and silent. Joel Hedley had suffered even more, as the synthetic material of his dinner suit had literally welded itself onto his body, in places melted right into the skin. His face was now unrecognisable. Had Godolphin Barnes not witnessed the whole thing, he would not have been able to tell who either of the victims were.

The horror of the men's burns was hidden slightly by the clumps of extinguisher foam dappled across them. Randall White's mouth kept opening and closing like a fish, as if he intended to speak, but nothing would come out. He turned to Barnes, but the policeman had his mobile phone to his ear.

'This is DI Barnes of Durham Police. We've got a major incident in Durham Castle. Significant fire, injuries . . .' He squatted down and put fingers to Armstrong's neck, and then shuffled over to do the same with Hedley. 'One close to death, one dead – we need ambulances very quickly, please. There may be other injuries among the guests, but the fire is out now. Send the brigade anyway, this'll need investigating.'

Barnes stood up, sniffed a sweet smell in the air and squinted at the charred remains of the haggis. 'We'll need a van load of uniforms,' he went on, 'the whole forensics team, and I'll get onto the DCI - he'll need to see this.'

Randall White had suffered a minor flare burn to the face. On his black skin it was visible as a fat red weal across his left cheek, running from ear to chin. The hair beyond the ear was shrivelled and brittle from singeing. He continued staring at the bodies, and Barnes took him by the elbow to guide the man away to sit down.

'Stay there,' he said, depositing Chef White in a chair several metres from the victims. 'We'll get someone to check you over in a few minutes.'

The detective inspector took charge, positioning himself, as much as was possible for a skinny man in a large room, between the crowd of Friends and the fallen Armstrong and Hedley, acting partly as screen, partly as bouncer.

'Ladies and gentlemen, please remain calm and take a seat,' he instructed in a firm and carrying voice. 'Ambulances and police will be here shortly. It's going to be a long night, so be ready for that. I suggest that in order to keep as warm as possible in the circumstances that one by one, at each table, you may go and fetch your coat from the adjacent cloakroom.' All those present knew Godolphin Barnes as a fellow member of the Society, and thus they knew his job – he had no need to introduce himself.

7

It was a freezing January night in Durham, and the fact that everyone was soaking wet kept them back from the exit, especially now it was a police matter. They milled around aimlessly before sitting down as instructed, while a few of the more adventurous souls edged forward or sideways for an angle where they could sneak a look at the little rostrum with the blackened presentation table and immobile bodies.

In a fresh horror, Joel Hedley's wife staggered forward and collapsed beside his body, her ululations of grief piercing the cavernous space. People had to put their hands over their ears at the shrill screams. Godolphin Barnes gently pulled her away, just as the Hedleys' two daughters arrived at the same spot.

'Genevieve, please. I'm sorry, you'll have to wait,' Barnes explained, as closely to compassionate as he could manage. 'We need to find out what happened to cause this and I must keep everyone away for the moment so the investigators will be able to do their job.' He looked at the two daughters. 'Beth, can you and Eloise take your mother over to that table and all wait there, please.'

The younger women propped up their staggering mother and supported her as they zig-zagged back to a nearby table and flopped her down, still wailing.

Barnes scanned the room.

Two Durham Castle porters, in their black suits, had appeared at the entrance at one end of the room. They loitered, seemingly unsure as to what they should do. In its recent history, the castle had not seen fire and death – the porters were more used to opening the keep door late at night for drunken student residents, and closing it during the day against unwelcome tourists. The policeman waved them to come and assist him.

He scanned the room again. Elspeth Armstrong, stiff as always, and in a thick mask of make-up, had not left her seat. She stared at her husband's body with a dour look, clearly in shock. A tiny couple – people in miniature, like well-dressed children – in the two chairs beside her tried to comfort the Friendship Society

8

President's wife. They looked panicked and more distressed than she did, but Elspeth seemed oblivious to their ministrations.

Mrs Elspeth Armstrong attended all events at her husband's side. The pair relished their status as a north-east power couple, a big business owner and the woman behind the throne. Their positions in and control of the Durham Friendship Society formed a complementary role in the social circles of the city: the bigwigs, in charge, and everyone was to know it.

If anything, Elspeth had been more involved with the organisation of the Burns Night Supper than Melville – standard practice. Whilst he stood in the limelight as President, Mrs Armstrong ran the show, proposing to him all the elements that he should insist on in the club committee, and then undertaking the management of the arrangements in a visible display of hard work on behalf of the Society. Durham City grandees by their own promulgation.

Two tables away, Genevieve Hedley drained a glass of white wine. Her daughters, one on either side, spoke to their mother and each put a hand on one of hers and an arm around her shoulder. All three were sobbing. Like their mother, the Hedley daughters were dressed drably. The glamour of a black-tie event did not appear to have registered with any of them. Durham City grandees, Joel and Genevieve Hedley were not. Mrs Hedley worked just as hard for the Friendship Society as Elspeth Armstrong, if not harder. As a lapsed librarian, Genevieve knew how to organise. She revelled in the times when her work neatly completed the administration of an event. However, her contributions followed Elspeth's directions. The wife of her husband's business partner made all the running.

Similarly, Joel Hedley lived, and had just died, in the shadow of his Falstaffian friend, Melville Armstrong. Over thirty-five years, the two men had started several businesses together, digging up sand and gravel from the Northumberland earth. Through a variety of sleights of business hand, Armstrong had managed to take the vast majority of the profits from these for

9

himself. Joel Hedley had repeatedly been pressured and tricked into working simply as the companies' geologist, despite their mutual commitment to partnership and equal shares. The structuring and re-structuring of the various aggregates businesses continually put the majority of ownership and financial benefits in the fat hands of Melville Armstrong.

Detective Inspector Barnes looked away from the sad Hedley women, his eyes flitting from table to table. He wondered how many mobile phones might still be recording. He wanted to hear the conversations.

Three

Saturday, 8.45 p.m.

Detective Sergeant Tony Milburn ran into the room, overtook the plodding porters and came to a halt in front of DI Barnes.

'Good God, Godolphin!' he exclaimed, then winced at his own crass alliteration. No light-heartedness had been intended – it never cut much mustard with Barnes anyway – but the words had just blurted themselves out at the sight of the disaster. With a pointed nose, and his hair always slicked back, the DI reminded Milburn of a rodent. In black tie, soaked to the skin from the sprinklers, he genuinely looked like the proverbial drowned rat.

Clearing his throat, Milburn asked more formally, 'What happened?'

The man showed no emotion as he replied, 'That's what you're going to have to find out.'

Milburn figured his superior must be in shock. He had clearly been present, so must know what happened.

'Perhaps you should sit down?' he suggested. 'I can take over here.'

Barnes squinted at him. 'Of course you'll have to take over. But first I assume you'll want to know what information I have.'

'Um, yes, of course. Shall we sit over there?' Milburn pointed to a table that had been vacated by its guests.

'Shouldn't you secure the scene first, Detective Sergeant? This is the primary location.' Barnes indicated the burnt table and slightly raised stage with Armstrong and Hedley lying motionless on it.

Milburn knew he would be wrong, whatever he suggested. This was not new territory with Godolphin, so he simply nodded and turned away to survey the crime scene. The close-up view of the victims nearly turned his stomach. He wondered again if

11

Barnes was actually in shock; the man often came across as simply inhuman.

Four paramedics loped up the central aisle to the dais, one carrying a rigid plastic stretcher. Milburn guessed the wheeled trolley could not be brought up the winding castle staircase. They dropped down beside the bodies of Armstrong and Hedley.

'This one's the one to work on. He's still alive.' Barnes pointed down to Melville Armstrong and then wandered away to sit at the table Milburn had suggested. He started to fiddle on his smartphone, while Milburn assessed the room further.

He saw a seated woman's head sway and then fall face down on the tablecloth in front of her. The two young women with her gasped and touched her hands, obviously fearful they might get no response.

Tony rushed over and blurted out, 'Is she all right?' The Hedleys' two daughters, Beth and Eloise, looked blankly at him. 'Sorry, I mean, what happened? Does she have a condition, or do you think it's just the upset of all this?' He put his hand to his chest and apologised again. 'Sorry, should have introduced myself. I'm Detective Sergeant Milburn from Durham Police.'

Eloise pointed over to the area of the fire. She spoke slowly. 'That's our father. This is our mother.'

'I'm so sorry. Should we get a paramedic over for her?' The three were saved from having to make any decision as the woman came to.

Milburn knelt on the floor, feeling the flood damp through his trousers. He squeezed into the gap between the chairs occupied by Beth and her mother. 'How are you feeling?' The volume of his voice was low and he spoke calmly. 'I'm a policeman, Mrs . . .?' He turned to Beth for help.

'Hedley. Her name is Genevieve Hedley.'

Tony mouthed silently, 'Thank you.' He turned back to reassure the widow. 'Can we get you a cup of tea?' Her hand lay on the table, and he gave it a squeeze.

Mrs Hedley's focus started to return, and she gave him a weak smile. Hot on the heels of her smile came red-faced rage. She tried to leap up, but the furniture wouldn't move and she was pinned in place. Instead, she shrieked and banged her fists down on the table.

DS Milburn swayed back a little, caught out by the sudden change in her mood. He assumed it was shock combined with the sudden return to consciousness. Having lost hold of her hand, he moved his grip to her upper arm, in an attempt to steady and placate Mrs Hedley with one movement.

'It was that woman, that bloody woman. She did this! Melville just wouldn't keep it in his trousers. My husband warned him it would end like this, but he just laughed. Not laughing now, though, is he?' Tony could smell the wine on her breath. 'But why did she have to take Joel too?' Her face collapsed into Tony's shoulder, and he held her for several minutes, letting the sobs flow. Eventually, Eloise peeled her mother away from the DS, and Beth slipped in as his substitute.

Tony stood and stepped back from the grieving family. He watched the three women hug and cry, occasionally looking over to the two burn victims, trying to figure out which one was this woman's husband. He made a note to find out later who 'that bloody woman' was, and what Mrs Hedley had meant about Joel's forewarning of this incident.

Uniformed officers were marshalling guests into groups around the dining tables. They sent the porters away to bring blankets. Despite the powerful heating system and roaring fire, many of the wet Burns Supper guests were in a bad way. Milburn could see two men trying to hold a conversation through chattering teeth, their white dress shirts slick to the skin.

More paramedics filtered through the space, instinctively assessing where they were most needed and spreading out to check on any wounded. Few present had suffered injuries from the fire: it had been large in its inception, but with the sprinklers successfully operating, it had barely spread from the podium

13

where the two men had been presenting the haggis. More injuries had been sustained in the initial panic to get up from seats and attempt to run for the doors.

Tony recognised Lord and Lady Sacriston, who were comforting Elspeth Armstrong. He had interviewed them in a previous case, and their diminutive stature made them unforgettable. Elspeth wore a stunning blue ball gown, which looked just as good wet as he imagined it had when she arrived. Her dark hair had blonde highlights subtly and elegantly traced throughout. The hairdo had not survived dousing, and it all stuck to her neck and shoulders. Over at the furthest table from the dais, the detective sergeant could see a tanned couple engaged in conversation with Alan, the hairdresser that Tony himself used. They were middle-aged and appeared Mediterranean, at a first guess, probably Spanish or Italian.

Tony was familiar with the Friendship Society but had never had any interest in joining. He had been invited to a couple of events in the past, but schmoozing with wannabe Freemasons was not his cup of tea at all. He was initially surprised that Alan would be into that sort of thing but, on further consideration, appreciated that the Society would probably catch all parts of Durham's business community.

Looking around the tables laden with bottles of wine and whisky, the DS mumbled to himself, 'Networking, I guess they must call this.'

Patting his jacket pockets, Milburn realised his radio was still in the car he'd parked with abandon on Palace Green, at the grand entrance to Durham Castle. He pulled out his phone and rang Sergeant Baz Bainbridge at the city police station. It stood perhaps only 300 yards away on New Elvet, across a deep-cut gorge of the River Wear. Tony, however, had been called from home and had driven hell for leather the mile downhill from Gilesgate.

'We're gonna need more officers, Baz. We've got a hundred or so shivering dinner guests who all need to give statements before we can let them go. And we need to cordon off the Castle completely. Should be the easiest cordon we've ever made – got its own giant doors and impenetrable walls all round. Have you got hold of DCI Hardwick yet?'

The echoey voice informed him that Hardwick was en route, and that he, Baz, would work on pulling in more officers, but the shift was short-handed anyway, so he'd need to ring around to call in more help.

Tony took a roll of blue and white tape from his jacket pocket and tied it around three chairs to form a barrier in front of the area Barnes had indicated as their main crime scene focus. Two crime scene investigators walked towards him in full white suits, hats, gloves and booties. They both carried a toolbox, and one had a large, professional camera slung around her neck. They handed Milburn a bagged set of the disposable white clothes. The paramedics had been working apace on Melville Armstrong at Tony's feet.

As he pulled on the white overalls, one of the paramedics looked up, saying, 'We're taking this one to hospital right now.' He pointed at Armstrong's unconscious body.

'OK. Bag all clothes you remove and anything else you find, please. Just one second, though.' Tony looked at the CSI with the big camera. 'Can you get some photos of this victim where he fell. Right now, please, as these folks need to get him down to the ambulance.'

Without a word the forensic photographer moved across, and the paramedics stepped back briefly to enable clearer shots.

The paramedic told Tony, 'We moved him a little, but not that much. Can't promise, but I don't reckon we'll have disturbed evidence any more than he did writhing about on the floor here.'

'How do you know he writhed about?' Tony asked her.

'I've never seen a person on fire, but it's what they do.' She pointed over to Hedley, who lay on the floor in a contorted position, as if he'd been breakdancing and had suddenly frozen in mid-action. 'We can't do anything for him. I'm pretty sure we haven't disturbed evidence on him at all. If you need us to give statements later, it's Ambulance 215.'

Tony nodded and thanked her. By now he had the arms of the overalls on, and let go of trying to zip it up, in order to take out his phone and make a voice memo of the ambulance call sign and the name stitched onto her green uniform.

'Right, on three.' The lead paramedic counted and the group of four strained to lift Armstrong onto the orange plastic stretcher. The patient did not stir. She counted to three again, and they stood up in unison, lifting the not-quite-dead weight. Milburn watched them shuffle between the dining tables and past the crowd of guests, many of whom shuddered at this close-up view of their President with a breathing tube and squeeze bottle hiding his face.

Milburn watched as the photographer's flash lit up Joel Hedley's body for the last time. He inhaled deeply then walked over to DI Barnes, some broken glass crunching underfoot.

Four

Saturday, 9.03 p.m.

DS Milburn indicated the inspector's wet black-tie outfit and asked, 'I take it you were at this dinner then.' It wasn't a question.

'Of course I was,' Barnes replied testily. 'I'm here every year. And that means I can't be involved with the investigation.'

Tony looked the man straight in the face. If it hadn't been so ridiculous an idea, Milburn might have thought that Barnes had engineered a history of attending the event annually in order to avoid the work of investigating this fire. This was the kind of case that DI Godolphin Barnes had a regular habit of dodging. He was so often off sick, or suddenly on some training course, that Tony had the DI pinned as utterly workshy. And yet a hundred witness statements, a dead bigwig, liaison with the World Heritage Site, probably the Health & Safety Executive too, and then most likely it would turn out to be a simple case of a candle setting fire to some old cloth. No, of course you won't be taking part in this investigation, he thought cynically. I should have guessed as much as I drove down here. This is a novel one though, gotta hand that to you. Milburn found his boss's excuses laughable, but he rarely laughed about it, as it meant twice as much work for him.

He set his phone to record their conversation, but also took out his pencil and notebook. 'OK, then, Godolphin, can you tell me all the information you have about what went on here this evening?'

'Your two victims are Melville Armstrong and Joel Hedley. They're President and Honorary Secretary of the Durham Friendship Society.' The inspector spoke calmly, seemingly unaffected by the horror he had witnessed. 'Armstrong owns Armstrong Aggregates, and Hedley is the chief geologist there. In

17

both areas, Armstrong is the gregarious face of the organisation, and Hedley actually does most of the important work.'

He went on, 'You've got Armstrong's wife over there with the Sacristons, and those two women with their mother are Joel's family.'

Milburn remained silent, noting the various groups as Barnes indicated each one.

'The two men were doing the ceremonial first cut into the haggis when the whole thing went up in flames and ignited their clothing as well. The fire spread a little, but the sprinkler system extinguished everything very quickly.'

Tony frowned. 'The haggis suddenly went up in flames? Is that what you're telling me?'

DI Barnes looked at Milburn. 'Yes. It was already alight. You douse it in whisky and set fire to it, ready for that first cut. That's a traditional part of a Burns Night Supper. However, when Armstrong put the knife in, there was what can only be described as a fireball. Flames shot out on both sides of the blade, which is how both he and Hedley got caught up in it.'

The younger detective looked over to the blackened area of the fire. 'It's just haggis we're talking about, isn't it – the Scottish food, haggis, right?'

'Yes, lamb and beef mince with oats and onions.'

'Has it got a whole load more whisky in there too?'

Barnes shook his head. 'This is arson, Tony, not an accident.'

'Arson? What makes you think that?'

'Can't you smell it? That sweet smell in the back of the nose. I don't know what accelerant it is, but that haggis also contained something highly flammable. So flammable that the tapestry caught fire just from Armstrong touching it.' He paused. 'Helluva way to go.'

DS Milburn turned towards the area he had cordoned off and inhaled deeply through his nose. There was a burnt smell in the air, but nothing he would label as particularly sweet. 'Accelerant?'

Barnes' rodent-like nose was twice the size of most men's, and he made a show of using it before declaring, 'Yes. It's not petrol is about all I can tell you, though. Get the CSIs to try and swab some from the floor or nearby carpet. Hopefully not all of it will have vaporised yet.'

As Milburn headed back over to the forensics team, he spotted DCI Hardwick enter at the opposite end of the room. The big boss made a beeline for Mrs Armstrong and Lord and Lady Sacriston. The sight of Harry 'H' Hardwick's full head of white hair caused Tony to stroke his own hair, conscious that the greying temples would likely spread, displacing the chestnut brown that held on for the moment.

He didn't head over to talk to Hardwick immediately but turned his attention to the main crime scene. He surveyed the remains of the ceremonial tablecloth and the plate of charred haggis, before putting on the forensics booties and gloves. His hair he secured with the stretchy white hat and then he stepped over his own tape cordon. Leaning down, Milburn tried to inhale any odour that might be left there. It just smelt like burnt barbecue.

'Julia, do you think there's an accelerant involved here?' Tony asked the Forensic Scene Manager. 'Can you try to swab up any that might be left? If it's an unusual one, that might give us a lead.'

He knew the woman from numerous cases. She was shrewd and insightful.

'Yes, don't worry, we're looking for it. You can definitely smell it, but it's an unusual one. I don't know if that's the whisky mixed in that's making the aroma a bit odd, but we'll find it. Whatever it is.' She was wrapping a bag around Joel Hedley's right hand and seemed distracted.

'You can't tell just from the smell?'

She looked up sharply, but Tony was grinning broadly to show that he was only teasing.

19

Dr Julia Sedgley returned to taping around the victim's wrist and taunted the detective sergeant back. 'I can only tell your Exhibits Officer. When the SIO has appointed one, send them over to collect my report.'

Milburn laughed and retorted, 'Oh, don't worry. Senior Investigating Officer – that'll most likely be me as well!'

DCI Hardwick caught his eye, and they met in empty space in the middle of the room, between the fire scene being processed by the CSIs and the milling, shivering crowd.

Harry said, 'We need to preserve this whole room. Can we get this lot moved to the main dining hall downstairs? It'll be safer too, in case there's still any fumes in here, or anything that might fall down.'

DS Milburn nodded. 'Yeah. The main hall is huge, though, so I expect it'll be even colder than in here. Can you wave your rank about to get them to turn the heating up in the dining hall, and to bring more blankets?'

Hardwick looked around at the collection of wet diners, seemingly using his dead, blind eye. Tony quickly realised that he was just on the wrong side of the boss and couldn't see the good eye taking in the traumatised, well-to-do crowd.

'Indeed. I think we've got another couple of uniforms coming over from Peterlee. When they turn up, get them to take names and IDs from this lot and send the witnesses home. We'll gather all the statements in the morning. Meanwhile,' he added, 'I'll take the Sacristons home and get statements from them straight away. I expect they'll be the most coherent of the lot. When I come back, we'll have a powwow about organising the investigation team.'

Tony peered straight at his DCI's bad eye, bemused at how Hardwick was so in thrall to the local landed gentry.

'Sure thing. Is that you leaving me provisionally in charge of the scene? And the investigation? SIO too, maybe?' His final question was dripping with sarcasm.

'I'll be back in two hours. Yes, of course you will manage the scene. I expect you'll end up as Exhibits Officer anyway.'

Tony looked over to the Forensic Scene Manager, but her head was down, closely examining the burnt material on Joel Hedley's legs.

Harry continued, oblivious, 'I'm sure I'll be SIO on this one. For now, if you can get the particulars for all these witnesses, get them out of here, and then secure the scene properly once they're out, that'll be enough for us to start. And that will definitely keep you and the uniform shift busy till I get back anyway.' He pointed at the white-suited group inside Tony's police tape cordon. 'They won't be done before I get back either, so keep them topped up with coffee, and we can debrief them together on my return. OK?'

Tony could have written the script himself, so he just nodded meekly before remembering: 'What about Barnes?'

They both stared over at the DI, who appeared to be playing a game on his phone. Hardwick had his arms crossed, watching the lanky detective, who looked like he had to fold himself up to fit in the chair.

'Give him coffee and a blanket too but keep him there. He won't be able to work on the investigation but will be vital for intel on this one. I want to take his statement tonight. And I want you and me to do that together, Tony. Don't let any of the PCs do that one. With him off the investigation team, I can see most of this whole thing coming down to you and me, so the more we're up to speed with it all tonight, the faster it should all go.'

The two men looked at each other, and once Milburn had nodded a final affirmation, Hardwick swept over to the tiny Lord and Lady Sacriston.

Five

Saturday, 9.41 p.m.

Tony's phone vibrated. Penfold's text message was in haiku form – they usually were.

> *a poet's fire burns,*
>
> *flaming haggis and whisky,*
>
> *is it best served cold?*

Milburn railed at how his civilian friend could have so much knowledge of this case barely an hour after he, as the on-call detective, had arrived on the scene. He messaged Penfold back to demand an explanation. The reply came immediately, and Tony rocked back at the audacity of the New Zealander.

> *I'm on Palace Green,*
>
> *hot coffee in each gloved hand:*
>
> *your Burns Night warmer.*

He looked out of the window, but the walls of the outer keep of Durham Castle blocked his view of Palace Green. The grassy square that had separated the cathedral from the castle for the last thousand years was a beautiful spot on a summer's afternoon. What his blond surfer friend was doing there on a freezing winter's night confused Milburn, especially as Penfold lived by the beach in Seaton Carew, more than half an hour's drive away.

He told PC Bob Smith to hold the fort, quite literally, whilst he went outside for a break. The man was such a giant of a copper

22

that Tony had a vision of him beating back barbarian hordes at the gate singlehandedly.

After signing out with the outer cordon officer at the castle's gatehouse, Tony went in search of the coffee and an explanation from Penfold. The huge gates to the castle keep were propped wide open. Three ambulances and a fire engine had had to ingress as close as they could to the danger zone. The small inner quadrangle could have held more, but not with enough space for the vehicles to leave again at speed.

Milburn's shoes were hurting his feet. As on-call detective, he'd rushed out of the house, putting on his stout Doc Marten shoes, but with no socks. The right shoe felt particularly painful at every step.

Other vehicles from all three emergency services stood scattered around the flat grass square outside, the cathedral towering up behind them. His swimmer's physique gave Penfold away, as he similarly loomed up taller than the majority of the emergency services personnel. Tony expected to receive only a cryptic rationale for the man's knowledge of, and appearance at, a difficult crime scene, twenty miles from his home. Nonetheless, details were inevitably circulating outside the castle walls, even those that only an information hound like Penfold could find.

'What are *you* doing here?' Tony asked.

Penfold sniffed theatrically. 'Here's your coffee. With some extraneous, distracting influences in it too.'

'Ah, the joy of take-away coffee – means I get milk and sugar with it,' Tony said. At his chilly house in Seaton Carew, Penfold would always serve coffee black, straight from the machine. There was never any milk or sugar on offer alongside. Milburn found it amusing that it was a filter machine. Despite Penfold's claim that he was all about the flavour of the coffee, he had not moved to the extreme of owning an espresso machine.

'Heathen,' Penfold quipped.

Tony cupped the cardboard vessel and sipped cautiously through the hole in the lid. He looked up over the escaping steam and reiterated, 'So, why are you here? Trip to the castle 'gainst the Scot for Burns Night?' He felt a bit of a glow at remembering the Walter Scott poem about Durham, until Penfold replied.

'Burns Night was the twenty-fifth.'

Milburn faltered, 'Oh. Well, I suppose you wouldn't hold a big fancy dinner on a Wednesday.' He turned the spotlight back again. 'So, what are you doing here?'

'A haggis mysteriously explodes in a fireball, killing two important local businessmen and threatening the fabric of our main defence against Scottish invasion these last thousand years. To my mind, that means you need my help.'

'Why would you possibly think I need your help?'

'Remember *The Case of the Drunken £50 Notes*?' It was Penfold's turn to gaze over the coffee cup at his friend. He raised his eyebrows, barely visible in the weak street lighting.

'Well, yes, but that's nothing like this,' Tony blustered. 'That was an actual mystery. This is likely arson, and there'll only be a handful of people who could have set it up, so it won't take long to catch them. Few would have been involved with the haggis or the whisky, I should think. Why they might have done it, or maybe even *how* they actually arranged everything, we might not find out so easily, but I don't really care about that for the moment.'

'The whisky?' Penfold echoed, raising his eyebrows again, this time to emphasise the question.

'Well, yeah.' Tony started to doubt himself but wasn't sure exactly how he could be wrong. He just knew that if Penfold was casually questioning something, it meant Tony was likely off course. He hated Penfold's supercilious, patronising approach and yet at the same time he admired the extraordinary intellect the Kiwi brought to bear on everything. He gave himself a little pep talk before continuing.

'For the flames to spread like that, it must have been sloshed all over.' Milburn remembered DI Barnes' comments about accelerant. 'And/or, given the smell of accelerant in there,

24

the whisky must have been doctored with something even more flammable.'

Penfold's head gave a little movement to the side. 'Have you seen the video?'

'*Video?* What video?'

'Well, you asked why I was here. This is on social media already.' Penfold held up a large-screen phone and replayed a video of the earlier fiery events. It spared the viewer nothing. The picture resolution was incredibly good, but the playback was silent. Tony winced at the imagery and then scowled at the idea that this had been posted online. He knew that some of the witnesses had been recording at the time but had specifically told PC Smith that all devices with a recording on needed to be collected, for the evidence team to download the video files.

'That's horrible. Who posted this? And how did it get past the moderators? I thought they were supposed to block graphic stuff like that.' Tony's stomach was churning again, but the coffee helped to settle it a little.

'Those are two wildly different questions. The latter is almost certainly irrelevant to our needs. The former though is pretty obvious.'

'None of this is obvious. What's obvious about the whisky? What's obvious about who posted the video? I mean, I see it's on the *@DurhamCastle* account timeline, but they must have lots of people with access to that account. It's a classic multi-user thing. Assuming it is actually the real castle account and not some fake one. Is that what you mean?'

Penfold shook his head and stepped slightly closer so he could point at details on the phone screen. The surfer wore cargo shorts, even though it was within a degree of freezing. Tony could feel warmth from the man's large frame, more so than what was left emanating through his coffee cup's thin shell.

Penfold scrolled the timeline up and down a few times. 'You see?'

'What? They seem to post very regularly. You think it's whoever is posting right now?'

'No, Milburn. It's automated. Every five minutes the account posts thirty seconds of video from one of the historic rooms. It just happened to perfectly catch your incident.'

Tony was highly sceptical that such a coincidence could be the answer. In his experience, all bad things had a human cause. Luckily, a lot of good things also had human causes.

'That still doesn't explain why you're here.'

'I told you: you need my help.'

'How so? I mean, any investigation needs as many hands as possible, but you're not a policeman, and you're not one of the force's civvy staff, so you don't qualify to get involved.' Tony was doing his best to be supercilious back, but his heart wasn't in it. Penfold had helped him in an unofficial capacity on several previous cases, but this was just arson. One and a half victims dead, and a weird venue for it, but still just somebody causing a big fire. Somebody who could be found, since the trail of evidence would point to a specific person.

'Did you watch the video carefully?' Penfold persisted.

Tony was getting fed up with this game now. Snatching the phone from Penfold's hand, he played it through again.

'*What?* What am I supposed to see here that amazingly closes the case?'

'Quite the opposite.' Penfold's voice was infuriatingly calm at all times. 'This blows the case sky high, if you'll pardon the pun. Watch the fire at the moment of the knife cutting in.' He used a tanned finger to slide the playback earlier, to the moment Melville thrust the blade down into the sheep's stomach outer lining of the haggis. 'See?'

'Well . . . his movement of the knife is what disturbs the excess whisky,' Tony said, adding, 'and/or accelerant. And so that's when the fire really kicks off and they get caught up in it. You don't think it was an accident, do you?'

'No.'

26

'No, of course, the smell of accelerant.'

'Smell? No. We'll come back to that. No, look here.' Penfold paused the video and slid back through the frames to the instant the knife had first cut into the haggis. A stream of clear liquid, part-ignited, appeared frozen in mid-air on either edge of the blade. It had escaped with force enough to form a jet in each direction, perfectly targeting Melville on the near side and Hedley on the opposite side of the small table. Each jet had a faint blue flame floating above it.

Milburn did not understand, so Penfold explained. 'The accelerant is *inside* the haggis. It squirts out when released by the knife's cut.'

Tony could now see this as clear and obvious, but he couldn't tell why it seemed so important to Penfold. 'Um, arson via a tampered haggis. How is that any more significant than arson with tampered whisky?'

'It changes the timeline. To fill a haggis with accelerant – that could be done days before the event. There are complications to it, of course: how did they stop it evaporating if it's that volatile, how did they ensure it didn't go up in flames in the oven, et cetera, but it's not the same crime at all.'

The detective sergeant shrugged his shoulders, replying, 'Fair enough. I'll keep that in mind when we work out a few hypotheses for the investigation direction.' He felt let down that Penfold hadn't cracked the case there and then, but also felt relieved that the man's information amounted to little more than a bit of conjecture. 'I'd better get my radio and go back inside. Thanks for the coffee.' He took Penfold's empty cup and his own, put them into the recycling bin nearby and turned to walk towards his car.

Noticing his limp, Penfold called, 'You hurt your leg, Milburn?'

Tony stopped walking, lifted and wiggled the right foot. 'I think these shoes must be rubbing. I didn't have time to put any socks on.'

27

'Put your foot up behind you.' Penfold went behind him and put his left hand on his friend's shoulder for balance, as he bent forward to look at the sole of Tony's shoe. 'One second.'

Glancing over his shoulder. Tony spotted Penfold's hand ferreting in the thigh pocket of his cargo pants and pulling out an evidence bag. He deftly turned it half inside out and then used it to tug on Milburn's shoe. The DI felt his foot being pulled hard and then suddenly released. He put his right leg back down and turned around.

Penfold had stood up and was sealing the evidence bag. Clearly visible through the plastic was a shard of thin glass, about two inches long, and curved in two dimensions at the same time.

'This is extremely lucky,' Penfold said. 'The way it was stuck into the rubber sole, it was held exactly in the gap by the heel, so it was protected from crushing. There's a second piece still stuck in there. It's larger and flatter, and the way it's stuck in will be what's given you a stone-in-your-shoe kind of limp. I can't get it out, though, I'm afraid, it's jammed in too deeply. We could either smash it and leave the sharp bit stuck in the sole, or maybe you should ask the CSIs to use some pliers to pull it out. They may well crush it anyway, but I myself can't get it out.'

'I don't think you need an evidence bag for that,' Tony said. 'There's a fair bit of broken glass on the floor inside. You can imagine the chaos of people in a fire.' He squinted at the bag Penfold held up to view. 'Yeah, that's probably a piece of a wine glass. The place was all set up for a big fancy dinner, and that looks a bit thin and delicate for a whisky tumbler.'

'Ah, OK. Well, hopefully you'll be able to walk with less discomfort soon, once the bigger piece is taken out.' Penfold put the bag with the glass piece into the same side pocket the bag had originally been in.

'Always a boon to be around, aren't you?' Milburn grinned and raised his hand in farewell as he dipped into his car to collect his police radio.

Penfold nodded. 'Here when you need me.'

Six

Saturday, 10.13 p.m.

The pathologist had parked up while Milburn had been chatting with Penfold. Tony followed him down the monumental flagstone drive to the castle's gatehouse. They talked briefly on their way up the historic, dark wood staircase that led to the kitchen end of the function room, now a crime scene. At the door, the DS pointed the tanned, salt-and-pepper-haired Andrew Gerard over to his colleagues on the forensics team, and then descended the staircase again to the main dining hall to check on the progress of his uniformed officers taking witness details ready for tomorrow morning's interviews.

He paused on the threshold, observing. Only a few steps inside, he saw the back of Police Constable Diane Meredith, and his heart sank. She stood relaxed and, despite the chunky stab vest, cut a vigorous, athletic figure. Meredith had dark hair, cut in a neat bob, which swayed ever so slightly. He wasn't sure if it was a slight movement of her body that made the hair move, or if his opening the large door had caused a draught. She held her police hat by the brim, down by her side, and as she spoke, it bounced gently against her left thigh. In front of her were a couple Milburn recognised from one of the tables upstairs.

'I'm Constable Diane Meredith,' she was saying. 'My body camera is recording our conversation. Can you speak clearly for the camera and tell me your full name, date of birth and address, please.' She lifted her right arm and Tony guessed she was pointing at the bodycam attached to her right pectoral.

The couple looked ashen. They stared at her chest and stammered their details. A quick calculation from their dates of birth told Tony they were around forty-two and thirty-nine, and with the same surname, he guessed at husband and wife. DI

Barnes ought to be able to fill in a lot of details about who all the guests were, assuming the majority were actually members of the slightly strange, almost-Rotarian club that Barnes belonged to.

As Milburn understood things from the occasional vague references he had heard about the Durham Friendship Society, it was a sort of networking social club. The members were from a wide variety of professions, and all sent business each other's way, helping out with contacts and expertise wherever it would benefit other members. He scowled. It was exactly the sort of thing Godolphin would revel in. He wondered how many times a Friendship Society member had had a speeding ticket go away.

Then Tony berated himself. *Cut it out!* He didn't think much of his boss but had no evidence that the man was corrupt. Tony believed strongly in 'innocent until proven guilty', so he was willing to give the DI the benefit of the doubt. He had never seen anything to even suggest corruption, but Godolphin Barnes was just a continuously dislikable bloke.

The couple quietly asked the DS to let them pass so they could go home. Meredith had dismissed them and moved away to the next disturbed-looking pair. She hadn't turned at all, so Tony had not had to make any sort of conversation, or even greeting. He was happy with that situation. Since all their trouble he had managed to avoid her most of the time. Occasionally their paths crossed like this, but mostly Milburn had been able to engineer things so that he could keep away from 'the Crazy Cow'. His other half, Kathy, had nicknamed her that during the period when Meredith had stalked them both.

After dating Meredith for just a short while, Tony had met Kathy, and she had turned his head. He immediately broke things off with Diane and started seeing Kathy instead. It had been enough to send Diane off the rails. She had sought to steal him back again, and her tactics had been unnerving – the very definition of stalking. Milburn smiled to himself, remembering how the whole series of events had brought him and Kathy so much closer.

30

BURNS NIGHT BURNS

Despite the trouble, the powers that be had insisted that Constable Meredith continue without detriment. Milburn had provided a lot of circumstantial evidence about her stalking, but nothing concrete. DCI Harry Hardwick had come to a grudging impasse with her: Meredith spent a period posted to a different police station then returned with a spotless record and a plan to move into CID.

Milburn watched as she moved on again to the next witness, flawless in her work, building a better and better reputation. It was only a matter of time before she could force a promotion and push her way into working in the same office as him. Tony despaired at what Kathy might say when that happened. He pictured his blonde-haired, hazel-eyed librarian partner seething about Diane's antics. 'The gall of that woman,' he visualised her saying over and over. His lips were still moving, mouthing Kathy's imagined commentary, when he looked up to see PC Meredith herself standing in front of him.

'Those two are just finishing up the last of the witnesses and then we've got all the names and addresses to catch up with them tomorrow.' She waved over a shoulder to indicate two additional uniform constables. 'Any idea what actually happened?'

The immediate thought that jumped into Tony's consciousness was to parrot the line, 'Can't you smell the accelerant?' However, this was very quickly superseded by the desire to avoid talking to Diane at all. He was saved by the radio. The information that a couple of homeless men were kicking seven bells out of each other in Durham Market Place came with a request for officers to attend. As everyone was at the castle working his crime scene, Milburn was legitimately able to choose who should respond. He sent another constable, who chewed his gum noisily whilst nodding at the DS's instructions, along with PC Meredith. She screwed up her face in contempt at being sent away but turned and left without actually saying anything.

Tony returned up the cold staircase to find out what pathologist Andrew Gerard thought of the geologist's corpse. From the entrance at one end of the long function room, he took in the scattered remains of a Burns Night Supper gone badly awry. Had he not known anything about it, and apart from the dead body, the room could easily have been mistaken for the remnants of a wild party. Some tables had been pushed out of their uniform spacing, with chairs scattered around, some of which were upturned. The odd tablecloth had been dragged off centre and its edge trailed on the wet carpet. Bottles and glasses lolled on their sides, abandoned by the partygoers. Only one punter in black tie remained: Godolphin Barnes, staring listlessly at the ornate coving in the wooden ceiling.

The two other people in the room were investigators. Pathologist Gerard stood beside the Forensics Scene Manager; they were studying the badly burned body of Joel Hedley.

The radio squeaked and DS Milburn received a message from Diane Meredith. She addressed him directly, albeit on a channel all the shift could hear.

'We've got two in custody, Tony. You'd better get down here asap. Got one dressed as a waiter. The other claims this waiter one had bragged about how he was going to come into money for something he was going to do at the castle tonight.'

'Really? Who is he, this waiter?'

'No ID. IC4 male, known to the other guy as Momo.'

IC4 meant Asian. 'Momo? Nothing else?'

'No. He ran off at the sight of us, but your mate rugby tackled the guy outside Waterstones when he saw me chasing him.'

'My "mate"?'

'That New Zealander who's always hanging around – the tall one.'

In the background, Milburn heard a voice clarify, 'My name is Penfold which, Constable Meredith, you very well know.'

'Says his name's Penfold.'

'God, right, I'll come down there now.' Milburn let go of the radio pressel switch, turned back and asked, 'You two OK to sort everything out here? I've got some people to talk to, hopefully at least vaguely connected with this.'

The boss of the CSIs nodded, and Andrew Gerard said, 'I should be able to get to the post-mortem on this one first thing tomorrow for you. Nine a.m. sound OK?'

Milburn shrugged. 'I guess so. We've got two injured up at the hospital: no news on Armstrong yet, and they took the chef up there for observation overnight as well. So, I'll need to visit early on anyway.'

Barnes called over, without getting up, 'You need to get fingerprints from that.' His long arm was outstretched, and a long index finger extended it even further to point at the discarded fire extinguisher which lay at the base of the wall by the smaller exit door, where the waiter had run out during the fire. 'I reckon that Asian guy she's telling you about is the same one who sprayed that and ran off.'

Tony turned to ask the team to secure the fire extinguisher as evidence, but the skinny woman in the white overalls had already started walking over to the red cylinder. A large plastic bag appeared in her hand, seemingly out of thin air, and she wriggled it up over the length of the extinguisher, doing her best to avoid touching the metal surface.

The DI finally stood up, saying, 'I can't be involved, so I'm going to go home and get some sleep. I'll come into the station tomorrow and give a statement. I may need some time off after that to process all this, but I'll see Hardwick there in the morning.'

Before Milburn could say anything in reply, Barnes had sidled away, out of the nearest exit in barely three strides.

Seven

Saturday, 10.51p.m.

'Get off me, you bastards!'

While Meredith shoved the handcuffed 'Momo' towards the open back doors of a Police transit van, DS Milburn was ensuring that the man didn't hurt himself by falling over or banging into anything. In a surprise move, their prisoner suddenly twisted a full 360-degrees, breaking free of the constable's grip, and ran off over the grey flagstones of Durham's Market Place.

Diane shook her hand in pain and held her right thumb with the other hand. 'Ow!'

With his hands cuffed behind his back, the prisoner was unable to move quickly. Milburn sprinted after the waddling Momo. The man had not even made it past St Nic's Church before the detective caught him by the upper arm. He turned and tried to kick out, but Tony held the short man at a stiff arm's length so his toes couldn't reach his shins. Diane caught up and they hauled him back up the slight slope to the Black Maria. They had thought that the suspects were well contained, so Milburn had sent the gum-chewing male constable back up to the castle. Immediately, Penfold stepped in. He held the van door open for them and then closed it behind the prisoner.

Again, the Kiwi surfer looked out of place, Tony thought, in his cargo shorts, rubber sandals and lumberjack shirt. Tony guided him to one side so they could talk privately. They took up the space in the doorway of Boots the Chemist. The Market Place branch had four steps up to the double doorway under an overhang. It made for an ideal private conversation space in the busy square.

'What are you playing at? You can't go leaping into police matters like that.'

34

Penfold's blond hair shone white in the light from the streetlamps, and his cheeks creased with a benevolent smile as he replied, bemused, 'Just doing my public duty, DS Milburn. I saw a police officer chasing a man and stopped his escape.'

'You can't do this,' Tony grumbled. 'H will kick you out of town if he hears you've been playing Clint Eastwood.'

Penfold mimicked a Wild West accent. 'Run out o' town by Dead Eye Hardwick, the share-iff kicked in the heeyad by his own hoss.'

'I'm serious. He hates me talking to you, as it is. Even now that we have civvies in loads of areas of investigations, he can't get his head around what you are.'

'Ha. Then my subterfuges are working.' Penfold was grinning widely. 'Look, I know the police are super-stretched every Saturday night, and here tonight you've got a big murder scene to deal with, so all your officers are busy with that. And that chap Momo is fit. He's not used to being homeless, I'd suggest. Not long out of the army either, if my guess is correct. So it was the right thing to do, to help out.'

Frustrated, Milburn left Penfold on the chemist shop threshold.

'Here when you need me, Tony,' Penfold called over, and Milburn continued over to the van, simmering.

He pressed his face up to the tinted glass in the rear window of the vehicle to try and get another look at the suspect. Although he was dirty, the man sat still and upright, staring straight ahead. A separately caged compartment in the van held another skinny, dishevelled man: Momo's opponent. This one was talking continuously, bobbing his tattooed face to gesticulate, since his hands were cuffed behind him.

Beginning to pull off his set of forensic coveralls, DS Milburn told PC Meredith, 'Right, Diane, can you take these two back to the station and check them in. Once they are checked in, transcribe those name and address details off your bodycam files.

I don't know if the DCI will have started setting up HOLMES and the case files, but you know the forms they'll need to go on.'

'Yes, I can do all of that.' She got into the driver's seat and gingerly manoeuvred the prisoner transport, with its blue and yellow markings, between the statue of the Marquis of Londonderry on horseback and a big stone bench. Milburn watched her go. When he looked back to the doorway where he had huddled with Penfold, the New Zealander was nowhere to be seen. Tony trudged up the cobbled streets back to his car on Palace Green. He felt that he would be most useful if he got some sleep. Only the CSIs remained on scene, and he would only hamper their work if he stayed.

At the red traffic light on Claypath, a small white hatchback van turned right across the front of Milburn's police issue VW Golf. It caught his attention partly because it was flying around a 90-degree turn, but mostly because it was emblazoned with the blue and grey logo of Armstrong Aggregates. The driver was not visible – the streetlights reflected from the window glass revealing nothing from inside the cab of the vehicle.

Arriving home before midnight made Tony feel guilty. He'd left a number of his colleagues working with many hours ahead of them. Kicking off his shoes relieved the rubbing sore that had been caused by the lack of socks. He muttered to himself, 'I'll be up by six and be better for the kip. There's nothing to be done before the forensics initial report and those injured are fit to talk. Early doors will work well.'

Milburn took out his radio and called the constable who had gone to the University Hospital, instructing that she should keep the two burn victims, Armstrong and Chef White, there until he arrived in the morning. Of course, Armstrong was severely burned and would be in no danger of leaving the hospital, but Randall White was a different matter. The reply did not sound promising: one near death and likely never to be able to speak, and the head chef claiming he needed a lawyer because the police were all racists.

As Tony turned from the line of coat hooks, he was kissed. Kathy's lips were soft, and he felt her arms move around him and her hands press into his shoulder blades.

'How was it?' she asked, maintaining the embrace.

'Pretty grim. I need to get as much sleep as possible. There's at least one murder victim, likely to turn into two, and lots of witnesses to work through to see if we can get any kind of handle on it. The chief scientist of Armstrong Aggregates burned to death tonight.'

'My God. What a horrible way to go. At the castle?'

'Yeah. Lucky the whole place didn't go up.'

'Gosh, yes.' Kathy released the hug. 'Go on then, you get up there and get into bed. I won't be long, but I'll put together some food in a Tupperware for you to take in the morning.'

Tony smiled resignedly as he slowly climbed the blue-carpeted stairs. That kind of planning and foresight was something he would never get the hang of, but seemed to just come to Kathy without any effort.

Tony was already half asleep when his partner slipped into their bed. She cuddled up beside him, resting her head on his shoulder and her hand on his bare chest. Kathy felt warm, and her hand felt still and stable. She always had a calming effect on him, and, once she had swept her long hair away to keep it from tickling his face, Tony fell deeply asleep.

Eight

Sunday 29 January, 7.51 a.m.

'Let me out o' here!'

Detective Sergeant Milburn had entered the private hospital room occupied by Randall White and reignited the man's insistence that he should be discharged.

'I'm sorry, Mr White. The doctors wanted to make sure you were definitely OK. They often keep patients in overnight after such a traumatic event. I think they call it "for observation".' He glanced at the constable beside him for a confirmation, but the young woman did not understand his cues and shrugged. She had been sent over from Peterlee station to help out at the castle and Tony didn't know her. It was unsurprising they could not blag the argument successfully.

'Don't patronise me, officer. Institutional racism, this is.' Randall White, head chef at Desanti's restaurant, was tall, lissom and black. His hair was cut very short. He pointed at the detective. 'You wouldn't keep a white guy in here overnight claiming to be looking after him while stealing his clothes.' White lay on the bed, wearing hospital-issue grey sweatpants and T-shirt. He had a large bandage across his left temple and ear, and a couple of small plasters on the jawline. His right hand was also bandaged.

'I can assure you this has nothing to do with the colour of your skin,' Milburn said firmly. 'It is more to do with the fact that a man is dead and—'

'Two.'

'I'm sorry?'

The young woman standing beside Milburn leaned in a little and whispered, 'Armstrong died a few hours ago.'

The DS nodded and pursed his lips to signal his thinking through this new information.

38

'Thank you. I'm sorry about that.' Turning back to the patient, Tony went on, 'Well, as you can see, Mr White, we have a significant case to investigate, and you were right there at the scene. As a witness you will have a lot of useful information about what happened. Right now, I need to talk you through that information . . . and then you'll be free to go.'

'And what about my clothes?' The chef pointed again, and Tony noticed that the little finger on the man's left hand was unexpectedly short; it appeared to have been cut off at the first knuckle. An old injury, it was fully healed.

The young constable jumped in. 'I told you, Mr White, when we took your clothes away, it was because we needed to check them for forensic evidence. You will get them back. I just can't say when. Any idea on that, DS Milburn?'

'I'm sorry, no. As my colleague says, they are your own clothes so you will get them back, Mr White. However, I'm afraid that in some cases, that return could be more than a year from now. That's rare, though. More likely it'll be much sooner, by which I mean maybe within a month.' Milburn organised his phrasing to gloss over the longer possibility by finishing with the quicker option.

'A month?' White squeaked, but Milburn sensed that it was exaggerated for effect.

'Yes. Sorry. As the officer said, two men are dead, and we need to make sure we find out what happened. So, if you and I can talk through your recollection of last night, we can get you out of here quickly, once the doctors have given you the all clear.' He looked over at the constable who had been baby-sitting Randall White.

'They haven't done their rounds yet, sir,' she said. 'I'll go and see if I can find one to come and do the paperwork.'

'Thank you.' Milburn sounded like he had dismissed her but gave a hidden thumbs-up to signal that he understood she had kept the doctors away up to that point.

White leaned over to the bedside table and took out a vape pen. 'They let me keep this, but insisted I couldn't use it in the hospital.'

'What, and you think I'm going to let you?'

The man grinned then took a big hit, blowing out an opulent cloud of steam. 'You will if you want me to talk coherently.'

Milburn couldn't tell if this was a threat to hold back his information, or whether Randall was suggesting that he would be unable to converse without the nicotine. In the end he ignored the rule-breaking, closed the door, took out his phone and set it to record their conversation. Like many coppers, though, he also held his notebook, ready to note down the most salient points with their timing in the recording.

After confirming name, date of birth and address, Milburn took the man through the previous evening's events. As his job was at Desanti's, not at Castle College, Milburn first asked why White was the chef for the Burns Night Supper at all. Laying the vape pen on the blanket beside him, the patient rubbed the little finger stump with the bandaged fingers of his other hand.

'I'm keen to join the Friendship Society, that's why. Mr De Santi keeps nominating me, but somebody keeps blackballing me.'

'I beg your pardon?'

White pointed his half finger straight at the detective. 'Mr De Santi told me they have this stupid voting system for those who want to become members. The committee pass two velvet bags around the table. Each person secretly takes a ball out of the yellow bag, either a white ball or a black one. They put it into the blue bag and pass on both bags. At the end, if the blue bag only has white balls in it, then they let you join the Friendship Society.'

Milburn stared through a window at the trees, in the misty January-morning light. He felt as if his brain was fogged slightly, too.

'Sounds pretty weird, I agree.'

'But if there's even just one black ball in there, you're blocked from joining. Bloody great word that – "blackball" – for their racism that's keeping me out.'

'If you don't mind me asking, why do you want to join if you think they're racist?'

'Well, they're not really. There's just one of the committee keeps doing that. Mr De Santi has been a member for years and speaks very highly of the club. And he's a very dark Italian. I mean, he's not black, but he is a foreigner, and he and I have talked about the prejudices we've suffered, and he reckons the Friendship Society's not a bad place for that. If you're my colour, you get trouble all the time. There's nowhere free from it, so you learn to go for the places where it happens less. I trust Mr De Santi, so I'll give it a go – *if* they ever let me in. You see, officer, this club's my ticket to the big leagues.' White became more animated as he explained, 'There's chief executives of hotels in it, one guy who runs cruise liners, even a national catering firm that's headquartered in Consett. I love Desanti's, but I'm destined for much bigger things than a nice little restaurant.'

'OK, sorry, but I still don't see why you were the chef at the Burns Night, if you're not admitted to the Society yet.'

'Mr De Santi set that up. He said that making a really good showing of the Burns Supper would be sure to swing my membership. Hah! That went well, didn't it!'

Talking through the events chronologically, the DS learned that Randall had arranged a significant amount of the food preparation at Desanti's and they'd driven it all over early in the afternoon. The restaurant had closed for the evening and all the kitchen staff had worked on the Burns Supper. The Durham Castle events team had supplied some extra waiters, but everyone in the kitchen worked for the restaurant, under Randall White's management.

Milburn asked about the setting up of the room and the names of people who had access to the area of the haggis presentation table on the dais. As the fire had started from

41

Armstrong's first cut into the haggis, Tony wanted to find out about its provenance and who had access to it. He had to stifle a smile at his own notes headline: *Timeline of the Haggis*. Never imagined that would be something he'd ever write.

The chef was eager to explain. 'Melville Armstrong himself sourced the haggis. He wanted to have one that was genuinely Scottish, apparently.' He shrugged. 'I make a damn good haggis, but clearly a black laddie from Newcassel could never do a good enough job for Armstrong.' White spoke with a light Geordie accent, but here he really emphasised the local pronunciation of the city name.

'OK, so where did it come from? And when did you take charge of it?'

'I was never told what company he'd bought it from, but it was first delivered to the Aggregates company offices, and then one of their vans brought it over to Durham yesterday, at about three.'

'And once you had it, what then? Who looked after it?'

'It's not a pet!'

Milburn nodded meekly. Hiding a grin, he wrote *Not a Pet* in *The Timeline of the Haggis*.

'Mostly, it sat on one of the workbenches in the box they'd brought it in. I put it into the oven, and I took it out.' He explained, 'It's best if you poach it for a long time. I had it in there for over two and a half hours, but it was a big one.' He looked sharply at Milburn. 'That's just the ceremonial one, mind. For that many people, you need loads of big ones. But you microwave the others in portions.'

'So did they all come in that same delivery from Armstrong Aggregates?'

'Nah. He didn't understand the catering needs. He'd ordered one that could only serve about ten plates, so I sourced a whole bunch more for the event. Armstrong only supplied the ceremonial one.'

DS Milburn looked at the bare branches of a beech tree, waving at him through the hospital's second-floor window. 'And you were the only person who had access to it after it was delivered, right up until the fire?'

Randall White rubbed his finger stump again, before picking up the vape pen.

'Er, no. No. Any of my staff could have accessed it on the workbench. No . . . I didn't see anyone touch the box before cooking, but then after taking it out of the oven, it had to sit for a few minutes.' He tutted. 'I don't know who could have drowned it in that much whisky. I only put the standard glassful on it. I'd have expected that much to be burnt off by the time Hedley had said the poem. I reckon somebody must have added a whole load of extra whisky when it was sat on the side in the kitchen, before I picked it up.

'I can ask the staff who that was,' he went on, 'but I'm sure they did it by accident. We'd talked about the whole haggis deal in the days before, 'cos it's not a dish we ever do in Desanti's, so I guess somebody must have taken it on themselves to add the whisky I'd talked about, and then when I added the glassful, that was enough to splash them both when Mr Armstrong cut down on it. It might have been one of the sous chefs. I'll ask them all.'

'That's quite all right, we'll ask everyone what they saw and did. But I will need a list of them all, please.'

'Yeah, Mr De Santi will have all the names and addresses, but we didn't know the castle's own waiters. They supplied six extra bodies for that, so you'll need to ask them to find out about their details.'

'But they could have had access to the haggis after it came out of the oven?'

'Yeah, they were all coming and going all the time just before the event started, taking out bread rolls and iced water and so on.'

Milburn nodded. Through the security window in the door, he saw the police constable returning with an accompanying doctor so thanked White for his help. He wasn't sure what to make of the man. The chef clearly had well-worn grudges but had also seemed calm and helpful. The guilty suffer either from over-confidence or extreme nerves. This chef had shown neither, but a nagging at the back of Tony's skull went along the lines that White hadn't seemed especially shocked or upset by the events.

As the doctor spoke to the patient, the police constable beckoned Tony out of the room.

'I just talked to the nurse who was with Armstrong. He only spoke just as he died, but she took care to remember it.' The young officer opened up her notebook and flicked through, trying to find the page with the note.

'Was there no police officer with him?'

She shook her head. 'I'm the only one here. We didn't have enough people, so I was sent to look after both of the wounded men, and I had trouble enough convincing Mr White that he had to stay put. Armstrong wasn't going anywhere and was unconscious all the times I saw him.'

Tony supposed that he should be grateful that Peterlee police station had supplied her to help out at all. 'OK, what was it?'

She pointed at her neatly written notes: *Find her cleaner dead e . . .*

'That's it?'

'Yes. She said he died during the last word, but it definitely sounded like it started with an e.'

Milburn spoke the deathbed statement aloud. '"Find her cleaner dead e . . ." What the heck does that mean?'

Nine

Sunday, 8.55 a.m.

'*Gooood* morning.' Andrew Gerard welcomed Tony into his underground world effusively.

The mortuary and pathology labs were built into the basement of the University Hospital of North Durham. Milburn had picked himself up a takeaway coffee, accompanied naturally by milk and sugar, and set it down on a spotless, stainless-steel worktable. Melville Armstrong had quickly transferred from the intensive care unit down to the pathology table. He rested, naked, on the nearest cutting table, ready for post-mortem.

On the other polished metal cutting table, Joel Hedley lay with strips of his clothing missing. The removed pieces of dinner suit, shirt and shoes were in various evidence bags, lined up along a side worktable. Gerard had clearly been in early to prep the bodies, so he could start the important stuff immediately upon Tony's arrival. He was meticulously neat, and the entire workspace was ordered to a point Tony often considered obsessional. Through the open door into the tiny office at the end of the mortuary, Gerard's influence was further evident. The books and files on the shelves filling the entire back wall in there were positioned so their spines were exactly level, and the size increased from smallest on the left to tallest on the right, regardless of the topic of the item.

'Back again, Tony. Can't keep away from the place, eh?' Gerard's middle-aged lab technician, Jan, rolled herself in, with the big camera dangling from the side arm of the motorised wheelchair. It was unusually tall, specially adapted so that she was high enough to photograph the bodies from whatever angles Gerard requested.

'Bad penny, I guess. I see they haven't let *you* out yet.'

45

'They keep the lift broken so I can't escape.' She was joking – Milburn had come down in the lift. 'But don't stay too long: after a certain time, the only way out is in a box.'

Tony flourished his coffee and theatrically made for the exit. Jan waved goodbye and logged in to the computer beside the evidence bags of clothing.

The joke was done, and Tony returned to stand beside her. He waved along the line of plastic bags. 'I'll take these away at the end if you want to sign them over to me.' She nodded but didn't look up, clattering away at the keyboard as the barcode scanner bleeped repeatedly.

Gerard wheeled over a tray of surgical instruments, which ranged from fine hooks, needles and scalpels, right up in scale to the hefty bone saw.

'All ready?' He switched on a bank of very bright lights overhead.

Jan swivelled and raised the camera. Milburn squinted at the sudden brightness, but he leaned back against the worktable and raised his paper coffee cup to signal readiness.

The hospital radiology department had CT scanned both bodies during the small hours, and Gerard already had a good idea what he was looking for in order to confirm the cause of death for them. He showed the scans to Milburn and explained how the various lines and shadows could indicate the most likely biological problems that would lead to death.

Two video cameras at different angles recorded the whole process, and Milburn watched most of the proceedings on big screens on the wall opposite the worktables. It took a little over two hours for Gerard to be satisfied that he had confirmed everything they needed.

Milburn asked, 'So, you're saying they didn't both die because of the fire?'

'No, of course they did. What I'm saying is that how that led them to expire is different in each case. This one, provisionally identified as Joel Hedley, died directly from his burns. The

physical trauma, and the pain, simply caused his heart to stop.'
For the post-mortem recording, Gerard chose his words carefully,
to emphasise that they had yet to make a formal forensic
identification. The victims had been identified by those who knew
them, but the pathologist was a stickler for protocol.

To illustrate the intensity of the agony Hedley would have
suffered, Gerard pulled on a large piece of trouser leg which was
welded to the thigh, strongly enough that the whole corpse shifted
from the force. Milburn grimaced at the thought of the extreme
temperature being sufficient to melt clothing into his skin.

Gerard swivelled to point at the other victim. 'This one,
provisionally identified as Melville Armstrong may well have
suffered more, given that he lasted longer. His clothing burnt less
intensely, being natural fibres, wool mostly, but his lungs were
filled with combusting accelerant.' The pathologist held up a
piece of burnt lung tissue in a pair of long tweezers then put down
that blackened slice of flesh and picked up another that looked
slightly less charred, but which was oozing white liquid.

'God, what's that?'

'When you burn the lungs that way,' Andrew Gerard
instructed, 'the broken tissues leak liquid into the airspaces, and
you essentially drown. You can see the fluffy-looking and
damaged areas on the CT scan there.' He waved the white blobby
lump of Armstrong's lung then put it back in the metal dish. 'They
took him straight to the oxygen tent on arrival last night, but he
died despite the interventions.'

'What's that on the image there?' DS Milburn pointed at a
white square on the computer-screen picture of the lungs.

'Pacemaker.' The pathologist used a different pair of
tweezers to lift a shiny little box from a different metal dish. It
dripped blood. 'Armstrong had had two heart attacks and the
pacemaker had been in for nearly ten years now. Actually, let's
check the serial number and get an ID that way.' He rinsed off the
device under a sluicing showerhead and dangled it in front of a

visualiser for Jan to copy the number from the big screen and type it into a database she had just opened.

She shook her head. 'Ooh, no, I can't tell a hundred per cent for certain. Look, it's been partially melted too. Only a tiny bit remains of the serial number. He was so overweight I'm surprised he lasted as long as he did.'

'The pacemaker makes sense,' Gerard agreed. 'The GP notes here say he was prone to a lifestyle of drink and rich food, little or no exercise, and had been under instruction to moderate it all since this was installed.'

He dropped the pacemaker into another evidence bag, which Jan had held up. She then sealed, signed and entered it into the computer log. She copied the details over on to a paper form she was filling with the details of the various bags Milburn was to take away.

The detective dropped his coffee cup into a bin by the door and summarised: 'OK, so we know that both their deaths were caused by the fire.'

Andrew and Jan nodded in unison and the pathologist confirmed, 'Yes, all correct. There's not much else, medically at least, that I can feed into your investigation. We'll give you all this evidence we've collected, and I reckon you'll have all we've got.'

DS Milburn had brought an empty backpack to carry away the evidence bags, and he and Jan exchanged signatures on evidence logs. He was now officially in charge of them until he could get the materials to the forensics lab in Wetherby. It was an hour's driving each way, and Tony did not want to waste his time doing that. He hoped he would be able to convince a traffic officer to take charge of that transportation, as part of their patrolling the A1(M) motorway down to North Yorkshire.

Ten

Sunday, 11.48 a.m.

Penfold regularly took a drink in what he called 'Durham's best little coffee shop', The Daily Espresso. The low lighting and dark wood, gentle jazz and buzz of conversation made it ideal for losing oneself in a book or having a discreet conversation. Tony Milburn walked in and immediately went blind. The crisp winter sun outside meant that, on entering the dingy grotto, his eyes had to adapt to the light level. Penfold took the same table 90 per cent of the time though, so Tony was able to head in the right direction anyway.

'All the fun of the fair up at Gerard's Butchers?' the Kiwi asked genially.

Milburn shuddered. 'Grim. Not a good way to go at all.'

'Fire and brimstone in this life as well as the next?'

Tony ran his fingers through his hair and wondered if he could combine a visit up Gilesgate to interview Alan, his hairdresser, with a quick trim. Then he remembered the brittle singed hair on the corpses and pulled his hands away from his own scalp.

'One of them drowned in his own secretions. You know that sort of pus that oozes from a burn?'

'Hmm. Drowning is one of the big, haunting fears for a surfer, but I never picture it coming to me from being in a fire. That is counterintuitive. You sure he didn't drown from inhaling water from the sprinkler system? I can imagine he might have been gasping for breath if there was a lot of smoke.'

Milburn scowled. He hadn't thought about this possibility.

'I don't expect Gerard has made a mistake,' he said grumpily. 'He did say that drowning in your own lung ooze is actually quite common for fire victims. And the bits of lung he

49

showed me were all white and blobby from the burns.' A waitress had just leant over to deposit his flat white, and she recoiled quickly at their discussion. Tony half-heartedly called after her, 'Sorry!' but she had already retreated too far to hear him.

'They might have been able to save him,' Tony went on, 'if they'd got him into a ventilator quicker, but I daren't think how long that kind of injury would take to heal.'

'Probably quicker than we imagine. Lungs are soft-tissue organs with an efficient blood supply, and I bet the doctors would have given him a ton of oxygen too. He might well have recovered, and surprisingly fast.'

Milburn shrugged. 'Maybe. I guess we'll never know. He made a bizarre last breath statement too.'

'Ooh, really? Do tell. Confession?'

Tony showed Penfold the photo he had taken of the police officer's notebook. The Kiwi stared for a whole minute, holding Tony's hand in place so he couldn't remove the image from Penfold's sight. '"Find her cleaner dead e . . ."' He let go and looked up at the detective, his tanned face quizzical, his eyebrows raised.

'Yeah, no idea. "Find her cleaner dead easily." "Find her cleaner dead even though I'm not." Could be anything.'

'Maybe that e sound at the end wasn't going to be an e word. "Find her cleaner dead in the cupboard." Dead "een" the cupboard.'

Milburn gave a little laugh. 'Well, exactly. Could be anything. But whose cleaner? If he said "Find my cleaner . . ." I could have worked with that, but we don't even know who it is who has a cleaner that we need to find dead.'

'You wonder, too, if he might just have been delirious anyway.'

'Exactly. Without any more to go on, I doubt I'll be wasting much time on that line of inquiry.'

'OK, well, let me tell you what I've found out.'

'What do you mean, what you've found out? I told you last night that Hardwick won't go for having you "consult" on any more investigations. He's adamant.'

'Look, I'll just scour through public domain sources and drop you whatever information I find. I don't need access to anything confidential,' Penfold looked pointedly at his policeman friend, eyebrows raised again, 'like post-mortem details. If anything helpful turns up, you can have it.'

'I know, but that's almost worse. The DCI gets riled up exactly because you're just playing at it. If you wanted to be paid, he might find it more acceptable. Like I said, we do have specialist civvy investigators these days, so it's more about your approach than the work.'

'Well, I can't alter my process. I couldn't work if I had to go to meetings and fill in forms.' There was a pause as they both mused on investigation methodologies. 'Like I said, if I find anything noteworthy, I'll give you the details so you can run with it, but you'll have the information sources and so on if you need to back stuff up in court.'

Milburn shrugged in resignation. 'Thank you, Penfold.'

'There's some stuff about the Friendship Society of Durham, and a whole load of company history about Armstrong and Hedley's sand and gravel quarrying businesses. Actually, a lot more about that: the Friendship Society don't seem to put much online.'

'Did you say businesses, plural?'

Penfold gave a big, slow nod. 'Oh, yes. These two have been in business together almost since they left university. And it's rarely run smoothly. Hedley was a very good geologist, picking absolutely plum sites for them to move their diggings around Northumberland. I was at school close to one of them, actually, and I remember the old ArmAgg logo on the fencing at the end of the top playing-field.'

'ArmAgg? Their company is called Armstrong Aggregates. I saw one of the vans last night. The logo definitely includes the full words.'

'Well, this is what I'm getting at. Hedley first worked for another company, and then he and Armstrong opened their own sand and gravel pit on land adjacent to Armstrong's family farm. They were partners – they'd been to school together in Alnwick, and then both at uni in Edinburgh. One at Heriot-Watt, one at Edinburgh Uni, different courses, but at the same time. That was AH Aggregates. After the 2008 crash, that business came under intense financial pressure, so they split the company and took one part each. These were Hedley Aggregates and ArmAgg. As far as I can tell, this was a financial trick to restructure the businesses and stiff a bunch of their creditors. At a guess, I'd put Melville Armstrong as the author of that plan. From what I can work out, Hedley was only a geologist, and Armstrong was the businessman.'

'I'm sure this is all very interesting, but business history from years ago isn't going to solve their murders yesterday.'

Penfold stretched his neck to one side and then the other. 'Maybe not, but if I spare you the company accounts and just give you the summary, basically Armstrong was a mean sod who took Hedley's expertise and milked him. He manipulated a string of businesses that they owned and split and partnered in and split again, always working things to his own advantage.'

'And yet they were still in business together, so it can't have been that bad for him.'

'Um, yes and no. They have continued to work together since all the way back, when their first company started in 1987. However, Hedley is only an employee of Armstrong Aggregates. He's listed on their website as Chief Scientific Officer, but that's still only an employee, not a part-owner of the business. Despite Hedley being the brains behind it all, the magic touch with finding places where aggregates can be cheaply dug up, the profits of it all have been pretty unfairly divvied up. The Hedley family have a nice home in west Durham, but Armstrong owns a million-pound house on South Street and owns the whole business. Joel's wife will get none of the business because of his death.'

'OK, but they were both murdered. Who has a motive to get them both?'

Penfold raised his hands. 'Nope, sorry, that I haven't worked out yet. I confess, Mantoro did most of the work to research that corporate history, but he offered no suggestions for wronged employees or similar as culprits. I myself have been working on family and social networks, but I haven't got much beyond the basics. I need to do a fair bit more research to see if there's something in this Friendship Society. That seems to be the main other crossover where they're both involved.'

The stocky South American, Mantoro, always intrigued Tony. He was a ubiquitous presence in Penfold's life, but their relationship was unclear. Penfold's throwaway reference to him here was typical. No indication of whether they were working jointly, or if Mantoro was an assistant, paid or otherwise. Tony shook his head. *He's just an enigma. About the only thing I can be sure of is that he has a massive mane of hair.*

Milburn was flicking through his policeman's notebook. He'd jotted down two or three things that Penfold had mentioned and was now looking at the family information he had gleaned thus far.

'I've got to go and talk to the families,' he said, 'so text me if you come up with anything I should particularly ask them about.'

'Will do. By the way, you know Armstrong had a mistress and a twenty-year-old son by her?'

Eleven

Sunday, 12.52 p.m.

After the ten-minute walk from The Daily Espresso back to the city police station, Milburn walked in the front door, still musing over the names Penfold had supplied him with. *Jacqui and Declan Tait . . .*

'The DCI wants to see you, Tony. And he's *not* happy.' Sergeant Singh was working the front desk in the station and gave DS Milburn a knowing look, a jerk of his head indicating upstairs.

Milburn imagined Harry Hardwick, grey hair perfectly ordered, sitting behind his large desk and staring straight at him with the eye that didn't work. DCI Hardwick had lost sight in one eye years earlier, after being kicked in the head by one of his horses, and he made good use of its strange angle and apparent blank stare to unnerve those he needed a psychological advantage over. Tony remembered the killer who had ended up in tears in an interview in which the DCI had not uttered a single word.

It worked well in interrogations, but Tony knew it could be turned against him too, if the situation warranted it. He was not afraid – there was nothing supernatural going on – but the eye was genuinely unsettling.

After climbing the three flights of stairs to the top floor of Durham City police station, a building that stood proud and bold in the middle of New Elvet, Tony was quite out of breath. He could hear the DCI on the phone and paused in the corridor to settle his breathing. He felt his jacket pockets, and when he realised that he'd left his mobile phone in the glove box of the car, he leaned up on tiptoes to look out of the corridor window down to the car park at the back of the building. A couple of Community Support Officers walked across the tarmac in glaring winter sunshine, and Tony reckoned there was little danger of a break-in to his black Golf. The only suspicious people he'd ever seen in the car park had been bundled out of police cars to be booked into the custody suite via its back door.

'Bloody idiot.' The sound of Hardwick's voice was muted by the door, but he spoke in a sufficiently stentorian manner that his words were clear. The sound of his phone being banged down on the desk did not encourage Tony either. He drew in a breath, knocked on the door and walked in.

'Good morning, sir.' Tony usually called the DCI 'H', but he felt that this moment could do with a touch of subservience. He had no idea why the boss might be in a bad mood, but Andrew Singh would not have commented without reason.

'Morning? It's bloody lunchtime.' Hardwick left a pause, and Milburn thought better of sitting down without invitation. 'Where the hell have you been? I've been trying to set up a murder team, and I've got no information from you, the principal investigating officer at the scene last night. No response to phone messages, and going to voicemail when I call. You need to be absolutely on it – you can't just go AWOL when you fancy it. Even Barnes was here at nine a.m.' The dead eye scorched a line of sight to Milburn, and he squirmed inside.

'Sorry, sir, I left my phone in the car, but I've been investigating all sorts of things. Lots to report. Apologies, it's taken a while to get it all.'

Hardwick squeezed his mobile phone, so it showed the time and waved it at the detective sergeant. 'At this hour, you'd better have the whole case wrapped up.'

'Ha, I don't think . . .' Tony stopped, realising that Harry's hyperbole was not meant to be funny but admonishing. 'Sorry,' he repeated. 'I've got a long way with a lot of things, but essentially, it's all created more leads to chase down.'

He continued by talking through the initial outcomes of the post-mortems, Barnes contributing information from the night before, and the initial forensics, which didn't amount to much

55

more than showing the social media video and explaining how it showed additional accelerant than just the whisky.

The chief inspector was sceptical, especially at the mention of Penfold. 'Are you sure that shows anything other than just whisky sloshing about and on fire?'

'We'll need to get the full forensics report, but the smell of accelerant, rather than whisky, was pretty strong at the scene. Did you not notice that? Barnes said it struck him immediately at the first whoosh of flames.' Milburn gestured in front of his face in a way to imply Godolphin's oversized nose.

Hardwick raised his eyebrows, but his expression appeared to have softened overall.

'Yes, he mentioned that this morning too.'

Tony continued, 'I spent most of this morning at Dryburn, observing the two post-mortems and interviewing the survivor, the Head Chef guy.' He referred to the University Hospital of North Durham by its old name, but Harry was long enough in the tooth to understand without a pause.

'And what did all of that turn up? A haggis that's been tampered with – I assume the chef is in custody now?'

Tony knew that the DCI would be aware this was not the case. H's sarcastic tone had returned.

'As expected, the PMs showed that the two men died from being set on fire, essentially. However, my morning has produced three important points that we need to look into.'

Hardwick waved his hand forward to encourage Tony to proceed.

'Firstly, Randall White told me that the haggis was not cooked by him. Armstrong had sourced it himself, and it had been delivered to the castle kitchens from being stored up at the aggregates company site. It was only delivered a matter of hours before the event and was kept in a busy kitchen the whole time. At the moment, I feel that any tampering with it would have been much more easily done *before* it was delivered.'

'OK, what else?'

'Right, yes. The second thing I found out was that Armstrong had a long-term mistress, and an illegitimate son by her. We should definitely find them and see what the story is there. Names of . . .' Milburn made a show of looking in his notebook '. . . Jacqui and Declan Tait. I haven't had time to do anything with those names yet, so I've no idea who they are, where they live, nothing yet.'

'You said there were three things.'

'Yes. The third one may be no help at all, but here it is: with his dying breath, Armstrong said to a nurse, "Find her cleaner dead e . . ." and that was it, he died mid-word apparently.'

'Hmm. What do you make of that? Who is "her"?'

'Well, exactly. I'll see if the wife has a cleaner. Or the mistress, or maybe she *is* a cleaner. Like I say, no info on Ms Tait just yet.'

The DCI mused, 'Her cleaner . . . *her* cleaner . . . her *cleaner* . . . dead. Hmm. Find her cleaner dead. What about if that's an adjective? Find her cleaner than when she was alive.'

'But we've got no dead women.' After a moment, Milburn added, 'Actually, Hedley's wife made an accusation. I mean, she was drunk, but she said something like "That woman did it." The exact quote is somewhere in here.' He started flicking through his notebook.

'Hmm.' Hardwick was noncommittal and then put his thoughts aside. 'Right, we need to get this murder team properly organised. Like you say, there's many different inquiries to follow up. I sent some uniforms out to pick up on all the witness statements. Did you see Meredith's collation of all the names and addresses? Very thorough work. You should take a leaf out of her book, Tony. She's meticulous to a fault.'

Even with only one working eye, DCI Hardwick could see the tension building in his sergeant's body language and expression and changed tack immediately, saying, 'Anyway, call a meeting for two p.m. in the CID office, and we'll collate everything we have so far, make some hypotheses and allocate people to follow up on the top priorities.'

As Milburn walked back down the stairs to the open-plan CID office, he muttered to himself, 'That'll be me collating everything, you making some half-arsed hypothesis, me allocating the two investigators I've got, and me following up on all the priorities. With bloody Diane sticking her nose in, no doubt.' He telephoned down to Andrew Singh, saying, 'I don't know who the DCI has negotiated for you to let us use, but any bodies you're lending us need to be at the CID office for a two o'clock briefing, please, Studs. Oh, and could you ping a message to the CID WhatsApp group telling them of the meeting – I've left my phone in the car.'

The Sikh had earned his nickname after several of the Police Football Fun summer seven-a-side tournaments. A very measured and stable man in uniform, and both calm and skilful on the hockey pitch, Sergeant Singh metamorphosed into a berserker, once he put football boots on. No fewer than three career-ending tackles were notched up on his studs, and his colleagues would never let him live it down.

'The DCI already messaged the group. And I can't say that "negotiated" is a suitable word for it, but you've got Big Bob Smith and Diane Meredith.'

'I knew it. I bloody knew it! Can't you send Diane out somewhere different and give us somebody else?'

'She's seconded to CID, Tony, you know that. It's probably not even correct for me to be saying I'll "let you have her". My shift is just one short all the time anyway because of her secondment. I don't know why you don't want her, she's an excellent detective.'

Milburn hung up without saying goodbye.

An email of initial findings from the Crime Scene Investigation Team confirmed fingerprint findings on the fire extinguisher discarded by the waiter at the fire: they revealed an ex-soldier called Mohammed Jackson.

'Bugger! Momo.' Milburn realised that the man would already have been in custody for twelve hours and that he'd need to get an interview organised for straight after the murder team briefing.

Twelve

Sunday, 2 p.m.

DCI Hardwick charged into the CID office moments before the murder team briefing was due to start and immediately took charge. The place was set up appropriately as a major incident room, but the team was sparse. With the DCI taking the job of Senior Investigating Officer, Milburn was then the second most senior on the team. The SIO would rarely leave the office, collating and directing things from there. Milburn could see that he was going to end up being expected to cover a host of admin work like the Exhibits Officer's organisation of physical evidence, as well as leading the investigating team out in the field. That part of the job was what he loved. The admin side of things not so much.

'Right, everyone, let's get going. Clearly we're way below establishment staff levels on this, but needs must, so let's start by confirming roles. I'm SIO on what we've got for now as a double murder investigation, and I'll be Office Manager and Action Manager. Tony here is my deputy, and he'll also be doing Exhibits and the Analyst job. Basically, I want Tony to lead on assessing evidence and hypotheses, which he'll feed to me to allocate Actions.'

Milburn was surprised and inwardly pleased at this role. With the DCI in the station all the time, dealing with much of the admin, Tony felt he would be able to really work the case.

'Diane Meredith is acting up as a Detective Constable still, so she'll be in charge of organising house-to-house inquiries – and there's a lot of witnesses to be tapped up, so big job that. And on the back of that, I also want Diane to be HOLMES manager.'

The assignments were getting better and better for Tony. Being in charge of the HOLMES computer system was a laborious, boring job that kept you stuck in the office a lot. He could also imagine Meredith struggling to manage both house-to-house work and keeping HOLMES up to date, and any opportunity for her to fail was a positive for him. She was allocated three uniform constables to assist with interviewing all the witnesses, but in this case, house-to-house was not along one street, they would be scattered across the county. Durham is a big county too. Tony did not even notice his own hands rubbing together with glee at the prospect of Meredith coming a cropper with her allocated tasks.

The station's civilian administrator was appointed to all the really tedious tasks like reading every document that came in and indexing all the information gathered. Diane was very solid and conscientious with such assignments, and Milburn could see that Hardwick would not actually need to do much of the work of Office Manager. He reckoned this would be a good thing, as he needed the DCI to be available to focus on the investigation in order to enable whatever actions Milburn came up with as plans for chasing up leads.

He was torn, though, in that the more the boss was tied up with procedural work, the less he would be able to worry about Penfold assisting on some elements. They had reached an uneasy truce about Penfold's free consulting work. The surfer could not be controlled, or even directed, but his contributions were always insightful, often to the point of breaking a case open.

The immediate outcome of the briefing was that Tony could go straight down to interview Mohammed Jackson about his sudden departure from the scene of the fire and the story about him suddenly coming into money. Leaving Meredith trying to allocate groups of dinner guests and staff that her house-to-house trio should go off and talk with, he made for the custody suite and got there just as the sergeants were changing shift. As he arrived, the two were stood behind the check-in counter, staring at the CCTV monitor. Milburn stepped around to join them and saw the screen fixed on one cell. The Asian man he had chased across the

61

market square earlier sat on the bed, feet squarely on the floor. He was straight-backed, legs perfectly parallel and bent exactly at a right angle at the knees: a formal pose. In the air above his lap, Mohammed Jackson waved his hands in a complex series of twists and turns. The gestures segued smoothly, consisting of a repeating set of sharp motions, with clearly defined start and end points. It reminded Milburn of tai chi but faster and more staccato.

The custody sergeants were mesmerised, silent. Tony pulled out his phone and recorded two minutes of video of the TV screen before interrupting them, asking, 'Is he OK?'

Without turning away from the screen, Baz Bainbridge replied, 'Been doing this for hours. He's mouthing some sort of incantation along with it – some sort of sorcery or voodoo shit, you think?'

DS Milburn scowled. 'Better hope not, or you'll be first to be cursed.'

Sergeant Andrew Singh scratched his turban with the corner of his clipboard, making no comment.

The detective went on, 'Has he eaten anything? He's been here sixteen hours now.'

'Yeah, no, he's fine. Really polite. Stops this business when you go to see him, calls you sir, and apologises all the time.'

Milburn turned to Bainbridge. 'Apologises? Not a confession, is it?'

Baz was a longtime boxer, with a permanently bent nose to show for it. He broke into a big grin. 'Nah, man. Apologises for troubling us, for us having to keep checking on him. Apologises for looking clarty, says he was in a fire.'

'Right, what about the other one? What was his name?' Tony thought maybe he should get some information from Momo's combatant in order to inform his interview plan for Jackson.

'Sniveller?' Bainbridge inhaled sharply through his nose to mimic the other suspect. 'He's in here often enough, he knows the drill. Had a kip, enjoyed breakfast, and he's now back lying down on the scratcher. Gettin' a bit antsy, though. Been asking when he can gan.'

'Is he awake now?' Milburn understood that there was little for prisoners to do other than lie on their bed.

The outgoing custody sergeant leaned forward and clicked the computer keyboard to change the camera view to showing all the cell cameras in a tile pattern on the screen. He pointed at one of the squares where the skinny man from the night before lay on a blue crash-mat style mattress.

'Right, I'll talk to him first and see if I can get him out of your hair,' Milburn decided. 'Is there an interview room free?'

Bainbridge nodded. 'I'll get 'im out. Interview One in five minutes, OK, Tone?'

Milburn just nodded, now mesmerised himself by Momo Jackson's hand movements, in the top left quarter of the screen. He sent the video of the fast tai chi with silent chanting to Penfold and clicked the CCTV viewer to show Interview One.

Sergeant Bainbridge escorted a very skinny, dirty man in and told him to sit down and wait. In the bright light of the small room, the camera showed up that he clearly had not washed himself or his clothes in a long time.

Tony made a few brief notes about the information he wanted to ascertain. Based on Bainbridge's assessment, he did not expect any criminal charges to come out of the altercation in the square the night before. The aim of this interview was more to prepare himself for interviewing Momo, with a view to finding out what he knew about the fire at the castle. A man running from the scene of the crime as two men were burnt alive seemed as good a place to start as any, in finding out who was responsible for their deaths.

Thirteen

Sunday, 5.02 p.m.

Penfold's earlier haiku text message had been taken by Milburn to be a cryptic invitation to visit the Kiwi's home. DS Milburn now parked the black car in the dark by Seaton Carew's promenade strip across from the Norton Hotel. Penfold's large, rambling house sat on one corner of a little green square back from the seaside hotel. Very few other cars took up spaces on the beachfront road in the early evening on a Sunday in winter.

As Tony walked up the deserted Promenade Square, the wind vied with the waves for which could be the noisiest. The waves crashed continuously on the sand, dark grey in the weak light from the streetlamps on the front. The cold January wind chased around him, louder when it gusted. Despite Penfold only serving black coffee, Milburn was already looking forward to its warmth.

As usual, he knocked on the big oak front door but entered without waiting for Penfold. The New Zealander refused to believe that he needed to tend to the door and told Tony he must simply walk in. A long radiator in the front hallway was rattling, and a full-length wetsuit on top of it steamed wisps that put Tony even more in mind of the coffee to come.

'Hey man, good to see ya.' The drawl sounded like it should have been coming from a Texan. In the dim threshold of the kitchen doorway, Tony could make out the figure of Mantoro silhouetted against the light in the room behind. His giant hair made it look like he had a lion's head. Milburn shook hands with the short South American and was handed a saucer of cashew nuts to snack on. They both went into the kitchen and Penfold stood up from the farmhouse-style dining table to pour a cup of coffee from the filter jug.

Mantoro made small talk. 'How's that gal of yours?'

Milburn smiled at the thought of Kathy and her lovely blonde hair and bright smile. 'She's good, thanks. Still smarting at the idea that I'm gonna have to work with Diane Meredith on this double murder that happened yesterday.'

'I bet. That bitch sure sounds *craaaazy*.' Mantoro stuffed a handful of cashews in his mouth and could not say anything more on the matter.

Tony gave a slight shrug of his shoulders. He didn't feel that he knew Mantoro well enough to have this conversation about his ex-stalker. This made a question occur to him, and he wondered in his mind, When does a stalker become an ex-stalker? How long would it be before you no longer had to watch everything you say, and think carefully about being in the same room with them?

His musings were interrupted by Penfold, and Milburn refocused on the kitchen surroundings. 'Got a few interesting bits and pieces for you,' the Kiwi told him.

'Yes, your text message suggested you had something for me to see here. I really need to get on to visit the two widows, though, so can we make it quick?'

Penfold waved for Tony to follow him, and they went along the hallway and around into the office workspace. Books and papers littered all the surfaces like a hoarder's paradise. As they walked in, Penfold called out, 'Trident, are you there?'

The furthest computer screen responded, 'As ever, big bro.' There was a manga comic-style image of a young woman on the screen, which was animated as it spoke. The mouth moved exactly as Penfold's sister said something at her end. 'Has Milburn arrived then?'

Tony stepped to one side of Penfold to wave at the camera mounted in the corner of the office above Trident's terminal. The manga girl on screen smiled at him. It was unnerving, but Penfold's sister always attended video calls as an avatar. Keeping her identity secret was vitally important to the queen of hackers.

He had seen her once in Penfold's car, and the doodle representing her on screen was not a close likeness.

Penfold launched himself down into a wheeled office chair which slid across in front of her, and he started tapping at a touchpad beside the keyboard.

'You got all your ducks in a row, Trident,' he asked, 'in a position to explain to Milburn? He's in a bit of a hurry, so remember brevity is next to godliness.'

'Yes, Ms MacAllister.'

In unison, Penfold and his sister's icon screeched, *'Penfold, stop it!'* They both sniggered and then Penfold turned to Milburn, who was looking nonplussed.

'Sorry, but old schoolteachers never die: they live on in parody forever. Are you ready?'

'For what?'

Tony nearly jumped out of his skin as Mantoro's voice spoke loudly behind him.

'Follow the money, man. Always follow the money.'

Tony whipped round but only caught the trailing edge of the huge hairdo, as Mantoro disappeared off down the hall again.

'Jesus!' Milburn exclaimed. 'Will you lot just tell me what you've found out, so I can get out of this madhouse.'

Penfold and Trident sniggered again, and she started to explain. They had indeed been following the money and discovered a variety of interesting things about the financial affairs of the Durham Castle fire victims. Trident controlled Penfold's computer screen, to show up various documents and emails. Tony wrote key points into his notebook, with the occasional asterisk for an urgent action to follow up the information.

He quickly realised that they were discussing the sort of financial records that were unobtainable without a court order, or a seriously good hacker. Trident was well known to him as the latter, but this would taint all the evidence for any subsequent court case. As was quite common with Penfold's assistance in police matters, Milburn would have to use this information to guide his inquiries so that he could turn up legitimate evidence as part of the correct police process. Sometimes this would stymie him significantly, but more often it meant that dead ends were ignored. Penfold and his sister, and also to an extent Mantoro, were sufficiently capable that they always worked out who was guilty and what they had done; the only difficulty, and this was sometimes insurmountable, was to navigate a route to nailing the guilty parties with useable evidence.

'I won't ask how you came to know these private matters about these people, but let me just confirm that I have correctly understood what you're telling me.' Tony scanned down his bullet point list, which encompassed both the dead men, their wives and businesses, a mistress and an illegitimate son. 'Blimey, nothing uncomplicated in any of these.'

Penfold nodded his blond head with a grin. 'Indeed. It's not really a surprise that somebody committed murder. It's more just a question of who. At the moment, I'm working on the how – I think that should be relatively easy to determine. If we're lucky, that'll point us to the who a bit quicker.'

'Right,' Tony said, 'and thank you for all your help. Now there's enough in this that I could do with some sort of push in one direction or the other. Looking at this lot, who do you reckon would be the highest priority for investigation? I haven't got time or the manpower to go off in all these directions at once.'

Penfold wheeled his office chair next to Tony and craned his neck over to peruse the list. 'Hedley doesn't appear to have any financial issues, or enemies. He's not received any strange emails. Niche geologist marathon runner seems like an unlikely victim.'

'Agreed.' Trident's disembodied voice echoed from the bare grey walls.

Penfold continued, 'Indeed, Armstrong seems far more likely the intended target. He was a pretty ugly character. Not dangerous, but selfish and brutish, conniving and manipulative.'

At that point, Milburn glanced at the time on his phone and saw that he had eighteen messages to deal with. 'Right, well, he was the victim, so can we stop eliminating and start implicating, please. I need to get back to Durham and make some headway. H will be doing his nut at my absence. There's only so long I can claim witness inquiries might take, unless they throw up something juicy.'

'Yes, of course.' Penfold put his finger onto the notebook page, near the bottom of Milburn's list. 'This one.'

'Declan Tait?'

Trident chimed in again. 'Agreed.'

'Their emails tell a scary, patriarchal story,' Penfold clarified. 'Armstrong held Jacqui Tait as his mistress for more than twenty years. In all that time, he gave her small amounts of money regularly. Enough so that she could get by, but he never arranged anywhere for her to live, and pressured her not to work so she could be available to him as and when he liked. She and Declan lived in a council house in Brandon ever since she was made to leave her job as a secretary at the aggregates business – that was the first one, AH Aggregates, which the men owned jointly.'

Tony inhaled volubly. 'Again, we're talking about other things, and not why Declan might murder his father.'

'Context, Milburn, context. Declan Tait is a very angry young man. He's quite the boxer and has been cautioned for assault before. His social media would suggest a bubbling resentment for Armstrong. Actually, resentment is not a strong enough word. He hated his father, and it would appear that the feeling was mutual. Tait spouts on about how he and his mother had been held down in the gutter, which is perhaps a little harsh for a commentary on Brandon as a place, but in his mind, Jacqui's career was squashed at its beginning, and they could have had a much better life without Armstrong. He even says once that the world would a better place if Melville Armstrong were not in it.'

'Hmm. He does sound aggrieved, but enough to commit murder?'

From the computer, Trident's voice reverberated. 'No will.'

'What?' Tony never found Trident's minimalist statements easy to follow.

Penfold responded on her behalf, 'Do not ask how, but Trident has strong information that Melville Armstrong died intestate. The son could have a financial motive in addition to his hatred of the man.'

'OK, I agree – there's good motive,' nodded Milburn. 'Have we got means and opportunity? Could Declan have spiked the haggis? What's more, did he have the technical know-how for the accelerant, as well as a chance to get his hands on the haggis in the first place, to tamper with it?'

The big Kiwi shrugged. 'Well, the accelerant's just methanol, which is widely available, and you don't need to be a genius to know that it'll set fire to the victims.'

'Whoa, hang on – methanol?' Tony said, putting up a hand to slow him. 'We've not had anything back from the forensics team yet about the identity of the accelerant.'

'Methanol burns exactly like in the video, with virtually no visible flame. Watch the video again. The only time the flames are visible is when something else catches light, like the tapestry and the tablecloth. And I found some on the shard of glass we took from your shoe.'

'Alcohol on a piece of wine glass? Duh!'

'Not any alcohol, this is industrial methanol – one hundred per cent methanol. That piece is a funny shape too, rounder than a wine glass.'

'All right, but what about access to the haggis?'

'No, I haven't worked that out. But here's an interesting one. Declan struggles to hold down a job. He's too mercurial for most employers. How it came about is not quite clear but about three months ago, he got a job as a delivery driver at . . . would you believe Armstrong Aggregates?'

There was a pensive silence.

After some further thought, Tony said, 'Hmm, when I was there last night, Genevieve Hedley bent my ear, saying, "It was that woman, she did it." Do you think maybe Jacqui herself might be responsible rather than the son? Presumably his feelings would have developed from what his mother said about Melville.'

Penfold squished up his tanned face in a thoughtful expression before replying, 'I don't know, but I'd say not. Jacqui Tait seems to just get on with things. She's not expressed any animosity toward Armstrong, and she'd maintained their relationship for twenty years as well. He hasn't forced or caged her into it, he just hasn't been very nice to her. I mean, quite a bit of that is speculation – her social media feeds don't say much about him at all. In fact she never names him, but often says things like "Went out for a lovely dinner with the other half". She always calls him that, as if she thinks they're in a monogamous relationship, but of course he spends most of his nights at the Armstrong family home.'

'How do you know that?'

Trident interjected, 'Satnav. His car told me where he's been all the time for the last six months. Occasionally he spends a night away, sometimes for work, sometimes some social do, sometimes at his flat on the Quayside in Newcastle, but mostly it's at home in Durham.'

'I was just thinking that maybe Elspeth Armstrong could be worth looking into, as the cuckquean wife . . .' Tony put in.

'Mrs Armstrong?' Penfold looked doubtful. 'I don't know. She wasn't her husband's biggest fan, but her life seems to be all about being the wife of a big business leader. She's President of the Bridge Club, Secretary of the Friendship Society, and big in Rotary and WI as well.' He mused, 'Probably not your classic chemical fire-starter either. Jacqui Tait, though, may suddenly have some financial issues. As I said earlier, Armstrong's been making regular payments to her – every month since Declan was born. Not a huge amount, but it seems those payments stopped three months ago. That could be something worth following up.'

Milburn nodded. 'Yep, first stop Declan Tait, and I'll see about catching his mother at the same time.' He closed up his notebook, pocketed it, and waved goodbye to the screen. 'Thanks, Trident.' Then he turned and headed briskly along the hallway to the front door.

As Penfold went to close the door against the wind that had blown a thick sea fret onto Promenade Square, he said one last thing.

'Oh, Milburn. That video you sent of Jackson in his cell waving his arms around?'

'Yeah, what is it?'

'He's repeatedly stripping, cleaning and assembling an imaginary rifle. A good soldier going through his daily routine. I imagine it's a sort of psychological stabilising ritual that keeps your consciousness running in a straight line. He's probably not even aware that he's doing it.'

'Hmm, interesting. Mohammed Jackson's his full name. Said he got the waiter's job through Colonel Griffiths: the Light Infantry boss was at the Burns Night Supper. Reckons the good colonel strives hard to get ex-army blokes work, and a lot of that comes through the Friendship Society.'

'Makes sense. It's kind of what the Society is set up for. You think Jackson's involved?'

'I really didn't get that vibe,' Milburn told him. 'He is trained in a whole host of urban combat activities, including Molotov cocktails-type stuff. He actually volunteered that in interview, which leads me to suspect him even less.' Raising a hand in farewell, Milburn walked out of the front door.

As Penfold closed the door behind him, Milburn pulled his coat tight against the wind and stole along the path to his car as fast as he could.

Fourteen

Sunday, 6.28 p.m.

Milburn sat in his small office just off the main, open-plan CID office. If Durham City police station had enough detectives, that central area would have been a hive of plainclothes officers. A couple were out interviewing witnesses still, and through the window in his door, Tony Milburn could see only two people. The civilian administrator was collating documents and filing them in various ring-binders. Acting Detective Constable Meredith was tapping away at her keyboard, feeding information into the HOLMES computer system as fast as she could. Milburn had to admit to himself that she was very adept at doing that. Hardwick had chosen wisely when assigning her the role.

Even as he thought this, Diane clicked the mouse briefly and then stood up. Working in CID, she was out of uniform and wearing a knee-length red skirt and a white blouse, along with nude tights and smart shoes the same colour as her skirt. As he spotted her striding towards his office, Tony quickly retreated behind his desk and touched his smartphone to start recording the conversation. He had taken to doing so every time they were alone, and he made sure that she knew he was doing it.

Diane entered his office and stood there for a moment before taking a step towards him, caressing the shiny hair of her perfect bob. As her hand reached her neck, she slid it down, dragging against the shirt between her breasts and then around her hip to come to rest on her left buttock, thrusting her chest forward.

'HOLMES is all up to date,' she said, before adding, 'unless you've got anything else you want to *stick in*?' She pulled at the sides of her skirt to raise the hem a few inches and gave a lascivious lick of her lips.

'I've got some leads that need to be followed up, but nothing that is ready to go into the system yet.' Tony did not react but spoke evenly. The information he had received at Penfold's Hartlepool home needed to be discovered by the police in the course of their inquiries before it would be legitimate enough to be recorded on the computer.

'Tony, why are you taking your shirt off? I really don't think it's appropriate for you to get changed in front of me.'

Milburn had not moved anything except his mouth since she entered. She was simply messing up his recording, throwing mud, so that any evidentiary purpose he might want to put it to would be tainted. He stood up and their eyes locked.

'Shut up, Meredith.'

'No, I won't shut up. It's this kind of casual sexualising of the workplace that gets people in trouble. If I don't do anything to call it out, people will say I was happy about it when I get molested by my colleagues. Well, I'm not standing for it. I'm telling you clearly *to put your shirt back on*!' She flicked her head slightly so that the bob haircut whirled left and then swung back forwards again. She grinned.

Tony's stomach was knotted tightly, but he was determined not to lose his nerve and to stand up to her. He picked up a sheet of paper from the desk; on it was written several names and points of 'clarification' that he wanted from follow-up interviews. Those being questioned had all given statements, but further questions, designed to tease out Penfold's information, were needed on the record. He turned the paper round and held it out for her to take.

For the brief period that Milburn and Meredith had been lovers, he had often told her how beautiful the curves of her neck were. To receive the paper, she bent forward from the hips and tilted her head to one side to reveal the creamy skin he had loved to touch. He was glad she could not spot the tremor in his legs, concealed behind the desk.

'Here are a few things I want you to go and check with these witnesses,' he went on coolly. 'If my hunches are correct, we'll

73

be able to eliminate some of them as suspects. That should then also confirm a couple of good hypotheses to use as the focus of our investigations from tomorrow morning. Can you get round all three of these this evening?'

She looked at the names and questions, the paper in her right hand, while her left hand casually cupped her neck. It was a thoughtful pose he had seen many times before. He wondered if she had stopped the coy nonsense and was genuinely interested in the new questions, or if it was some sort of double bluff. One thing was certain – Diane loved the job and was very good at it. She was so good at the job, in fact, that he and Kathy had never been able to prove any of her stalking. He could easily imagine new leads distracting her from her shenanigans, but Tony was equally wary of everything she did.

'The Hedley women and Mrs Armstrong I can see as needing more interrogation,' Diane replied now, 'but who are Jacqui and Declan Tait? I don't remember seeing their names on the guest list.'

'Jacqui is Melville Armstrong's mistress, and Declan is his son by her.'

Meredith's face lit up. 'Oooh.' Milburn assumed that the disruption and trouble that a love triangle with an illegitimate child could cause would be right up her street. She folded the paper into quarters and swapped it for one identically folded that had a corner sticking out of her skirt pocket.

She handed her paper over to Tony, and he asked, 'What's this?'

'Well, if you're going to give me these interviews to go and do, I've got one for you to follow up. The DCI says we need to get over to the castle and find out about the sword that's apparently gone missing from the function room where the fire was. He specifically said it should be you as you're Exhibits Officer and ran the crime scene last night. I got the impression he thought you'd let somebody run off with it whilst you were standing there like a tit in a trance.'

74

'What the fu—' Tony remembered the recording and stopped himself, although he'd forgotten that he couldn't use it. 'What on earth are you talking about?'

'Some big antique sword from the wall of the castle. You know they've got loads of suits of armour and stuff. Well, a sword got nicked and you need to go and sort it out with the university and the Master of the college.'

'Right.' Tony exhaled heavily. 'Have you got the list of all the dinner guests, and all the staff as well?'

Diane stood up, swivelled neatly on the spot and sashayed to the door, smiling sweetly over her shoulder.

'I'll print a spare copy, just for you, Big Boy,' she purred.

The door swung closed behind her and Tony was left wondering what exactly had just happened. He felt as if he was trying to investigate a double murder whilst swimming through some psychedelic dream, both helped and hindered by a beautiful, poisonous madwoman.

The silence in the room was suddenly broken by a clicking and whirring as the printer on the table in the corner revved itself into life and started spitting out sheets of A4 listing the Burns Night Supper witnesses. He caught them as the fourth page tried to shove all its predecessors off the plastic tray and onto the floor.

Once reshuffled into order, he scanned through the list of names. They included addresses and a brief summary of their interactions with the police and the essence of any information they had provided. Most told the same story about the fire itself, with little more of interest. A few had more details, if they knew the victims or were related to them. He noted that Genevieve Hedley had also mentioned Jacqui Tait in her interview with Diane Meredith. Moreover, she had clearly explained that the woman was Armstrong's lover and had told of their son Declan's existence as well.

Tony squinted through the small glass window in the door, watching Meredith's every move as she buttoned up her coat to leave. She didn't look across to him. She had sounded both

75

surprised and excited to hear about the mistress, but it seemed from this that she had already known the story. *What are you up to, Diane?*

Deep into winter, the night shrouded solidly, chilling to the bone. Tony checked his watch: a quarter past seven. Emerging from the police station, he headed for Kingsgate Bridge, the high pedestrian walkway onto Durham City's peninsula. The far end of the concrete bridge incongruously connected to a medieval cobbled lane between two of the university's fabled colleges. The streetlamp glow that lit his route gave the night a ghostly feel, and Tony shivered. He told himself that it was just because the heat of the CID office had fooled him into leaving without a coat. The darkness, barely held back by the weak lighting on the lane, was almost more penetrating than the cold. Sometimes this walk could be magical. That night, it felt deathly.

The top of Bow Lane spilt out onto the narrow street called South Bailey, and noisy groups of students meandered past in both directions. Their presence gave reassurance; he was no longer alone in the wicked dark. Some were on their way to the evening meal in their college dining hall, while others were crossing the road back to their accommodation block after eating the institutional catering. Durham University students tended to be wealthy. These ex-public school types lived full board in their colleges. *Lazy buggers.*

The east end of the cathedral loomed up in front of Milburn, and he gazed up at the rose window dominating the huge wall. In the half-light, it looked like a massive stone and glass pizza slapped on the end of the building. That reminded Tony that he had not eaten since Kathy's Tupperware of breakfast on the way to the hospital that morning; no wonder everything was reminding him of food and the student meal-goers were winding him up.

He walked up Dun Cow Lane, another cobbled alley beside the lumbering cathedral. Crossing the frozen lawn of Palace Green took the detective sergeant to the lodge in the castle gateway. The bearded porter telephoned for the Master of University College, as Castle was formally known, and Tony wandered across the keep to visit the crime scene again.

On the ground floor, students were eating their evening meal in the grand hall where Meredith had taken witness names and addresses, laughing loudly with all the exuberance of those anticipating brilliant futures. Milburn flashed his warrant card at the entrance to the kitchens and asked if they could offer a hungry bobby a sandwich. He came away with two roast beef rolls. On biting into the first one, he had gravy running out and down his little finger. Nothing was wasted – he sucked the finger clean.

As the detective arrived at the threshold to the Fellows' Meeting Room, the uniformed constable on watch at the entrance door nodded to him. Tony made the man's evening by handing over the second beef roll, and the officer confirmed that the forensics team had finally left, a good ten hours earlier. As they had worked through the night, Tony wasn't surprised that he had not yet received their initial report. He looked at the time on his phone and decided it was too late to call the Forensics Scene Manager.

Walking through the large room, it looked much the same as when he had left the night before. The CSIs had taken a few things away – he particularly noted the absence of the fire extinguisher by the rear exit door – but mostly everything was as he remembered. Tony then went and looked closely at the small stage area around the haggis's ceremonial table. He squatted down and pushed a few small pieces of glass a few inches along the floor, but it was impossible to tell if there was anything significant about them. After all, a broken wine glass is just that – a broken wine glass. Unless you were Penfold, in which case it'd probably tell you the migration patterns of ancient nomads in Iraq, he thought to himself and stared across the room from his squatting position.

The quiet was occasionally broken by laughter floating up the old wooden staircase from the hall below, and Milburn pictured the glamorously dressed diners from the night before. He imagined them looking towards him and remembered the video of the blaze where he now crouched. The assembled group must have looked universally horrified and stunned, especially given that the victims didn't really appear to be on fire. They batted themselves as if they were, but the damage must all have been done in the instant of the first fireball.

Tony shook his head to try and dispel the images. It was a horrible way to die, and he felt a deep-seated need to solve this case. A person willing to kill in such a callous way needed to be taken off the streets.

He stood up again, knees complaining after the exertions of his Saturday-afternoon football matches for the police team. He normally only played for the Sunday Morning Idlers, as they liked to be known, but the end of January always held an inter-nick tournament against other police stations in the area. That had meant three, albeit shortened, games in a row the day before. Milburn squinted slightly at the aching joints and hoped that when he caught the killer they would not run away. Catching Momo had been easy, but somebody willing to plan a murder like this would be more serious about making a run for it. At that moment, he realised that he had already discounted Mohammed Jackson as a suspect.

Out loud, Tony told himself, 'Not so fast,' and then mimicked Penfold's slight Kiwi accent: 'Follow the evidence, Milburn. Wherever that takes us is the way to go. And right now, we have nothing confirmed. Double blind confirmation, remember?' The final phrase was uttered with the sort of patronising tone that always annoyed him.

Somewhat louder, Tony uttered, 'Well, screw you, Penfold. I don't think he did it, whether there's evidence for my gut feeling or not.' He then glanced towards the doorway to check whether his outburst had attracted the attention of his colleague, the constable on watch, but there was no sign of him. No doubt he was busy polishing off the beef roll.

Feeling somewhat guilty about following his gut instincts, Milburn looked around to see if he could spot any useful evidence to point him along a suitable investigative path. Carefully, he stepped over to the charred wall-hanging. It had been a huge piece of red velvet, with gold tasselled edging. Much of it had fallen away as ashes, and the burnt edge was black. Frowning, Milburn compared it to the cotton tablecloth which was barely burnt at all. It had smouldered and then quickly been doused by the sprinklers.

Every table had had a glass candleholder, but the one from the table on the dais was broken on the floor. He picked a piece up to examine it closely and wondered how it might compare to the fragment they had found in the sole of his shoe. The candleholder was a different shape to the wine glass, so maybe that accounted for Penfold thinking the glass was somehow different. Tony photographed it and sent the picture to Penfold.

'Sir.' The constable stood at the threshold accompanied by a woman in a business suit. 'This is Mrs Landrey, from the Bursar's office.' She and Tony strode towards each other.

'Detective Sergeant Milburn, good evening. I understand you're inquiring about something that has gone missing?' the woman said briskly.

He was relieved not to have to deal with the college Master. Landrey appeared straightforward and to the point. He needed efficiency from her so he could file the sword thing away and get on hunting for a fire-starter. Godolphin Barnes had been office-bound or just plain absent so much over the years that Milburn had mostly learnt the ropes directly from DCI Hardwick, and when dealing with people associated with a case, he followed his precept to the letter: 'Always be vague, even when you know some information already. The gaps will tell you as much as the facts.'

Tony held out his hand and the woman smiled pleasantly and shook it with gusto.

'I'm seconded to the Bursary here,' she explained, 'but I actually work for the World Heritage Site. Essentially, my role would be as curator of the castle. It's all complicated by the fact that this is a working college in the university, and then there's UNESCO's oversight and the triple ownership of Durham's peninsula, but basically, I manage aspects of the castle as if it were a museum.'

'Nice to meet you.' But what about the missing item? He wished she'd get on with it.

'Your officers have kindly allowed us to assess the fire damage, working around your crime scene as best we could. I hope we didn't disturb anything – apparently the forensic team had finished before we were allowed in.'

Milburn could play nice when he needed to. Hardwick had also taught him diplomacy; the police had to interact appropriately with all levels of society.

'Not a problem at all,' he said, then joked, 'The forensic team love to say: "If the CSIs have left the building, then so has Elvis".' He became serious. 'Please tell me what the problem is. Do we have a separate crime, or do you think something else happened during the fire?'

'There has very definitely been a theft.'

'Why do you say that?'

The wall opposite the dais area had small leaded windows looking out onto the courtyard. She pointed to the corner near the entrance door.

'You see where we have a sword hanging between each of the windows? Well, over there – that empty space between the last window and the door – was where another sword hung. Sometime before the dinner was the last time the college porters were in here. They'll always notice any slight change in the decorations or furniture because they often have to search out some item that drunken students have moved. This is not normally a student area, and the tours come through this room, so we use it as a place to display some of the more important historical pieces. So, we must assume the sword was still in its place before the Burns Night Supper.'

Milburn nodded and made a show of writing notes in his book. He made eye contact again to urge Mrs Landrey to continue.

'The missing sword is not the finest piece, but it is very old. It would be worth somewhere in the region of thirty thousand pounds.'

Hardwick's gruff tones went through Milburn's mind again, memories of some of his earliest interviews in CID, watching and listening to the older detective. 'Always play Devil's Advocate in as simple-minded a way as you can get away with. If people think you're stupid, they'll elaborate much more.'

'Hmm. I'm guessing that it was metal, and if it was hanging on that wall away from the flames, we don't think it was consumed by fire?'

'That sword, the battle sword of Thomas Malory, has survived two fires before,' she said, smiling. 'Once during the Wars of the Roses when Dunstanburgh Castle in Alnwick fell, and a second time during a probably more intense fire in a storeroom annexe here about a hundred years ago. As you say, it is all metal, including the hilt.'

'And it was just hanging up, with no security measures, despite being worth thirty thousand pounds?'

Mrs Landrey nodded resignedly. 'It had two metal strand cables fixed around it to the wall. They look as if they've been cut, so I agree it clearly wasn't sufficient to deter a thief. The problem in Castle's thinking is probably that it's a little-used function room, and normally college staff would always be here with any group. This dinner was unusual in that the Friendship Society insisted on bringing their own caterers. I understand that the group's president held enough sway with the Master of the college to be able to organise that.'

'You think one of the catering staff took the sword?'

'I've no idea who took it. What I mean is that we didn't have college eyes in this room at all times. I think the Society may have used a few of the student waiters and waitresses, but nobody who would have noticed the absence of the sword.'

Milburn remembered the video Penfold had shown him.

'Are you sure? I've seen footage from an automated camera in here.' He scanned the room to try and spot the camera and finally pointed at a plastic hemisphere above one of the windows opposite.

'Unfortunately, that doesn't cover the whole room. It does swivel to show off different things, but it can't see all the way along the same wall. And before you ask, it's the only one in here, and we haven't yet found any footage from other cameras that shows somebody carrying a long sword. Which is actually another reason for the lax security – you'd have to carry it out through the gateway, past the porters' lodge. A castle is an inherently difficult place to steal from. That's really the point of it.'

Tony nodded to show he understood – although he didn't. The fact that a sword had gone missing showed up the fallacy in her suggestions. However, Hardwick's lessons in diplomacy had taught him that a sympathetic approach always led to greater co-operation, which one might need to leverage at a later stage.

She added, 'I don't know if the thief would have intended to kill people, but a big fire at the opposite end of the room would certainly have made for a good distraction as cover for taking it off the wall.'

The DI paused for a moment to make a show of mulling over what to do next.

'Right. Here's my card. Please will you email me some photos of the missing item, plus any descriptions you've got. I'll see if we can get one of the CSIs back to have a bit of a look around that area where it's gone missing from.' He reverted to a questioning tone of voice. 'I assume that it'll be a fairly small, niche kind of market if you're going to actually get thirty grand for it?'

'Yes, and I'm already connecting with those auction houses that would be a target for selling on an item of this nature.'

'Great. Well, I'll also feed the information you send me into the National Crime Agency. I take it this would be classified as sort of a fine art theft?'

'Sort of, yes,' she agreed. 'You'd call it a "Cultural Object", and the National Crime Agency are likely to be the best support to call on. Not many forces have a Heritage and Cultural Liaison Officer, so bring in the big guns, I'd say.'

Milburn had never heard the phrase Heritage and Cultural Liaison Officer and glossed over her comment with a knowing nod.

'OK, well, if you can email me those details, I'll set all the other wheels in motion.'

He then headed for the door, with a theatrical pause at the wall with no sword, before heading back down the wooden staircase, his footsteps echoing.

Fifteen

Sunday, 9.12 p.m.

Detective Constable Madeline Aria tied her auburn hair back into a practical ponytail then sat down next to Diane Meredith, both of the women facing Milburn across a table in the CID open-plan office. They compared notes about the various witness statements that had been gathered, and Tony drew a sort of cloud chart on a large sheet of paper taken from a flipchart in one of the meeting rooms.

The HOLMES computer system was open on the terminal beside Acting DC Diane Meredith, with the screen positioned so they could all see it. The software was set up as a screen full of text in a database-style format. In order to make investigative connections, Tony preferred to draw out a little cloud for each person or event, and connecting lines with a brief note along the line to say how the things were connected. The visual representation helped him make connections that a screen of words simply could not.

A man called Harry Carruthers was included on the list provided by the university as being a member of the function room serving staff at the Burns Night Supper last night, but so far he had not spoken to any of the police investigators. The implication of the blank spaces on the list for his address and date of birth was that Carruthers had not been present once the police had taken charge. On arrival, Tony himself had stationed a constable at the main gate to ensure nobody left until their details had been recorded.

'Why did no one speak to this Carruthers? The instructions were very clear that you should get the address and DOB details for everyone.'

'We have been and spoken to everyone who was present on the night.' Diane looked Tony straight in the eye. 'If Carruthers was there, we spoke to him. His absence from our witness statement records means he was not in the room once I arrived. I believe *you* were controlling the crime scene until that point.'

DC Aria shifted her large bulk in her chair and looked decidedly uncomfortable at the conversation. Few people, and no police officers other than Milburn, Meredith and Hardwick, knew of the stalking complaint Tony had made against Diane. As far as Madeline understood things, this was two colleagues arguing about the quality of each other's work. It was not helpful towards the investigation. She tried to mediate.

'Sounds like we do need to go and find this Carruthers. He was probably ill and never showed up for work that night or something, but if he's on the list, let's get him eliminated so HOLMES can make some useful hypotheses. Let me put myself down for that.' She copied his name from the printed list they were working from.

Tony followed up with, 'Good, that's a positive approach. I've been needing to go and find Declan Tait.'

Diane countered, 'Declan Tait? We've already established that he wasn't there. It's not him.'

'How can you say that?' Milburn retorted, stung. 'We've found no evidence of an alibi, and there's plenty to show that he hated Melville Armstrong. I intend to interview him and see if he hated his father enough to kill him. Who knows how far in advance you could tamper with the haggis so it would cause this fire. Would you need to actually be at the dinner?'

His nemesis obstinately shook her head. 'It's more than just motive and opportunity though, it's—'

'Means is easy. Any idiot could get hold of methanol and would know it would cause a big fire,' Milburn interrupted, hot-headed. He wanted to crush Meredith, and with DC Aria sat right there, she wouldn't be able to assault him or threaten anything, or even let on that there was more to their conversation than professional differences of opinion.

Diane remained calm, and her head gave a tiny, inquisitive twist to the side. 'Methanol? Have you had the forensics report back already? What makes you think it's methanol?'

'Just an educated guess. That sweet smell at the crime scene gave it away.' Tony looked over to Aria to see her take on his 'educated guess'. Her face gave nothing away, however, and she quickly looked down at her notebook.

Acting DC Meredith came back at him again.

'No. The accelerant might be easy for him to source. He might even have been able to use his company ID badge to get in and tamper with the haggis, if Armstrong was running the organisation of the dinner. But that's not the key. My point is that Declan Tait is an aggressive thug from a Brandon council estate. He won't know what goes on at a Burns Supper. Never in a million years would he come up with the idea to add accelerant to the haggis because they'll pour flaming whisky over it and then cut it to release the accelerant. Nor would he know that Armstrong would be the man doing the cutting.'

DC Aria looked back up at Milburn and he scowled. Meredith had a point, but Tait seemed so much to be the perfect fit as a suspect.

'Well, as Madeline says, we need to eliminate everyone connected with this whole thing. I'll go and see both the Taits so we can do that. Maybe his mother put Declan up to it.'

'You're wrong,' Diane said. 'If Declan Tait wanted to kill Melville Armstrong, he'd just batter the fat old sod with his fists.'

Aria looked back and forth between the two of them, and this prompted Tony to defend himself further.

'I'm not so sure about that. We don't really have that much information about Declan, beyond his caution for assault and being a boxer. There may be a lot more to him than we know so far.' He went back on the offensive. 'You must stop making assumptions about people based on where they've come from.'

'Whatever,' Meredith replied rudely. She turned the computer screen back to face herself directly and started tapping at the keyboard. After a moment she looked around. 'Well, go on then, you two. If you think you'll find out anything useful from Carruthers or the Taits, be my guest – get out there and get interviewing. Do make sure you message me back any information that'll help in here.' She pointed at the screen.

Diane had made him mad, and Milburn pulled rank without thinking it through.

'No. We'll go together, and we'll find out what makes both the Taits tick. Leave that,' he ordered, gesturing at the computer. 'We're going to see them right now. If you think I'm so wrong about them, come along and confirm it with me.'

DC Aria jumped in with, 'It's a good idea, Diane. We need this case to go somewhere, and you two work well together. I reckon, between you, you'll see the wood through the trees. I can carry on with inputting all this stuff.' She waved at the piles of papers and the computer in front of Diane.

'I'll meet you at the car, Diane.' Tony got up and marched out of the room, berating himself and wondering what he'd set himself up for.

On his way down through the quiet police station building, Tony messaged Penfold the essence of Meredith's objection. Penfold had definitively pointed the finger at Declan, but Diane had assessed the man accurately. From what Milburn had learned of him, his modus operandi would not be a subtle and secretive booby-trapped haggis. They needed to gather some first-hand up-to-date information about the young man in order to confirm this, but Tony did not expect to discover that Declan now had a chemistry PhD and the finesse of a Professor Moriarty.

As he turned the key in the ignition, Penfold's reply lit up the phone sitting in the car's cup holder. Meredith had seen the notification come up.

'Penfold on the payroll now, is he?' she said bitchily.

Tony paused to read another haiku:

boxer's brain damage,

morals drop: murder OK,

cinch to learn arson.

'Until we get enough proper detectives on our team, we've just got to make do with all the help we can get.' Tony was being both defensive and aggressive at the same time. Diane ignored him and started tapping away at her own phone. He didn't exactly squeal the tyres, but he flew out of the tight police car park much faster than was safe.

As he turned right onto Old Elvet, without looking up from her phone, PC Meredith muttered, 'It's quicker the other way.' This prompted Tony to speed up and roar down the hill towards the red traffic light by the City Hotel pub.

Sixteen

Sunday, 9.50 p.m.

They pulled up to the kerb in a poorly lit street of social housing in the village of Brandon, four miles from Durham City police station. Tony parked behind a white van with signage for Armstrong Aggregates painted on the sides. He was convinced it was the one that had shot past him the previous evening.

The houses were all box-shaped and semi-detached, made of modern red brick with grey roof-tiles and gravel for driveways. The house they had parked beside had three old wooden pallets leaning up against the front wall, and a scrawny greyhound shivered underneath them. In the darkness, it was difficult to get a sense of the atmosphere of the locality, beyond the bits of old junk festooning front gardens, and the battered nature of the few vehicles parked there. Except for the white van, which looked new.

Although it was nearly ten o'clock at night, Milburn and Meredith knocked on Jacqui Tait's black front door, with the aim of discussing the arson double murder. When she opened it, with the chain across the narrow gap, Tony saw a woman with a tanned face and look of weariness and strain that fitted her surroundings. Diane immediately stepped forward in front of her boss.

'Mrs Tait?' she asked. 'We're from the police. We're detectives investigating the fire and deaths up at Durham Castle last night.'

Tony bristled at her claim that they were both detectives. He took every opportunity to emphasise that she was only an *Acting* Detective Constable. On this occasion he knew better than to intervene – and he expected that Meredith knew he would not. Rapport was much more quickly built if a female officer could

89

take the lead with a female interviewee, especially so late on a dark night.

'It's "Miss", and I don't know what you're talking about.'

There was a long pause, the police officers inwardly assessing Miss Tait's claim of ignorance. If she genuinely knew nothing and was Armstrong's long-term mistress, then the news would be a significant shock to her.

Meredith replied quietly to impart the gravity of their visit: 'In that case, Miss Tait, I think we had better come in so you can sit down.'

The woman unhooked the chain and opened the door. Jacqui Tait was the same height as Diane and dressed in tight leggings and a loose white hoody. She was thin and attractive, of mixed race, it now became apparent, and she wore a full face of make-up.

The three sat on a sofa and armchair in front of the gas fire in the woman's small lounge. The fire was on maximum heat, but the room remained cold. The officers kept their coats on, and Jacqui wrapped a blanket from the sofa around herself. Tony assumed that the social housing landlord had never invested in decent insulation for these houses.

Meredith gently explained the basic circumstances of Melville Armstrong's death, and it was obvious that the news came as a shock to Jacqui Tait. She wailed and argued and cried, blamed the two police sat in her front room, and buried her head in the blanket. The cold in the room meant that her sobbing included a significant runny nose, and the blanket received a large smear of snot.

DS Milburn had given families news of deaths several times before, and Jacqui Tait came across as genuine and convincing. In his opinion, it was a significant blow to her. He sent Diane out to find some tissues and make them all a cup of tea, and he began, compassionately, to get some details from the bereaved mistress.

'How long have you known Mr Armstrong?'

'God, more than twenty years. Since before Declan was born.' She wept quietly.

'Is there somebody we can call to come and support you?'

'My son will be back soon. He's at boxing practice, but he lives here, so I'll have him.'

'That's good. What do you do for work? Do we need to let them know that you'll need some time off?'

Jacqui's face peeked out from the stripy blue blanket as she explained, 'I don't really work. I do occasional house cleaning, but it's not like a job. I've got nothing on tomorrow.'

Milburn cocked his head slightly to the side. 'You're a cleaner?'

'Oh God, no!' Tait wailed again, and tears began to slide down her face. 'Please don't tell the social – I'll lose my benefits and I can't afford that. Melville cut off my money months ago, and I only really eat now when he takes me out to dinner. Oh God, how will we survive? How will we eat?' He could see that she was clutching the pendant of a necklace she had pulled out from under the hoody.

'Please don't worry, Jacqui.' Tony held up his hand in a placatory gesture. 'We're not interested in any way in your benefits situation. We're only looking to find out some background about Mr Armstrong.'

No sooner had Diane plonked the teacups down and handed Jacqui a roll of toilet paper to blow her nose with than the front door banged open, so she went to meet whoever had come in. Before she even left the lounge, the large bulk of Declan Tait burst in. He had a round, closely shaven head, with one ear sporting a chunky square earring, which Tony assumed was zirconia rather than diamond.

The man stepped nimbly into the space between his mother and the two police officers. He wore a grey hoody emblazoned with a boxing club logo and sweaty grey shorts. At the hem of the shorts' legs was a sheen of ice where his sweat had frozen. His stocky legs had a bulldog tattoo on the left calf and finished with white socks in white trainers. His skin was brown but somewhat lighter than his mother's.

Milburn and Meredith had passed the boxing club, or at least a sign for it, by a door on a bare breeze-block building, near the turn into the housing estate.

'What are you two doing, upsetting me ma?' He held an aggressive stance, hands balled into fists, but he kept them down by his sides.

Meredith's body was taut, ready to leap at Declan, if necessary, but Milburn remained seated and made his placatory hand gesture again.

'Please, we're police, and we're here to help. Your mother has had a bit of a shock about Melville Armstrong, and we want to make sure she's all right.'

'What's that ballbag done now?' Declan's voice was loud, and he half-turned so that the question was addressed to his mother as much as to the officers.

The detective sergeant maintained his calm, even tone.

'Perhaps, would you mind sitting down – Declan, is it?'

The young man dropped into the empty space beside his mother, and she wept, clutching his big bicep.

'He's dead. What will we do now?'

'What do you mean?' her son challenged her. 'Armstrong was no good for us. He held you back your whole life, Ma.' There seemed to be no shock, concern or even surprise in his voice at the news of his father's death. Milburn and Meredith caught each other's eye.

The DS asked, 'Declan, how did you know Melville Armstrong?'

'Ah work at Armstrong Aggregates, don't Ah. The clue's in the name, isn't it?' His demeanour was unnecessarily aggressive.

'He's Declan's father,' Jacqui said. 'That's how we know— oh . . .' she gave another quieter sob '. . . how we knew

92

him.' She blew her nose with a stretch of toilet roll and glared at her son.

Diane squatted down, positioned across the white coffee table from Jacqui. She spoke with a soothing tone.

'I'm so sorry that he's gone. I like your necklace, is it significant?'

The grieving woman had been clutching the pendant all the while and opened her fingers to look at the polished grey stone attached to the silver chain.

'Melville gave me this when I left the aggregates office – I used to work there as a secretary. That was in the first business when he and Joel were partners. He said it was a symbol of what had brought us together.' She held it forward for Meredith to admire. 'It's one of the first stones that came out of the ground at that first site.' She smiled, remembering her long-time lover. 'Mel had a lot of flaws, but he could be so romantic.'

Declan looked sideways at his mother, muttering more curse words under his breath. She ignored him, lost in gazing at the small round stone.

Taking Diane's cue, DS Milburn came in with the more business-like questions. Not exactly Bad Cop, but they were playing a subtle double act.

'You said you were worried about money for food, Mrs Tait, but Declan works for Armstrong Aggregates.' He wanted to ask irritating questions, without saying anything unprofessional, things that might rattle a cage. 'It's not my place to ask about your family finances, but doesn't that mean that there is money coming into the household?'

Jacqui looked at Declan, seemingly unsure how to answer this. From her expression, Milburn wondered if it was the first time she'd actually considered why she was struggling financially in such deprivation with a working son living with her. Declan had not smiled once since entering the room. He looked at the large television, switched off in the corner.

'Ah've got expenses,' he said brusquely.

'That's true, he does,' Jacqui said wistfully, almost to herself, and nodded as if this explained everything completely.

Milburn continued, 'Declan, can you tell us what exactly you do at the aggregates company?'

He gave the detective a suspicious look, answering, 'Driving mostly. They gave me that van out there, and they send me out on deliveries. Not the stones, they use the big trucks for that, but taking things to the post office, or sometimes around the site. It's a big area and things need moved around all the time. That's what Ah do.'

With an understanding nod, Meredith remarked, 'Sounds like it's more interesting than most driver jobs would be. Do they use chemicals in the mining? I dare say you have to drive that dangerous stuff around the site sometimes – or are they just getting you to take coffee round the place?'

Declan's shoulders relaxed and he actually laughed briefly.

'Ah did have to take coffee out one time, yeah, but the quarry workers all bring their own Thermoses, and their own food. But, yeah, there are some chemicals that go out round the site.' He flashed a sudden look at Milburn. 'They divvent let me carry any explosives though.' His Geordie accent became stronger as he became more defensive. 'They divvent do much blastin', but that's really controlled, driving that stuff about. It's always the engineers and geologists sorting that.'

'What about methanol – is that one of the things you transport?' Milburn tried to make his voice soothing like Diane's, but his persona in this room had already been established as more abrasive.

Declan's face dropped to looking serious again. He hesitated and stuttered slightly. 'Ye-yeah, but Ah only do what I'm told to with it. They say to pour it in the ponds to keep away the algae, so Ah pour it in the water.' He held up an imaginary bottle and tipped it over to act out pouring methanol. 'An' they're right – there's no algae in any o' the ponds.'

94

'Sorry, I'm not sure I understand. They use methanol in the quarry ponds to stop algae growing?'

The young man nodded his round head, eyes widened to confirm. 'But Ah'm not to blame for owt with that. Ah just do what Ah'm told.'

'Surely that's not good for the environment?' Tony directed his next question at Diane.

She shrugged and took the chance to reinforce her positive position in the good-cop, bad-cop set-up.

'Probably not, but that's not Declan's fault, is it? The environment agency must have scientists who should be clamping down on Armstrong.'

'Well, sure, but . . .' Milburn looked back at Declan. 'How is the methanol stored? Do you keep it locked up?'

'Oh, aye. There's a metal cabinet and the key hangs up behind reception. So there's always someone there with it.'

'And you have to sign the key out to use it?'

'Well, no, but they see who uses it.'

Meredith came in helpfully again, with, 'Are you OK? Some of those chemicals can be pretty nasty. What else is in that cabinet you have to go in?'

'Ah dunno. All sorts. There's mebbe eight bottles in there, some big old tins, too. They've got a lab in one o' the Portakabins. Mr Hedley is always gannin' in and out of the chemical store. For his rock experiments.'

DS Milburn had been taking notes throughout, and repeated this back out loud as he wrote it.

'Eight bottles of unknown chemicals, plus several larger tins of unknown chemicals. Joel Hedley has the details.'

'Do you ever remove any of the chemicals off site? Maybe for a little party?' Meredith grinned and wiggled her hand to her mouth to mime taking a drink. 'Methanol's quite a strong alcohol.'

The stocky young man folded his arms and looked put out, saying indignantly, 'Ah divvent drink. I am an athlete.' He unfolded his arms and mimed back to Meredith a pugilist pose with fists in front of his face.

Jacqui had been still for some time, but now she sat bolt upright and shoved her son.   'You liar! You're always having a beer. I bet you went to the pub after training tonight.'

'Well, mebbe, Ma. But Ah only have a beer or two. Nivvor the strong stuff. Ah hate spirits.'

'That's true.' Jacqui nodded and turned to Diane. 'He was really ill after drinking vodka when he was fourteen, and he's never touched the hard stuff since.'

'Sounds like a good learning experience, even if it was grim at the time.' Diane smiled warmly. She glanced at Tony who gave a little nod, and they both stood up. 'We need to go and carry on with our investigations. I'm so sorry for your loss, Jacqui. I'm sure Declan here will help and support you over the next few days and weeks.'

The woman started crying again, and as her son enveloped her in his bulky embrace, DS Milburn and ADC Meredith showed themselves out.

Seventeen

Sunday, 11.17 p.m.

The road up the hill to Neville's Cross traffic lights brought them into Durham on the side of town known as the Viaduct area. Here, all the old, terraced houses had been taken over by landlords to accommodate a dense population of students, just as in the past, the same streets had been full of miners' families, most of whom took pride in keeping their homes spick and span.

Times had changed. Tony turned left at the historic Colpitts Hotel pub and drove into one of the narrow streets with cars parked on both sides and up on the pavements. Groups of students weaved around the parked cars and the slow-moving, unmarked police Golf with equal disregard. Wheelie bins with poorly tied black sacks and green boxes overflowing with empty bottles further blocked the road and the pavements. Every house seemed to have produced an incredible volume of rubbish.

Milburn shuddered slightly at the neglect, the litter and the shabby corners full of weeds. An earlier rain shower had left the place damp and, despite the warmth inside the car, he could feel the chill. Even with numerous young residents wandering along the roadway and pavements, the whole place felt abandoned.

How is it worse here than Brandon?

'What's up?' Meredith asked, noticing the shudder and turning to look at him, instead of out at the milling, tipsy young people.

'Just thinking how these kids are all so rich, and yet they choose to be crammed up together and leave the place filthy all the time. It makes me mad and sad at the same time.'

'Student life,' she shrugged. 'It's always been the same. This place will be a total ghost town in the summer vacation.'

Tony grumbled, 'Look at this lot. It's Sunday night, for God's sake. Have they got nothing to do tomorrow morning?'

She laughed. 'They're a lot younger than you are, Tony. They'll manage fine, I'm sure.'

No parking spaces were available, so they just parked in the middle of what had effectively become a pedestrianised area. Harry Carruthers lived in a mid-terraced house. Once inside, they discovered that what had once been a two-up, two-down had an extension into the back yard and rooms cut in half so that it now housed five members of the university hockey club: Carruthers and four of his mates.

A floppy-haired, tall and athletic young man answered the door. He did not seem perturbed at the arrival of the police.

'Harry Carry? Sure, he's in his room.'

He shouted up the stairs that the feds had finally caught up with Harry. An assured, entitled approach to life exuded from this student, barely more than half Milburn's age. The hallway was blocked by an array of tall, fat sports bags, with shoulder straps. The officers helped the youth to shift them into a neat line-up, so they could all squeeze along to a communal area around the kitchen table.

Almost immediately, the hockey player who had answered the door was replaced by a similar-looking individual with an ironic mullet cut into his blond hair.

'Hi. What's up?'

'I'm Detective Sergeant Milburn, and this is Acting DC Meredith,' Tony told him. 'Could you sit down, please.' He waved to a seat in front of unwashed dinner plates. The detectives seated themselves to prompt him to join them.

'What can I do for you, officers?' His body language was open and compliant, but his voice exuded the same sort of entitled contempt that his friend's had.

Meredith started off in her same good-cop role. 'You're in Castle College, right?'

He nodded. 'Right.'

'The college told us that you were scheduled to be working a function there last night as a waiter. Is that correct?'

Carruthers jerked a look over his shoulder to the empty hallway, stood up quickly and closed the kitchen door. He sat back down and replied, quieter now, 'Well, yeah, but the dinner was cancelled because of the fire.'

'You know about the fire?' Milburn asked, his notebook poised.

'I was there, so of course I know about it,' the boy said rudely.

'It must have been awful. Are you all right?'

Harry looked at Diane as if she was mad. 'Yeah, I'm fine, why wouldn't I be?'

She returned the same look back at him.

'You were in a fire, where two people died. Even if you avoided physical harm, which it looks like you did, that must be a pretty traumatic thing to experience. Are you sure you're OK? We could point you towards some counselling for that sort of thing. The effects often don't manifest immediately, but it's worth being ahead of when they do. Post-traumatic stress can be a pretty serious mental-health issue. I wouldn't want to deal with it without help.'

'Honestly, I'm fine,' Harry insisted. 'I left almost as soon as the fire started. I could see I wouldn't get paid because the whole thing would be cancelled, so I headed down to the bar.'

Milburn confirmed, 'The Undercroft Bar in Castle, you mean?'

'Yeah. We had a good win on the hockey field yesterday afternoon, so the boys were all in the bar.' He glanced at the closed door. 'I'd been pretty gutted that I'd only be able to join them later. I'm captain of the team, so I really should have been leading the celebrations. Plus, I'd left my hockey stick bag down there, so I had to drop by the bar even if they might have moved on already.'

The officers left a quiet pause before Milburn stated, 'I find it very difficult to believe that you witnessed two men being burned alive and casually went downstairs for a couple of pints.' There was another significant silence. 'Unless you knew it was going to happen. Maybe somebody paid you to arrange the fire?'

'Sir, that's a bit of a stretch, isn't it?' Meredith faked shock. She indicated Carruthers with her hand and turned her head to look at Tony. 'This is the captain of the hockey team, not some sort of hired killer.'

The student's eyes were wide, and he looked back and forth between the two detectives repeatedly.

'No, *no . . . what?* I had nothing to do with that.' He stopped speaking and stared at Milburn for a few seconds. Those brief few moments were enough for him to regain his composure, and the cocksure confidence returned.

'I was never near the end of the room where the fire broke out, and I never had anything to do with the flambé they put on the haggis. If there was too much whisky there, it was nothing to do with me. What even makes you think it wasn't an accident?' He paused long enough to emphasise the question but briefly enough that there was no chance for either police officer to speak. 'I had nothing to do with the fire, and as a consequence you cannot prove that I did.'

Diane was good at this kind of parrying. She continued addressing Tony.

'See? I told you there was no reason to disturb Harry here.' She looked back at the blond youth whose chest had swelled as she spoke. 'Sorry for my colleague. He always goes off the deep end.' As she said this, she wagged a dismissive hand in her boss's direction. 'Now, we do need to eliminate from our inquiries everyone who was there last night, which we've now done with you.'

She ran through his name, address and date of birth with him, before continuing to interrogate in the guise of friendly chat.

'Working as you did, sort of behind the scenes, you probably had a good chance to see something that might help us, most likely without even realising you had seen it. Some details can be really important even though they seem insignificant at the time.'

Milburn noticed the young man's shoulders relax.

Harry then shrugged insouciantly and said, 'I'll help as much as I can, but I'm pretty sure I didn't see anything untoward going on.'

Meredith continued, 'Well, exactly. Let's run you through the timeline of your activities and if I note it all down, we may spot something in it later on that helps our inquiries no end.'

He shrugged again.

The DS leant back in his chair and watched ADC Meredith at work. She was more than a decade older than Carruthers, but she managed to flirt with him and make the arrogant athlete feel so at ease that he spewed out no end of information about his life and his Saturday night. Tony could see much to be feared in Diane. She could manipulate people to an extraordinary degree.

Harry Carruthers, it turned out, was from a relatively poor family – both of his parents were merely teachers. In Castle College, that counted as poor: both financially and also poor form. His colleagues came from families who owned shooting estates in Scotland, chateaux in France, mews terraces in Westminster. Their parents were in the House of Lords, ran banks in the City, captained aircraft carriers and directed multinational companies.

They learned that Harry was out of his depth trying to appear their equal and had blown his entire student loan for the term by going on the university ski trip, in an attempt to keep up with the Cholmondley-Joneses. These were difficulties that his friends and housemates could never find out about: his having to work as a waiter was a secret he kept tightly locked up, yet Meredith had extracted it all from him in the space of five minutes.

As they walked back to the car, the detectives compared notes. Milburn thought there was more to Harry's account of

101

events. The tale of poverty amongst the rich rahs of Castle was plausible and well told, but Tony had a gut feeling that the young man actually felt he *could* compete with his colleagues. He had seemed strangely optimistic that his ship would come in, and that he would be able to stand shoulder-to-shoulder with those who owned Caribbean islands. Milburn suggested Carruthers was deluded.

Meredith was more succinct in her disdain. 'What a dick.'

'Agreed. But was he involved? I don't feel that he was, but I do feel as if there's something going on.'

'Everything is about money with him,' Diane snorted. 'Did you notice how he mentioned the price of everything? That fancy new hockey stick he showed us, his mate's skis, the rent for their house, even that old pizza slice he munched down.'

'He's struggling for money.' Milburn was pragmatic. 'All students struggle for money, but he's convinced he's worse off than most, and that's because he chooses to hang out with kids who are absolutely loaded. It's not surprising he sees the cost of everything he looks at. But none of that is criminal. Like you say, he's guilty of being a dick, but do you think there's anything more than that?'

'He's studying chemistry and is desperate for money. A *lot* of money. Hired killer-type money. Think: means, motive and opportunity.'

'Hmm.' Tony pondered on what she'd said as they walked the remaining steps in silence and got into the car.

'It does seem a bit too much of a coincidence to be true, though,' he said slowly, once back behind the wheel. 'You think that lad might be willing and able to do an assassination job, and here you have somebody wanting Armstrong or Hedley killed, or both. You've got Carruthers happening to be studying in this college, and working as a waiter there, and the Friendship Society Burns Supper is also taking place in the castle. It all seems a bit convenient, with the employer and employee finding each other, and then having the stroke of luck that the victims are dining in his college.'

Diane frowned. 'Well, maybe it didn't go down exactly like that. There's definitely something wrong with that boy, but you're right, perhaps it is just the fact that I don't like him which is making me put him in the frame for this.'

There was a lot to think about on the short drive back to the city station.

Eighteen

Monday 30 January, 12.30 a.m.

In the CID office, DS Milburn and ADC Meredith set to work reading through the statements of the eighty-three witnesses. Tony split them unequally, taking more himself and setting Diane to also look through the CCTV footage supplied by Durham Castle. As it was fresh in their minds, she was particularly aiming to follow Carruthers' movements.

DC Aria had gone home, as had the civilian administrator: the CID section was empty. The two sat at separate desks in the open-plan office. After about an hour, Milburn had made some notes of consistent points that several witnesses had independently put forward. It didn't amount to much that he thought might be useful, but the process was the point. Following the police's murder investigation manual had been shown to be both successful in working up useful hypotheses, and also in making sure the evidence was collected in a manner that was impregnable to defence lawyers. Well, maybe a bit less pregnable at least, he mused internally, before nearly jumping out of his skin. Diane had plonked herself down beside him, her hand had grabbed his thigh, and she leant in so their shoulders were touching.

Once he had realised what was going on, he stuttered, 'B-bit of space, please,' and tried to lean away from her.

She swapped the hand gripping his thigh so that she could turn to face him, but still grip him tightly. In typical Crazy Cow fashion, she had a couple of buttons on her shirt open and her smile was disturbingly alluring. Penfold had once warned Milburn to beware her siren song and, in this moment, he saw himself tied to the mast of a ship crashing on the rocks.

'Stop it!' He pulled her hand off his leg, stood up and moved around to the opposite side of the desk.

She leaned forward to give him the perfect view down her cleavage, but it was all business when she spoke.

'I've pieced together the various cameras around the castle, and Carruthers' story fits exactly with the video evidence. There's bits where there are blind spots, but when you connect it together with the time it would take to move between cameras, it all fits.'

She went on: 'He exits the stairwell doorway down from the Fellows' Meeting Room, and then cuts across the few yards to the entrance to the Undercroft Bar. That has CCTV inside, so you see him come in and go and sit with two other students. After about ten minutes, he buys a round of drinks, which they all down pretty quickly before they all get up and leave. The three of them go through the little door in the castle's giant gates and away up the drive. I could see if we can get some footage from out on the streets, but I reckon his story checks out.'

Tony was on his mettle. He was barely listening to her, trying to spot the next danger. The incongruity of her body language compared with her spoken language he found difficult to process.

'There is one little thing that doesn't look quite right, but I can't see it being significant.'

Tony latched on to this. 'OK, tell me.'

'You remember he showed us his new hockey stick on the way out?'

'Obviously I do.'

She manipulated the computer mouse on his desk, looked up and then patted the seat next to her, the same one he had so quickly vacated. Tony made a show of getting out his phone and setting it to record their conversation. He moved around the desk and stationed himself out of reach from her, but standing in a location so he could see the computer screen.

Meredith ignored his performance. The screen showed a still of Harry Carruthers entering the castle courtyard from the little staircase doorway, down from the scene of the fire. She pointed at the sports bag on his back.

'He said he had left his hockey bag in the bar, but he has it here before getting to the bar.'

'Like you say, not really a significant anomaly.'

'No, and he goes into the bar toilets to change, before meeting his friends, which all makes sense.'

'They have cameras in the toilet?'

'No, they're just inside the entrance from the courtyard into the bar area. So, we see him go in, and then five minutes later see him enter the bar on the camera in there, having done a quick change from waiter's outfit to team captain.' She worked the video software forwards to the point where Carruthers entered the Undercroft, now clad in his hockey tracksuit, matching his two mates. A slim, neat finger touched the screen. 'That logo with the two elephants on the bag is the same as the one he showed us the new stick from in his hallway, so it all matches up.'

'Yep, even the cockiest can just misremember things. I can't see anything in that video that puts him in the frame for arson and murder. Maybe you should search out what he was up to early on. When did he arrive? Did he go near the haggis? That sort of thing. I'd like to eliminate him completely. He rubbed me up the wrong way, so let's make sure that's all it is.'

Diane stared at him. 'Already done. Like I said, that bag not being in the bar is the only anomaly. He arrives at the castle for work at about six, has to change into his smart serving outfit, which he does in the same toilets down by the bar. He appears to get bollocked for being late – there's no sound – is pretty slow and lazy in his work generally but does what he's told and is in place with the rest of the serving staff following Randall White to the threshold of the kitchen as the chef carries the haggis out. The camera in the kitchen then loses the boy when he goes out to the dining area. And he never returns. As he appears out of the stairway door downstairs, he must go from the dining room straight down there when the fire breaks out.'

Milburn cut in, 'Which, to be fair, is exactly what he told us.'

106

Diane nodded. 'Yep.'

Tony picked up the papers he had been working with and withdrew to his own office, firmly closing the door behind himself. He watched through the little window in the door as Diane moved back to her own desk and continued reading through witness statements.

Tony's eyes slid closed, and he started sharply. At 4.20 a.m. it was time to get some sleep. He locked his computer and walked zombie-like through the office, passing Meredith with no more than a grunt. The brisk, cold air shocked him awake at the back door to the station, and he felt safe to drive the mile or so up the hill to home. Once there, he crept into the hallway, pulled his shoes off quietly and slinked up the stairs, skipping the sixth one that tended to creak. A text message from Penfold lit up the phone in his hand.

methanol glass blown:

seals in heat and pressure. Cut

glass blows methanol

By the light of the phone, he scooted around their bed, ready to dump his clothes on the floor, ready for a quick get-up in just a few hours' time. Kathy stirred and turned towards him. Her soft skin appeared pearlescent in the dim light, and Tony flopped down to kiss her cheek. The mattress bounced her, and she gave a little squawk of surprise.

He gently pushed the blonde hair from her face and whispered, 'Sorry, go back to sleep.'

As he leaned to kiss her again, Kathy woke and sat up straight, saying groggily, 'What time is it? Where have you been?'

Milburn was completely thrown. 'It's n-not quite five,' he stuttered. 'I've been at the station working on this case.'

'What – all through the night?'

'It's the job, Kathy, you know that. I'll get the time back in lieu, but when the investigation's hot, you've gotta work it immediately.'

'When the Crazy Cow's hot, you mean.' Kathy's voice raised in pitch and volume. 'Her smell is all over you. Do you think I'm stupid?'

'Whoa, whoa.' Tony sat up and leaned away from her slightly, her jealousy taking him completely by surprise. 'Meredith is seconded to CID, so she's working the case too.'

'Working you, more like. I can't believe this! How long have we been fighting her, just for you to succumb to her again. What was it, a quickie in your office?'

Exasperated, Tony groaned, 'Where is this coming from? I've had to spend most of this evening with her, but I've kept my distance and as much as possible have set her to tasks where we don't need to work together. There's nothing going on. I'm not that stupid.'

'No, Tony, *I'm* not that stupid. Can't you smell her? It's like you've been rolling in her. Her stench has filled the room.' He went to put his hand on Kathy's arm, but she recoiled at the touch. 'No, get off me. And get out! I don't want you in here.'

'What? Kathy, honestly, we've had to work together tonight, but nothing else. I don't understand why you suddenly think there's something going on.'

'Get out! Just get out.' Kathy slapped at his arm, without looking at him. With her other hand, she pointed towards the door.

Tony was utterly lost. He started to question his own memory of the evening. He even lowered his face to try and smell his own shoulder. There was no detectable odour.

'Go!' He half-moved, and Kathy continued, 'I don't want you to be here tonight.'

He stood on the landing, listening to his partner snivelling quietly. *What just happened?* Tony could imagine that he might well smell of something due to close proximity to Diane over several hours that evening, but Kathy's overreaction had come

108

completely out of the blue. *Why won't she listen to me?* The bedroom door closed firmly and loudly at his back and he jerked in shock.

Well, screw you then. Milburn stomped along the landing and down the stairs, making no effort to avoid the creaky sixth one. He was no longer tired, just very confused. And frustrated. And angry.

Driving to Hartlepool in the dark, through a very gusty wind, focused Tony's mind on the road, and gradually his anger subsided. Confusion and frustration remained, but he gradually stopped shouting at the occasional other vehicle.

Penfold's house was dark and forbidding. Ignoring the fact that parking on Promenade Square was not permitted, Milburn stuck his Golf half on the road, half up on the grassy central area. The wind whipped off the sea, and he launched himself through Penfold's front door, which was unlocked. The lights were on, but the gloomy old house seemed to absorb most of the illumination. Day or night, summer or winter, the rooms and corridors Penfold inhabited remained murky, with the exception of the laboratory in the cellar. The place was quiet and chilly.

Stopping by the kitchen, Milburn helped himself to a cup of the filter coffee but could not find any milk or sugar. He had been thwarted in that search many times in the past, and this January morning was no different. The door from the kitchen down the stairs to the basement formed a bright portal at the end of the room.

'Hellooo!' Tony called down the echoey staircase.

'Come on down, Milburn, we're just about ready for you.'

Nineteen

Monday, 5.40 a.m.

'OK, what are we doing down here? I haven't got time for you to show me a load of fun experiments or your new perpetual motion machine.'

'Very droll.' The big Kiwi led Tony over to a pair of large glass bulbs resting on what appeared to be a baker's cooling tray. They were slightly different sizes, but approximately equivalent to a pair of glass rugby balls, albeit with slightly more rounded ends. 'It took a while to get the technique right, but I managed to blow these this morning.' Penfold pointed to the glass eggs without touching them. 'I think we could be on to something.'

'What, are you opening a glass sports shop?' Milburn said tiredly. 'I know Kiwis love their rugby, but what possible purpose could these serve? Would anyone really buy decorative glass sculptures like these?' He went to pick one up, but Penfold grabbed his wrist and pulled it away.

'It'll be a good twenty-four hours before they've set completely. They're incredibly thin and may well be crushed if you grab hold now.'

Milburn frowned, even more confused.

'That glass fragment we took out of your shoe.' Penfold held up the evidence bag containing the shard from the base of Milburn's work shoe. 'It had been hand-blown.'

There was a pause in which Tony felt he was supposed to understand some important point that escaped him. 'OK . . . ?' He spoke with a hesitating, questioning tone.

Mantoro sat on a bar stool in the corner, snacking from a saucer of cashew nuts. Penfold held a cup of coffee in his hand, but more like an accessory – he didn't lift it to his lips. Neither he nor Mantoro responded. They just eyeballed Tony, so he stumbled on, trying to work out what they expected him to glean from this information.

'Um, hand-blown glass,' he tried. 'That means particularly fine stuff, right? The sort of wine or whisky glasses that a function in Castle's Fellows' Meeting Room would demand?'

Penfold's head flicked a little, and he pointed at the glass rugby balls.

'Do these look like drinking glasses?'

'Obviously not – but so what. What are they? Come on, get to the point.'

'Here, my friend, are your accelerant delivery vessels.' The Kiwi flourished a hand towards the cooling glass, and there was a theatrical pause for it to sink in.

'You what? The haggis was the source of the accelerant! You showed me it jetting out beside the knife blade on that video.'

'Indeed, but the haggis was steaming hot. It would have been in the oven for a couple of hours, and methanol vaporises at sixty-five degrees. There'd have been none left.' After another brief pause, Penfold continued staring almost gleefully at his glass eggs.

Milburn followed his gaze, then jumped up and went to look in detail. On closer inspection, he could see that both the cooling glass vessels were three-quarters filled with a colourless liquid. And each had a small, sealed projection close to, but not quite at, the pointed end of the rugby ball shape.

'Inside – is that what I think it is?'

'Oh, yeah.' Mantoro's gravelly baritone was loud in the basement lab.

Penfold nodded and waved Milburn to follow him, as he sauntered to the other end of the room. Mounted against the wall was a large cabinet with thick Perspex walls to allow you to see inside: a fume cupboard or chemistry demonstration cupboard of the sort that Tony remembered from chemistry lessons at school. A fat white pipe exited through the side and climbed upwards and through the ceiling. The tall surfer reached up to a switch high on the wall beside the pipe, and an industrial fan started whirring in the big cabinet.

'This one is not nearly so cleanly blown, but it should work for the purposes of this demonstration.' Penfold pointed inside the chamber and Tony could see a third glass egg resting on a large silver salver. The platter was itself resting atop a laboratory tripod, and a Bunsen burner sat beneath it, heating from below. Standing beside it inside the cabinet was a bottle of Johnnie Walker Black Label, along with a whisky tumbler, a carving knife and a box of matches.

'What exactly are you going to demonstrate?' Tony asked warily.

Penfold slid the front Perspex door upwards eight inches and pulled on elbow-length leather gloves, warning Tony, 'If you could just step back a little, Milburn.' He turned the gas tap to extinguish the Bunsen burner. Tutting to himself, Penfold then had to remove the gloves again in order to pour a glass of whisky and slosh it over the liquid-filled glass. He then struck a match and ignited the whisky.

Quickly reinstating his fireproof gauntlets, and with one arm twisted up inside the door, which was pulled as low as he could get it down onto the crook of his elbow, the Kiwi held up the knife and gave a swift stab into the glass container. A mini fireball exploded glass shards all around inside the chamber. Milburn flinched and cowered at the incredible sound. He was aghast that Penfold continued to hold his arm inside.

He stepped forward, put a hand on Penfold's shoulder, asking, 'Are you OK?'

'Perfectly fine, thank you. I need to wait, though, until the methanol is all burnt out.'

'It's all out now.' Tony could see no flames.

'No, Milburn, the flames are invisible. After the first fireball, you can continue to be on fire without being able to see it at all. That can be a real danger in motorsports.'

'What – they use methanol in racing?'

112

Penfold nodded casually. 'Sometimes, yes. And if there's an accident, a driver or mechanic can be on fire and nobody else realises why they're screaming and running around. Rather like in our video of the Durham Castle conflagration.'

'Hmm.' Milburn stared into the chamber to try and see if there was any indication of fire. Nothing.

Mantoro chipped in with, 'Pretty wild, huh?'

Without warning, Tony reached a hand in under the sash door to the cabinet, to pick up a piece of the shattered glass. Penfold watched like a hawk, and exhaled volubly when the hand came back out unburnt. Tony nodded sheepishly, like a foolish schoolboy who had got away safely but only by pure good fortune.

He glanced across to the evidence bag lying on the white worktop in the middle of the lab. The piece of glass in his hand closely resembled the piece pulled from the heel of his shoe on Saturday night. He held it up to Penfold, who remained with his gloved hand held inside the downdraught chamber.

'Are you trying to tell me that this . . .' Tony waved the sliver around, indicating the insides of the chemistry demonstration cupboard and then more widely towards the two further examples still on the cooling tray '. . . this is how somebody arranged for the fire to start? And that they expected this to be sufficiently well targeted to ensure that both Armstrong and Hedley were killed?'

Penfold closed the chamber door fully. He spoke whilst removing the gauntlets and moving over to an open laptop.

'Yes, that is what I'm suggesting, Tony, but I remain unconvinced that the killer intended to kill both men. My estimate is that Melville Armstrong was the target, as he would likely be the one wielding the *sgian-dubh* – the ceremonial dagger – to cut the haggis. I suspect your arsonist had no idea that the methanol would squirt out on either side of the knife and engulf them both.'

'Yes, why did that happen?'

'The glass vessel is ingenious. The fact that the haggis would need to be cooked for hours beforehand, with the glass

113

vessel already inserted inside it, means that the methanol would likely be at a huge pressure inside there. The glass would be ready to shatter at the slightest touch from the knifepoint. Actually . . .' He googled some graphs then leapt up from the stool by the laptop and picked up the plastic evidence bag. After scrutinising it for some moments, he turned and said, 'We got this quite wrong, Mantoro.'

'Whaddaya mean, boss?'

Boss? It was the first time Tony had ever heard from Penfold or Mantoro any kind of description of their relationship.

'The vessel glass used for the murder is about twice as thick as the ones we made.' He turned back to the policeman, waving the bag containing the glass fragment. 'This would be much easier to make. True, it would still need to be hand-blown, but there was no need to make the glass so fine. Any amateur glass-blower could create your bomb.'

Tony failed to focus on the implications for the case; he was bemused by the way Penfold had implied that he himself was *not* an 'amateur' glass-blower.

Penfold continued, 'However, the delivery method remains the same, and I still think it was not intended to take out Hedley as well as Armstrong. The vessel containing the methanol must surely have been built into the haggis long before it arrived at the castle. My recommendation is to follow its movements from the original manufacturer. Who could have interfered with it between then and its arrival at the kitchen on Saturday night? And when could they have accessed it for long enough to replace most of the contents with the glass container?'

Mantoro rejoined, 'Or done a good ol' Tijuana Switcheroo.'

Penfold nodded, and Tony immediately grasped Mantoro's meaning.

'You're thinking that they may have created an entire fake haggis with this glass vessel containing the methanol inside? The chef wouldn't know what to expect 'cos Armstrong was sending it from an external supplier. Why go to the trouble of doing

114

surgery on the real one, when even Armstrong himself wouldn't know the difference when it was presented for the ceremony? Yes, you're right – it would have been so much easier and more practical to just swap the real one for the Molotov version. That definitely makes sense.'

Mantoro nodded vigorously. DS Milburn felt so enthusiastic about his deduction of the Tijuana Switcheroo reference that any scepticism of the entire exploding glass receptacle concept was banished. This was now his working theory of the crime.

'Breakfast?' Penfold suggested.

Tony looked at the time on his phone and yawned, explaining, 'I need to go and interview the Hedley and Armstrong wives, but I really can't go disturbing them much before eight.'

'Ah right, yes, you probably should go home and get some sleep and see Kathy. An hour or so won't be much, but better than nothing.'

'Please – don't go there. I'm not Kathy's favourite person at the moment.' Milburn spoke with clear irritation in his voice. 'Breakfast is definitely a plan. What did you have in mind?'

'Well, if you need to be back in Durham to interview the widows—'

'Don't tell me, The Daily Espresso!' Tony interrupted.

'They do have wonderful croissants,' Penfold said mildly.

Tony looked at his phone again. 'Are they even open yet?'

'They unlock the doors at seven, but I'm sure they'll let us in if we're a few minutes early. We may have to wait for the croissants to bake, but you'll be finished well before eight.'

Milburn sighed. He had little doubt that the baristas would open up for Penfold at any hour.

Twenty

Monday, 7.17 a.m.

Penfold was right about the breakfast croissants in The Daily Espresso. He treated his policeman friend to as many as he could eat, and Tony drank three large lattes in the forty minutes they were there. Following the excitement of the exploding glass haggis and a delicious free breakfast, Tony was buzzing. Without even considering DCI Hardwick's objections, he invited Penfold to tag along for the visits to Genevieve Hedley and Elspeth Armstrong.

Lowes Wynd on the west side of Durham City, close to the Duke of Wellington pub, held a small collection of large, detached houses. They had been newly built about twenty years previously, and commanded high resale values. Not as high as South Street, however, and this disparity made the status difference between the Hedleys and the Armstrongs stark, blatant.

As they rolled down the dead-end street trying to spot house numbers, Penfold's attention was distracted by the fact that it was recycling collection day. Each home had a wheelie bin with a blue lid outside, some lids sticking up a little with pieces of cardboard nosing out. On the ground beside each wheelie bin sat a green plastic box for glass recycling.

Counting down the numbers, the detective sergeant guessed that the last house on the right would be the one they wanted. Twenty yards ahead, he saw the back of a woman he vaguely recognised walk to that driveway and turn into the property. He stopped the car, and the two men climbed out. Penfold scooted back along the pavement to examine the previous three houses' piles of recycling while Milburn paused by the gate to the front garden. The woman had vanished, most likely through the side

116

gate. Was it the younger daughter Beth, or . . . God, what was the other daughter's name? Milburn searched his memory – Elaine?

He watched his tall, surfer friend catch up. Penfold scanned the expansive front garden, more than half of which contained a rockery of boulders and succulents spaced with gravel.

'Where did Eloise go?' the Kiwi asked.

'Eloise, that's it!' Milburn paused. 'How do you know her?'

'I don't, but her picture came up several times when Trident and I were researching the victims.'

'Of course it did.'

Tony winced as the doorbell played its way through a tinny rendition of 'Greensleeves'. Eloise answered the door, her hair still untidy from the windy conditions outside. Milburn introduced himself, and covered Penfold's presence using the word 'associate'. The Hedleys' older daughter showed discomfort at their arrival but could not quickly come up with an objection as to why they should not enter. She placed them in the front lounge and excused herself to find and fetch her mother from upstairs.

After several minutes, Beth Hedley entered and offered to make tea or coffee. Both guests declined, with Penfold's excuse being that he had already drunk so much coffee that morning he could do with using the toilet. The daughter led him away, and Tony spent a few minutes wandering around the room, taking in the trappings of a modern, middle-class guest parlour. Tastefully co-ordinated furnishings looking like Next or Laura Ashley designs softened the distressed wood furniture and shelving, minimally adorned with photographs of the family and small potted plants. The overall impression was of the same sort of room that Kathy would aim to put together in their own detached house a mile on the other side of the cathedral.

Genevieve Hedley eventually came in, supported by Eloise. Mother and daughter looked very similar, Tony noted. Their clothes were uniformly low key, in drab browns and beiges. What's more, they were the same height, had identical noses, and

117

the two pairs of brown eyes looked at him almost as if all four were on one person. The two women also sported very similar haircuts, both unkempt in a similar way.

Eloise spoke. 'It's very early, Detective, are you sure this is necessary now?'

'I am sorry for the intrusion, Miss Hedley,' Tony said, 'but we're working all hours to find out what happened to your father and Mr Armstrong.'

Genevieve seemed out of sorts, as if she had just woken up. She lifted a dismissive hand towards her daughter and dropped on to the sofa.

'Please, Mr Milliband, do sit down.' At the end of the sentence, she gave a small, nervous laugh.

He did so and began gently. 'It's actually Milburn, but not to worry. Once again, I'm so sorry for what happened to your husband. I trust we have had Family Liaison Officers connect with you? They can arrange counselling and victim support services for you, too.'

Mrs Hedley appeared distressed but answered stoically enough, with, 'We've received some business cards and leaflets from them, but I have my daughters to support me. The girls have been wonderful, even though they have lost their father. Really, what would help the most will be for you to catch the bastard who did this.' Her voice cracked at the word 'bastard', and the nervous laugh came again when she finished speaking.

Milburn talked with them for nearly twenty minutes, discussing Joel Hedley's work, and the state of the aggregates business. He asked about business or financial troubles, and any enemies Joel might have had. Genevieve dismissed this as the most ludicrous idea she had heard in a long time. The picture she painted of her husband was of a bespectacled – she said this as if it were a character trait – scientist, who liked long-distance running through the rocky outcrops of Northumberland.

The large, square lounge had cream wallpaper with blue fabric threading through it. The full length of the back wall consisted of patio doors, built to fold as you slid them open, so the room essentially became open onto the garden terrace. Along half of the adjacent wall, chestnut-brown shelving in a modern asymmetric style held a large collection of old bottles and vases. This area seemed much more densely packed than the rest of the room. The detective sergeant stood and wandered along the shelves, admiring the collection and occasionally leaning forward to look closely at a particular vase, without touching any of them.

'These are wonderful,' he smiled, turning to Mrs Hedley. 'Are you a collector?'

'They were another hobby of Joel's.'

'Oh, really?'

'Yes, it was a geological thing. He always said that most of the earth's crust is made of glass, and he loved how people took that and manipulated it into beautiful objects.'

Penfold and Beth finally re-entered the room and sat down without interrupting. Tony assumed they had been chatting after the young woman had shown Penfold where the bathroom was. Tony then spread the questioning to include both of the daughters, recapping some of the questions their mother had already answered. The answers described a loving father devoted to his work, taking great satisfaction from extracting the secrets hidden underground across north-east England.

All three women were scathing of their father's business partner. Melville Armstrong came across as a selfish and unscrupulous boor. The three expressed a joint sadness at Joel's lack of willingness to stand up for himself in dealings with the man, and they had a special contempt for the way Melville always gave Joel just enough salary, so he could lead a comfortable life and not feel the need to rock the company boat, whilst Armstrong himself made millions from their sales of sand and gravel.

Finally, Milburn addressed the outburst Genevieve had made on the night of the fire.

'Mrs Hedley,' he began, then flicked through a couple of pages of his notebook. 'You said, "That bloody woman, she did

119

this." You blamed Melville and said your husband had warned him it would end like this.'

'Did I? I really don't remember. Sorry, the shock of it all was so great, I probably said a lot of things that didn't make much sense.'

DS Milburn frowned. He maintained a silent pause in the hope that somebody would feel forced to speak to break the awkwardness. Nobody did. Penfold caught Milburn's eyes and flicked his own towards the door, indicating they should talk outside.

Tony said his goodbyes, thanked the family and ended with: 'Once again, I'm very sorry for what happened. We'll do our utmost to find out who is responsible, and I'll make sure the Family Liaison Officer keeps you all in the loop on our progress.'

The three women stood, and the men walked out of the room and straight out of the front door, back to the car. Once inside, Penfold handed over a plastic evidence bag containing a toothbrush. He pulled a geological hammer out of his pocket by its head and slipped that into a larger plastic bag but held on to that one. Tony scowled.

Indicating the toothbrush, Penfold reassured him, saying, 'Don't worry, I got Beth to hand it over willingly, although we've only got her say-so that it belonged to her father.' He then held up the larger bag. 'This one I'll pass on to you if it proves important, so let's say I gave it to you now.' Luckily for Penfold, Milburn was distracted, hung up on the conversation with Mrs Hedley.

'Doesn't remember? Is it just me, or did you think she was being obtuse, trying to avoid answering?'

'She's a drunk, Milburn,' Penfold said matter-of-factly. 'A serious alcoholic – I suspect she really doesn't remember.'

'You know what, I did see her knock back a full glass of wine at the crime scene, and she was behaving very strangely. I just put it down to shock.' Tony's eyebrows scrunched up. 'What makes you think it's more than that?'

'Did you spot the glass-recycling boxes?'

'Yes, of course – what of them?'

'It seems that everyone in the street drinks exactly the same wine. Half a dozen bottles of Marks & Spencer pinot grigio in every one of those green boxes.' He was facing Tony from the passenger seat and waved between their headrests, gesturing up the street. 'Coincidence? This week's bargain at M&S, and everyone in the street took advantage of it? Not at all! When we arrived, we saw Eloise returning to the house after ditching her mother's stash of empties in the neighbours' recycling. Beth told me they are at their wits' end – they've been covering for their mother for twenty years. She's a functioning alcoholic, but only functioning with their help and support. It's the main reason neither of them is married.'

'How do you know all that?'

'Beth and I had something of a heart-to-heart in the kitchen. She's desperately worried about what they'll do, now that Joel's salary will stop. The only upside for Beth is that they're no longer balancing on the knife edge of the divorce threat anymore.'

'Divorce?'

'Yes. The Hedleys got together at university, and Genevieve continually reminisces about those halcyon days. She was a shy, bookish sort until then, and Joel's attentions completely turned her head. Beth and Eloise are convinced that Joel's intense devotion in their early courtship, followed by years of indifference after they married, influenced their mother towards her alcoholism. They needed a way to shock him into paying Genevieve, and I think also themselves, considerably more attention, hoping this might help the drinking to stop. Deluded, obviously, but they had convinced their mother to threaten him with a divorce. She told him on New Year's Eve. Presumably when drunk.'

'What did he say?'

'Well, this is where the knife edge comes in. It worked to a certain extent, with Joel contriving some family days out and so on, but his heart was never truly in it. Nobody really wanted any

121

divorce. It was a bluff, and you can imagine how difficult it must have been to keep the drunken Genevieve from blurting out the truth.'

'Oh man, what a can of worms. The daughters as well?'

Penfold immediately understood Milburn's concern at this piece of information offering up additional new suspects.

'I thought about that too, but patricide? I don't think so. I can't see those women plotting to kill their father.'

'That doesn't rule it out, though.' Milburn felt suddenly exhausted. 'Why does this case just keep expanding?'

Twenty-one

Monday, 8.45 a.m.

The narrow cobbled South Street was one-way and descended steeply from the boarding houses of Durham School down to the city centre, where Framwellgate Bridge met Crossgate and North Road. Cobbles and houses lined the uneven streets. Tony half-expected to meet some filthy serf driving a horse and cart the other way.

The Armstrongs' expensive home stood at a narrow part of South Street, and DS Milburn had to park his black hatchback mostly on the pavement in order to be right outside the front door. It was a grand townhouse of dark brown Victorian brick. The front door was half as wide again as Tony's own at home, and it had pillars and an arch of sandstone framing the old oak door.

The place reminded him of Penfold's house, but there was a significant variance. Rather like the social differences between Hartlepool and Durham City, the surfer's house rambled around its poorly kept garden, with cracks in the paintwork and some rot in the window-frames. This South Street home was pristine. Despite its age, the place had been meticulously maintained to a high standard.

The wind continued to gust, but the morning sky was clear. The view to Durham Cathedral was breathtaking. Penfold and Milburn stood and stared from the doorstep back across the River Wear, well below them in the steep valley. At roughly their level, the west end of the cathedral had two square towers, anchoring it to the rocky peninsula that St Cuthbert's entourage had carried his body to, back in the tenth century. The riverbanks on both sides were steep and thickly wooded. Through the vegetation, they could just make out some of the castellations on Durham Castle's long side above the medieval Framwellgate Bridge. A single bird's chirping came through the chill morning air. Nothing indicated modern times – the scene invoked hundreds of years of history.

The sun had been up for half an hour and peeked over the Cathedral's huge central tower, golden rays radiating like in a child's picture. Neither man spoke, but simply stood in awe. The warmth of the light made Tony wonder what a religious experience would feel like.

'I'm sorry, you can't park there.'

The voice from behind made Milburn jump, and they both turned to see a woman standing in the doorway of the Armstrongs' house. She was wearing a cleaner's tabard and yellow rubber gloves on both hands.

After flashing his warrant card, and introducing himself and his 'associate', Tony asked to see Elspeth Armstrong.

'She's not here. She's been staying at her mother's apartment in Jesmond since the fire.' The stout woman displayed no emotion at the mention of the tragedy.

'Terrible business,' Penfold said, shaking his head slightly.

The woman ignored him, so Milburn asked for the Jesmond address, and whether any other members of the family were at home. He was briskly informed that her instructions were to deep clean the whole house. The missus wouldn't be back for at least a week.

She concluded with, 'There ain't no other family. Least, not legit ones. None that live here. Or ever visit.'

By the time the door was roughly closed on them, and the two men turned back to the car and cathedral view, the sun had risen a little further. The spiritual moment had passed.

They exactly hit the rush-hour traffic jam as the A1(M) motorway split from the A194(M). One road went east, and the other went west to circumnavigate Newcastle. The traffic queued daily at that point, adding at least twenty minutes to the drive to Jesmond. Heading over the Tyne Bridge was similarly snarled up.

In the end, it took them over an hour for the journey only to find that the widow Armstrong had eluded them again.

Her mother appeared at first to be a genial and dynamic eighty year old. However, despite her charm, the woman took the opportunity to bend Tony's ear about the disgrace that had been Melville Armstrong. Throughout her polemic against her recently deceased son-in-law, Milburn winced inwardly, silently repeating to himself, *She can't be another suspect; she's too old; she can't be a suspect.*

Elspeth's mother, Dorothy, espoused the idea that her daughter had, through 'this good fortune', been given the chance to make her own success in life, instead of simply being the wife of a successful businessman. The man had been a no-good philanderer who deserved what he got, she ranted. Elspeth was only fifty-five and knew enough of the aggregates business to run it far more successfully than 'that lazy fat bastard ever had'. Dorothy's diatribe finally made its way round to the fact that her daughter was not at home, but up at the quarry site, working to keep the business going, despite the terrible state Melville was bound to have left it in.

It took Milburn another few minutes to get the conversation anywhere near to asking for the office address. That was when Penfold held up his phone, displaying the address details for Armstrong Aggregates. He simply interrupted the woman, in mid-flow, to confirm that that was the location where they would find Elspeth.

Another thirty minutes north into the wilds of Northumberland took them to a large site with chain-link fencing. The place was open for business, so the old gates, also chain link and metal, were thrown back, one leaning against the fence and the other against a tree that seemed to be propping it up from falling off its hinges. The vehicle barrier was up, and the sentry station was empty.

The sun that had bathed Durham in spiritual glory was absent in this part of central Northumberland. The dark green fields and stands of trees made for a beautiful panorama, but the sky here was overcast, and the January wind blew strong and cold.

The aggregates site was very open. Gravel roadways, rutted and scattered with large puddles, added to the chill Tony felt as he stepped from the warm car. They had parked outside a pair of double height Portakabin offices, reached by a set of steps, fifty yards into the site. As they emerged, a white van with the Armstrong Aggregates logo drove between a hard standing with piles of different grades of sand and a hanger of a garage, and disappeared behind the brown metal-sided building.

The wide gravel tracks continued further from the road and split away to several more distant areas where cranes and trucks moved around, presumably lifting stones and then ferrying them away for sorting and then transport off-site. The whole place seemed a bit of a blot on the wonderful countryside. Milburn was unsure exactly how far they were from the edge of Northumberland National Park, but he hoped they weren't actually within its boundary.

The group of office Portakabins had no organised car park, just a bulge of extra gravel to one side of the main track, halfway from the public road to the quarry area. Four temporary buildings, barely larger than shipping containers, sat next to each other, end on, with an identical four on top to make a second storey. Each hut had a door and a window filling the short side facing them.

They climbed four steps that led up to a walkway along the front of the lower four buildings. It reminded Tony of a wild west town, with a raised verandah walkway to keep fine skirts out of the mud in the street. Access to the doors of each of the upper offices came via four staircases that climbed up the front like vines.

It was ten-thirty by the time the two men entered the door marked Reception, to find two women tapping at computer keyboards in the neat but spartan workroom. DS Milburn introduced them both to the young receptionist, before Penfold headed to the rear to talk to the older of the two office workers.

BURNS NIGHT BURNS

Tony quickly gleaned from the young receptionist that Mrs Armstrong was in Melville's office, which consisted of the upper part of the two Portakabins directly above. The young woman was upset by the deaths of the two business owners and sniffled throughout her conversation with Milburn. His questions about problems at the company, financial or otherwise, did not improve her emotional state and Tony quickly wound up the discussion. It was obvious that she knew nothing that would further the investigation.

As they moved along the raised walkway in front of the prefab buildings to Joel Hedley's office and lab next door, Penfold was coy about his dialogue with the other woman, who had turned out to be Hedley's PA. Tony had seen them look over some paperwork, but he received no explanation. She had been similarly upset by the deaths, and Penfold's take on how her information might contribute to the investigations was unclear.

'She gave me a few odd bits and pieces to check up on, but I'm not sure there's anything that you need to follow up too specifically.'

The geologist's office consisted of neat areas and parts that were untidy to the point of chaos. After a couple of minutes taking in the whole scene, Tony realised that the science-y parts of the room were meticulously well-ordered, whilst the more business-oriented sections were the uncared-for areas. Dominating the centre of the space was a large conference table, with a pair of maps displayed on it, sellotaped in place. The title of the nearest one said *Geological Map of Northumberland*. It was the sort of thing Joel Hedley should have in his workplace, Milburn thought approvingly.

Under the window beside the door was a desk with a computer and printer. Scraps of paper and sticky notes covered the surface, the keyboard and much of the screen. Piles of receipts cluttered the mouse mat, and a variety of pens and pencils worked as paperweights to keep things in place.

A larger desk filled most of the opposite end of the Portakabin, positioned under another big window. On it was a complicated electronic microscope, with a screen attached, and an Apple MacBook. By comparison, this computer vastly outdid the old black box on the desk beside the door. That one looked so ancient that Milburn wondered if the business computer was powered by steam.

It came as no surprise to him that someone with his own underground lab would be attracted straight to the scientific investigations. As Penfold fired up the microscope and opened the silver laptop, the detective went over and picked up a handful of the notes scattered over the smaller, messy business desk. Occasionally a Post-It note would be written in a neat, orderly hand. From the contents, Milburn deduced that they had been written by the Personal Assistant Penfold had spoken to next door. The untouched reminders of meetings and reports that were due, interspersed with phone messages and requests to call people back, gave him the distinct impression that Joel had paid little attention to the commercial activities of the firm. He was Chief Scientific Officer, after all.

Some of the notes were written in another's handwriting, presumably Hedley's own. Mostly these were reminders to himself, To Do lists, references to look up, even a couple of shopping lists. The largest and best-organised hand-written sheet was stuck on the wall to the side of the desk. This neatly structured matrix of information had no title. After a few moments attempting to decipher it, Tony worked out that it was a runner's record, including distances and times and the dates of the runs, going back three months. He scrutinised it closely, and the times seemed to get much longer since the beginning of January.

'Overdid things at Christmas, did we?' Tony mumbled out loud.

He looked across to Penfold, now sitting at the silver laptop, clicking the touchpad and opening and closing windows in rapid succession.

'Whoa, put some gloves on, will you?' Milburn called over.

'Apologies. I didn't think this was a crime scene, but you're right – best practice and all that.'

'If that's Hedley's laptop, it'll need to go in to forensics. Who knows if there's a threatening email or something on it.'

'Very true.' Penfold pulled sky-blue disposable gloves on. 'Do you have an evidence bag this size?' He closed the lid and brought the machine over and placed it at the end of the map table whilst Tony fumbled around in his jacket pockets for a large forensics bag printed with information spaces.

The maps had attracted Penfold's attention. He leant over the middle of the table, his fingers sliding along coloured sections on the largest map. In places, coloured dot stickers had been attached, and Penfold slowly built up a situation where his fingers were spread over the map, touching numerous dots. At that point, he looked around at how the web of fingertips compared with locations on the smaller-scale map that sat adjacent.

'What do you see?' Tony half-joked. 'Does X mark the spot?'

'What?' Penfold looked up with a confused expression. 'No. But just look at this.' He pointed at two places, one with each index finger.

In each spot, a small area had been scribbled over in black pen. Next to the scribble, the word *arsehole* had been written in the same hand as the shopping lists and personal reminders that Milburn had just seen. Tony leaned forward to take photographs: one of each scribble marking, and a broader shot of much of the map, encompassing the whole area with the two fingers.

'Weird,' he said. 'What do you make of it?'

Penfold stood back to his full height and folded his arms across the chest of his blue T-shirt.

'Difficult to second guess a mind like this.' He released one hand to give a wave around the Portakabin interior. 'However . . .' He gestured at the OS map. 'This is where we're standing now.' The temporary structures forming the offices had not been marked on by the cartographers, and he pointed to a green area abutting the small road outside the fence, saying, 'Which is here on the geological map.' He used his other hand to point at an area shaded in ruddy-brown, to represent some particular mineral type.

'OK.'

'If you look at the scribbled-out places, they're here and here.' The Kiwi moved both fingers on to separate spots on the regular map.

Tony leaned in to see what was in these locations. Nothing obvious. One was the same light green as the rest, and one had a shading like small pine trees. 'And they are?'

'This one,' Penfold stabbed his left forefinger down, 'was the site of ArmAgg. And that's the site of the old Hedley Aggregates.' His right finger pointed down emphatically.

'Ah, I hadn't realised that those different companies were in different physical places,' Tony said, enlightened. 'I thought your explanation yesterday meant that they'd simply re-registered the companies for tax breaks, and for Melville to take the lion's share each time.'

'Yes, bits of that, but they've been steadily working across this yellow line on the map. You see this? It's deposits of river sand and gravel, perfect for aggregates, but this shows there's only a thin range of suitable locations.'

Penfold stepped around the central table and unhooked a large piece of floppy plastic from the wall. It turned out to be three separate thin transparent sheets, each with different coloured tracings on, and three different headings. The transparencies could be overlaid on the geological map, to highlight different things in relation to the sand and gravel deposits. Penfold flipped them on and off, one after the other, before laying down all three and aligning them exactly. Milburn followed the red titling.

'So, the red outline shows where permissions for quarrying are in place, whether or not there's an active quarry.'

'Right, and then blue shows land ownership, and yellow is the outline of the National Park.'

'Is the National Park important?'

'I assume so, if there's a transparency for it. Maybe you're not allowed to do any new quarrying inside the park boundary.'

The two men stood bemused. In black, the scribbles and the annotated words, *arsehole*, stood out brightly.

Tony confirmed, 'So these two places are where their previous digging sites were, right?'

'Yup. And in each case, Hedley did all this work, they made a lot of money, and then Melville essentially robbed him of the proceeds.'

'Sounds like more than merely an arsehole to me.'

'Agreed – but looking around at the mind that organised this room, I suspect that Joel was well beyond his swearing comfort zone writing that word down. To then write it a second time, he must have been really angry. Look there.' Again, Penfold pointed at one of the annotations. The same black pen had started to cross out one of the *arsehole* words. The pen had hesitated and then abandoned its course, as if Hedley thought to erase his angry gesture but then decided to stick with it. The second *arsehole* had no additional markings. 'He struggled to air his rage aloud, to leave it in the light of day.'

Penfold returned the plastic sheets to their wall hook, and the two men headed out to drop the laptop in the boot of the black police car. As they walked back to go upstairs to Armstrong's office, Tony asked about the signs and clues that his friend had seen inside, and which had given him that insight into Hedley's psyche. The answers, though, were vague and highfalutin. Before Milburn could quiz the aloof surfer any more deeply, they had reached the door at the top of the staircase.

Twenty-two

Monday, 11.14 a.m.

Despite being not much more than a furnished shipping container, the main director's office was luxurious. Tony could see Melville Armstrong's personality displayed in full force. The room was designed to portray the working environment of a highly successful leader in business. Straight ahead of the entrance door was a large photo of the late Mr Armstrong shaking hands with Tony Blair beside one of the excavators he had seen outside. Judging by the ages of the two men in the picture, Milburn assumed this would have been taken when Blair was Prime Minister, paying a media-friendly visit to a region relatively close to his Sedgefield constituency.

'Detective Sergeant Milburn. And . . .?' Mrs Armstrong was standing at the other end of the office. Pencil thin, she was leaning over another desk with a large map on it, to which she had affixed a number of Post-It notes with brief pen marks on them. Her eyes though were fixed on Penfold. The tall man had had to stoop to pass through the Portakabin door, and even once inside his short, blond hair was worryingly close to the ceiling.

'My name is Penfold. I'm an investigative consultant with Durham Police. We're looking into the tragic death of your husband.'

Elspeth appeared sceptical, and Tony was furious. He kept his feelings hidden, but Penfold's claim was unhelpful at best and probably criminal at worst. He was helping Detective Sergeant Milburn investigate, but not in any official capacity, and Tony needed to keep his involvement very much on the qt.

He intervened, saying smoothly, 'Once again, Mrs Armstrong, I'm very sorry for your loss. Is it a convenient time for us to ask you some questions?'

132

'Happy to help as best I can.' The woman put down the pen and waved the two men to a green chesterfield sofa, seating herself in its partner armchair. She was calm and composed and did not appear to be suffering from grief.

Milburn set his phone to record on the arm of the sofa and supplemented it with his notebook in hand.

'I hope my questions don't cause you too much upset, but in cases of this kind, we need to establish a picture of who might have wanted to hurt your husband.' The first thing he wrote down was how unaffected the widow seemed to be at the loss of her husband.

Elspeth Armstrong's highlighted hair looked expensively done, but the grey roots were just visible, as it was all tied back in a tight, businesslike bun.

'What? Do you think the fire was started deliberately?' She seemed shocked. 'Surely, it was just an accident? I can well imagine Melville adding too much whisky – to make a really big show of the flames, I expect.'

Penfold intoned, 'Rest assured, we know it was murder.'

'Yes, sorry, we are investigating the possibility of this as deliberate.' Milburn gave Penfold a hard stare, but the Kiwi was focused on Elspeth. 'Do you know of anyone with a grudge against your husband, or somebody who might have wanted to do him harm?'

Mrs Armstrong held her hands neatly in her lap, sitting straight up. Her face remained serious in expression as she answered, 'Where should I start? Perhaps we should go alphabetically.'

A smile flickered at the corner of Penfold's mouth. Tony ploughed on.

'Perhaps we could begin with you telling us about anyone who had made explicit threats.'

'Well, I'll discount myself,' she said. 'Every time I threatened to kill him, it was just a way to vent my anger or frustration. Melville could be a very difficult man.'

'Please, can you think of anyone we should talk to?'

'Yes, of course, I'm just getting started. Top of the list would be Declan Tait. He hated my husband. Even giving the boy a job here hadn't placated him at all. He and that woman, his mother, seemed to think they had some right to inveigle themselves into our lives.' She gave a scornful laugh. 'As if.'

Penfold asked, 'Declan was Melville's son by Jacqui Tait. You don't think that gives them any sort of place in your husband's life?'

The scornful laugh came again. 'Jacqui was my husband's plaything. He never had any love, or even concern for her. I washed my hands of the whole affair many years ago.'

Tony was sceptical about this. From his own dealings with Jacqui, he considered that she was probably a bit blinded by her feelings for Melville, but she wasn't stupid. She was never going to stick with him for twenty years without some sort of expressions of feeling from him. With his minimal financial contributions, there had to be more to it for Jacqui to stay with him.

'And the Taits knew the situation: they're not our sort of people. He could never invite *her* to the Burns Night Supper, for example.'

Almost under his breath, Penfold responded, 'Perhaps that's the point.' Tony quickly jumped in, hopeful that only he had been near enough to hear his friend's comment.

'OK, we've interviewed those two, but we'll revisit that.'

'They've told you a pack of lies, I expect.'

'Like I say, we'll revisit the Taits. Anyone else to consider?'

'If he hadn't died as well, I would have suggested you talk to Joel. Melville had bent him over a barrel so many times over the years, frankly I wonder why the man didn't just leave. But he was a bit strange. Very insular, wouldn't hold eye contact and always muttering to himself. *Very* strange, actually. Too quiet. You always wondered what he was planning. You know the sort,

134

where the neighbours say on TV, "Oh, he was very quiet and kept himself to himself". Until he shoots his whole family.' She looked at the others as if that concluded the case for the prosecution.

'As you said, Joel Hedley was first to die in the fire. He's not a suspect. Can you think of anyone else?' Tony's mind went to Randall White's accusations of racism. 'Perhaps someone in your husband's social circles that he might have had conflict with? Maybe in the Friendship Society? After all, that's where the . . . incident took place.'

'Really, Sergeant, whilst he was annoying and arrogant, my husband was the toast of the Friendship Society. Why do you think they kept voting him in as President? No, no, they loved him there. That sort of thing was his forte. He knew how networking like that, amongst real highfliers, could keep the wheels of business turning. Not only for us, but for all the Society's members. Everyone there was grateful to Melville for the success of their own businesses.'

Milburn could see Penfold's face struggling to maintain a blank facade. He could tell that the tanned cheeks would crease with laughter at any moment, so he diverted matters.

'Your husband said a few words just before he died, and we're not really sure what he meant by them. I wonder if you might know what he was trying to say?'

'Well, let's see. Go ahead.' Elspeth Armstrong lifted an encouraging palm to DS Milburn, and he flicked back through his notebook.

'He was speaking to a nurse at his bedside in the hospital and said, "Find her cleaner dead e . . ." He didn't finish that last word, but the nurse says it sounded like it would start with an e. Do you know of a cleaner, perhaps, who died? Or who might be the woman that he refers to as having a cleaner?'

Mrs Armstrong stared out of the large window, slowly shaking her head, and then turned back to the detective.

'No, I'm sorry, that doesn't make any sense at all. But if he was on his deathbed, perhaps it is just rambling nonsense.'

135

'We met your cleaner at the house in South Street this morning. You don't think he might have meant her, could he? Did you organise the cleaner?'

'Melville considered that was part of the wife's responsibility in our marriage, organising the cleaner, the gardener, any decorators and builders, and basically anything to do with the house. But as you saw, my cleaner is very much alive.'

'Well, thank you for your time. If you think of anything else, please give me a call straight away.' They all stood up, and Tony handed her a business card. 'One other thing, though, before we go: is there any item here that might have your husband's DNA on it? The pathologist will need to do a test to dot the i's and cross the t's on the postmortem report.'

The bereaved widow did not question the request. The fact that she had seen her own husband in the fire and could confirm his identity did not seem to cross her mind. 'What did you have in mind?'

'A toothbrush is the usual, but I don't suppose he kept one here, did he?'

'Not to my knowledge. He was a stickler for keeping his hair neat, though, so it wouldn't surprise me if there's a hairbrush here somewhere. That's an acceptable alternative, is it?'

Penfold pointed at the portrait mirror above a tallboy with tumblers and two whisky bottles on its top.

Elspeth either knew her husband well or got lucky, as the hairbrush was in the first drawer she opened in the tallboy – the second one down. DS Milburn held a hand over the drawer to stop her touching it and produced an evidence bag.

Once they had descended the white metal stairs outside the cabins, they spotted Declan Tait driving towards the exit in his works van. He stared at Penfold and Milburn and sped up towards them, wrenching the steering wheel round so that the vehicle was aimed right at them. Penfold pulled his friend back and the van missed him by barely a foot. Declan almost banged his head on the roof as the vehicle bumped through a sludge-filled pothole.

The two men watched him go as muddy water splashed their legs and dripped down onto their shoes.

'Bloody hell!' Tony shouted and turned to check Penfold was unharmed. 'Suspect number one, I reckon.'

From the step above and behind, Penfold put a hand on his shoulder.

'You had convinced me he was innocent, but I'm not so sure now. Although I definitely can't see him as capable of blowing a fine glass vessel.'

'Nor could he think up such an elaborate plot,' Tony grunted. 'As Meredith pointed out, he'd just give Melville a good kicking.'

'I think most importantly, though, his job here was contingent on Armstrong's staying alive. That money supply will run out once Elspeth gets round to firing him.'

'Well, he's clearly erratic and dangerous.' Shaken, the detective sergeant reached for his radio, but it was not in his jacket pocket.

Penfold then asked, 'Did you see the photo of Melville in his kilt at Balmoral?'

'I didn't realise that's where it was.'

'The Royal Standard wasn't on the flagpole, so it's clearly just for show. His *sgian-dubh* - the dagger – looked the same as the one from Saturday night.'

Driving back towards Durham past the Metrocentre, the traffic was much less hassle than on the way up. Tony's mobile rang, and the voice of Sergeant Singh came loud from the hands-free system.

'We've got an incident at the Moranne Private Bank on Old Elvet. Can you attend, Tony?'

'Well, I'm up in Newcastle at the moment, so can't somebody else attend? I'll be at least half an hour, and I'm deep in interviews about the castle fire.'

'Some bloke's holed up in there. It's only a small office, but he's barricaded the door and basically got the three staff as hostages. He doesn't have a weapon, but they called us on fraud prevention whilst he was in there. He was trying to move forty-three grand that belonged to your man Armstrong, out to some offshore account. He asked the teller to make an electronic transfer out to this Cayman Islands account, which apparently you can do if you go into the bank in person and have the right ID and paperwork. Which he does, and which he's waving around like a letter from his mother excusing him from PE.'

'OK, well, this seems like I should look over the information once he's been dealt with, but I can't see that it needs me to attend. Get uniforms to arrest him, and I'll interview him later about it.'

'I think you're going to want to go to the bank now, Tony. You see, the man trying to withdraw the money is Melville Armstrong.'

Twenty-three

Monday, 11.50 a.m.

'This I gotta see.' Penfold's face was practically pressed against the car window glass to stare out at the solid stone bank facade.

Given the Kiwi's eternal stoicism in all things, good and bad, Milburn was surprised at this display of enthusiasm. Penfold actually seemed *excited*. It was the most eager he had seen his friend since the previous spring's talk of the twenty-year storm bringing huge surf waves to Seaton Carew beach.

Milburn screeched to a halt outside the Hotel Indigo. His radio flew out from under the seat and cracked Tony in the ankle. Picking it up, he winced: his lower limbs had taken a few knocks over the last three days.

The beautiful red-brick Victorian hotel building sat resplendent, occupying a large chunk of Old Elvet. Opposite, in a huge stone-built townhouse with a plaque outside, was the grand entrance to the Moranne Private Bank. The plate-glass door was piled high on the inside with a barricade of desks and office chairs.

Three Panda cars, with reflective blue and gold chequer pattern livery, blocked off the street in both directions as well as the side road, Territorial Lane. Big Bob Smith formed an additional police barrier to the public, and he explained the situation to DS Milburn. Penfold lurked out of the way, but within earshot of the giant constable's information.

The bank staff were in phone contact with Hardwick up at the station, but they could not convince Melville Armstrong to talk on the phone. They had grown suspicious of the money movements he was requesting and contacted the police without his knowledge. The young receptionist had lost her nerve as Armstrong became agitated with her stalling, and that was when she had blurted out that they had called the police on him. This had precipitated the man to barricade them all inside, leading to the current stand-off.

'Has anyone out here actually seen the man?' Penfold asked PC Bob Smith, and DS Milburn gave a brief nod to the uniformed officer to confirm he was OK to answer.

'Not out here, but he has ID apparently, both driving licence and his credit card issued by this bank. They say the picture on the driving licence is a match.'

Tony and Penfold stared at each other.

'So, who died?' the New Zealander mouthed silently.

The three turned to stare at the door with the office furniture blocking any view inside the premises.

'Do we know if he's armed?' Milburn asked. 'What is the danger to the employees?'

PC1184 Big Bob Smith replied, 'Nothing reported.'

Tony looked Bob up and down. 'You reckon you could shift that door open if it's unlocked?'

The lifelong rugby player grunted, 'I went through Jarrow's entire front row on Saturday. That looks like less weight than they were – fat muppets.'

Using the radio, as the DCI would hopefully be on the phone to the bank staff, Milburn asked, 'Delta Charlie Alpha, any report of weapons or a threat of violence? And can you ask if the front door is locked or just blockaded?'

The radio beeped. 'Wait out.'

The sixty seconds before Hardwick's next message seemed like an eternity.

'No weapons seen, door not locked, suspect seems calm and amenable. He's adamant he can't be arrested but has not issued any threats to the staff. The hostage situation is about avoiding the police and nothing more. What are you thinking, Tony?'

'Permission to barge through the front door and arrest him, sir?'

'If you think it's safe. Suspect and three hostages are all in the main room behind that front door.'

Tony looked at the time on his phone and grinned, pressing the radio talk button. 'Delta Charlie Alpha, be advised, we'll breach at noon exactly.'

'Like I said, Tony, make sure it's safe. Let's not get anyone hurt here.'

'H, they're being held hostage by a ghost – Melville Armstrong is dead.'

'Safety, Tony, first priority, and that's an order.'

DS Milburn nodded towards the bank and he and Smith stalked to the door. Tony held up a flat hand to Penfold to stay put at the police car blocking the road. He then waved across to the other three constables maintaining the cordon around the bank and they all gave a thumbs-up. Everyone had heard the radio conversation.

At the glass door, the two stood on either side of the stone door frame rather than in front of the glass itself. They peeked through the gaps between bits of stacked furniture. Occasional limbs and heads could be spotted, and Tony convinced himself that they were all far enough back from the door to avoid being hit by a chair falling from the pile.

He looked at his phone again and gave Smith a thumbs-up. Five splayed fingers held high started a countdown so all could see it, four fingers, three fingers, two fingers. After the single finger curled closed, Milburn pointed at Smith, who launched himself like a charging bull into the glass door right by the long metal handle. The thick glass would never break at such an attack, but he strained to move it open at all. Like he'd seen rugby forwards do on the television, Tony took up a similar bullish stance, wrapped an arm around Bob Smith's pelvis and together they drove the heaped furniture backwards. It only needed a couple of feet before they could surge through the gap and enter the bank.

141

As reported, the three bank staff sat on the green and yellow carpet beside the front reception desk. As the two police officers crashed through, a corpulent red-faced man in a blazer turned and ran down the corridor towards the rear offices. Bob Smith was now in full rugby mode, and within five steps, he'd propelled himself to tackle the waddling suspect. The corridor was narrow given the bulk of the two men, and they landed in a heap on the plush floor.

Milburn radioed that the police could now remove the roadblock and come inside to help with witness statements and the arrest. He photographed the man lolling on the floor by Bob Smith and sent the photo to Penfold. The staff assured him that they were unhurt and barely even felt threatened. The man had been polite, if rather arrogant, but not one of them had ever imagined he would attack.

Penfold's message came back.

Melville Armstrong? No,

check the soft underbelly,

barely a disguise.

Milburn turned to the tackled man and held out his hand to help him up, saying, 'Are you hurt, Mr Armstrong?'

With a heave, and Bob Smith's assistance, they righted him, up onto his brown loafers.

'My lawyers will work that out, you pair of oicks,' the fellow puffed and panted. 'What the hell do you think you're doing?'

'Sorry, it is Melville Armstrong, is it?'

'Yes, it is, and I'll thank you to let me on my way now.' The well-dressed fifty-something flourished a fat black wallet from the inside pocket of his jacket and left it in Milburn's hand.

He made as if to stride towards the door, but Smith was fleeter of foot and blocked the exit like a bouncer.

Tony scanned the man's figure from behind and could see a ridge around the waist. He pushed a hand against it and the flab squashed in like the side of a bouncy castle. The suspect appeared not to notice and was more interested in boldly chastising the large police constable blocking his way.

Again, Tony pushed his fingers into the blazer at about kidney level. It felt strange, unlike flesh, more rubbery. The man still did not notice, and Tony lifted the hem of the blazer and the jumper underneath it, to reveal a nude-coloured wall of latex. It reminded him of a sumo suit, the oversized rubber outfits for playing daft party games.

'You're under arrest, whoever you are. At the very least for false imprisonment, and potentially other offences. Bob, can you tell him his rights and take him across to the nick for processing, please.'

'My pleasure.' Big Bob Smith took the man by the wrist and led him outside, reciting the arrest spiel as they went.

Tony waved two other constables inside to help the bank staff, and he walked out to meet Penfold in the shadow of the hotel that had once been Old Shire Hall. He put on blue evidence gloves and, as he wandered out, the leather wallet flopped open in his hands. He pulled out a card at random – a NatWest debit card – and, sure enough, it displayed the name Mr Melville Armstrong. Sliding it back in, he searched through the wallet and found the driving licence. If it was a forgery, it was a good one. Even Penfold could not point to any inauthenticity in it.

'That guy really looks like this photo,' DS Milburn said in wonder. He and Penfold stared at it. 'Burned beyond recognition would be a good way to start a new life, but I can't believe that both DI Barnes and Mrs Armstrong could be fooled into thinking he was the one that caught fire. And how would you convince an actor to stand in for you on an occasion like the Burns Night Supper, let alone your own immolation?'

'Listen to yourself, Milburn,' Penfold chided him. 'Armstrong did die in the fire; this one's the imposter. Why else would he wear the fat suit today?'

'Of course.' Tony shook his head to flush away the confusion. 'I haven't slept - think I need more coffee. I'll get one back at the station.'

Penfold took his leave and Tony tiredly got back into the car and headed for the police station.

Twenty-four

Monday, 12.50 p.m.

The police station car park was full. The defunct bus stop across the road that the police often parked in was also full. In the end, Tony had to squeeze into a space at the old driving test centre on Hallgarth Street, the place where candidates used to wait for the examiner to come out to their car.

'Would have been better leaving it blocking the road outside Hotel Indigo,' he muttered.

DCI Hardwick's office was the biggest in the building but was still not huge. Durham City police station, as a repurposed and refurbished Georgian building, suffered from an acute lack of space. Milburn often wondered how they might cope if any of the shifts actually had the full complement of officers it should have. Unfortunately, the compact office meant that Harry could give you his deadeye look more easily and more intensely than in a bigger space.

'Where the hell have you been?' he snapped at Milburn. 'You're the second-in-command in this double murder case, and I haven't seen you for twenty-four hours.'

'I've been out investigating, H. I've spent all of that time confirming alibis and witness statements and so on.'

Milburn then realised he'd been far too quick to defend himself, and too quick to be overly friendly with his boss, using the diminutive 'H' to address him. Had he let the boss's rhetoric wash over him, he might well have escaped the DCI's wrath. As it was, Hardwick seethed through several minutes of non-stop complaints, ending with Milburn's lack of meticulous procedure-following.

Tony stood silently listening to the litany of remonstrations until Harry finally ran out of steam and left the final rhetorical question hanging. Milburn did not attempt to answer it. The variety of things he had failed to do were, of course, correct protocol according to the manual – but equally they would have taken his time away from the investigative steps he had followed. The work he had done had followed the manual's procedural steps, it was just he had not recorded the details in the system.

Unless we get more police, something will always have to give. I can't do the work of three men. These thoughts did not surface out loud. Instead, he moved to explain the progress he had made in the hope that it would appease Hardwick to see that the case was being thoroughly investigated, even if not totally by the book. Once Tony had recounted his activities and the position of the various suspects and witnesses, Hardwick revealed that he had received the forensics report.

'Dr Sedgley has confirmed the use of methanol as an accelerant but says there's a huge inconsistency about how it might have been delivered. Her report says they may never find out how it hadn't evaporated before the ignition. Off the record she told me that she'd once seen a movie where a criminal used a sort of CamelBak-type tube thing up their sleeve to squirt methanol on victims. Here, though, neither of the victims had any strange apparatus hidden in their clothes, and the video evidence from the various phones shows Randall White standing too far from the haggis for such a thing, and not obviously behaving strangely. She says it's a mystery.'

Tony's stomach was somersaulting. He knew the answer to this conundrum but was also aware that Penfold's involvement would sour the delivery of the information. Biding his time on this would help, but he would have to inject the concept of the glass vessel by the time they came to hypotheses of suspects to home in on, or the investigation could go in the wrong direction.

'There is also the very slightest trace evidence of,' Hardwick sounded out the syllables, 'A-Cryl-A-Mide. Based on our victims, she's written that this is often found around sand and gravel quarries, some sort of environmental pollutant.'

146

'You mean that's been brought in by Hedley and Armstrong, or is Dr Sedgley saying it's connected with the fire?'

'Yes, the fire. These traces were in the tablecloth where the haggis was sitting. So not just off people's shoes.'

Milburn nodded. 'Ah, now, Randall White said that the haggis had been brought in separately from everything else, on the orders of Armstrong himself. It was delivered to the castle from Armstrong Aggregates on Saturday afternoon. I wonder who handled it there? I'd guess that's how it got the acryliwotsit on it.'

'Well, yes, look into that delivery. That's another time when it could have been tampered with. The CSIs are also going to the aggregates site to do some comparison swabs. Apparently, they'll be able to confirm that the site is definitely the source of the acryl chemical.' Hardwick moved on. 'Dr Sedgley is waiting on the DNA test results for a hundred per cent ID on the victims, but the eyewitness IDs seem solid enough to use for now. I mean,' he added, 'I'd have said it was Melville Armstrong just from looking at the body. And the only fingerprints on the dagger they used on the haggis were Armstrong's.'

With an unnecessary flourish, Milburn took out the toothbrush and hairbrush in their evidence bags. He picked a biro from a pot on Harry's desk and completed the relevant details on the bags' white spaces.

'I'll pretend I didn't see this.'

Tony tried to deadeye his boss but knew it would never work. The master would never become the apprentice.

'Both these widows watched their husbands burn to death. I wasn't about to stand in front of them for five minutes filling in the forms on these bags just because procedure says you have to do it at the moment you seize the evidence.'

'That's why I'm happy to gloss over it,' DCI Hardwick said.

Milburn felt the full force of the DCI's one-eyed stare. And then a nagging thought entered his tired head and came into focus.

'Wait! Armstrong's fingerprints were *on file*?'

'He had a shotgun licence.'

The DS subsided. 'Of course he did.'

'But the body at the scene had its fingerprints burned too badly to compare for ID.'

'I agree, though, if that dagger only has Armstrong's prints, it's a reasonable leap to put them as those of our dead man and run with that as an ID for him.'

There was nothing further in the forensic report that Milburn did not already know. Having carefully omitted Penfold's involvement and over-emphasised how difficult it was to work with Diane Meredith, he moved quickly to the most recent activity with the mysterious imposter at the bank. This left a good space for Tony to excuse himself to go down and interview the interloper.

As he descended the stairs, Milburn texted Kathy with a message of love, hoping it might help with reconciliation when he got home at the end of the day. That was followed by a message to Penfold to ask him to upload the video of the exploding glass container in the fume cupboard, so that Tony could show it to Hardwick as something he had 'found' on YouTube. Penfold replied straight away to confirm he would edit out himself and any of their conversation that had been captured before uploading it to YouTube.

The bulky Armstrong look-a-like was still holding forth at the custody suite's reception desk when Tony arrived. He asked Sergeant Singh if the interview room was free and led the man along the short corridor. They sat opposite each other, and DS Milburn indicated that he was starting the video recording.

'No need for a lawyer, thank you,' the man said pompously. 'I'm sure we'll be able to clear up this misunderstanding pretty quickly. It's not unusual when you deal with large sums of money to have to explain these things to the police, so I'll be happy to put you in the picture.'

148

Tony had brought the man's belongings in their evidence bags. He signed the one containing the wallet and opened it up to look through it in front of the suspect. The real Melville Armstrong's burnt wallet was still at the forensic lab in Wetherby, so the detective was winging it slightly.

'I'm a little confused: your wallet was burnt beyond recognition in a fire at Durham Castle on Saturday night.' After a brief pause in which the suspect did not respond, Milburn looked him in the eye. 'As were you.'

'I'm not quite sure what you mean. As you can see, I am quite fit and healthy.'

Milburn managed to keep a straight face at the overweight man's claim of being fit, with a bulbous nose pockmarked by years of drink.

'Very fit and healthy, considering you were killed in that same fire, Mr Armstrong – or whoever you really are. And here you are, two days later, brandishing the dead man's wallet and identification at his bank, trying to remove a large amount of money. You can see how this might cause us some confusion.'

Before he had a chance to challenge the fellow further, Andrew Singh entered and handed a print-out to his colleague.

'You just gave your fingerprints to the custody sergeant, and you have been identified as Franklin Veitch. Well, this makes a lot of sense. "Franklin S. Veitch, taking money by deception, eight counts of fraud, illegal wire transfer, money laundering and so on." And that's your history, before we even start with today at the bank. You're nothing but an old-school conman.'

'Please do call me Frankie. It's a pleasure to meet you. I'm sure we can clear up this misunderstanding somehow.' He hammed up a big wink.

'Are you looking to add "Attempting to bribe a police officer" to this list?'

The round face grinned. 'Of course not. Perish the thought. No, I'm thinking more about my supplying information that will help you catch the real criminal here.'

149

The appearance of Armstrong's miraculously unburnt wallet was bizarre. It looked the same as the one they had found at the crime scene, and all these IDs appeared to be the originals. Nothing had survived the fire in the wallet Julia Sedgley had logged at the scene, but here was Armstrong's driving licence, intact and original. Milburn's interest was piqued as to whether there was an underlying conspiracy or whether this lifelong confidence trickster was trying to deceive his way out of this arrest.

'Mr Veitch, you are currently in the frame for a double murder, so I reckon you had better start talking if you have information about the crime.'

'What if I suggested looking at the Merry Widow Armstrong?'

'I'm not sure what you mean.'

'I'm saying nothing more till we get a deal in place.' The big man grinned broadly again, enjoying the verbal fencing.

Milburn put his hands behind his head and yawned loudly.

'A man of your history – a career criminal – knows very well that we don't make deals in this country. That's not a thing.'

'Oh, I'm sure a detective sergeant has been in the job long enough to know that there's the official position, and then there's how life really works.' Veitch was still smiling.

'Well, I can always take a proposal to the DCI, who is the one to make recommendations to the CPS. I doubt that this can just disappear, after the hoo-ha at the bank today, but no money was actually transferred, and the staff never felt threatened, so I suspect we'll likely be able to come up with something minor. What have you got to tell me?'

'Not so fast, Detective. The information I have is my lifeline here. I'm not giving up the details in the hope you'll be above board and tickety-boo.'

'Well, you get a copy of the recordings, and I am on record here as saying that I will petition the Detective Chief Inspector to explain your immense help to the prosecutors. We both know the courts are overworked and underfunded, so they're always looking for any opportunity to avoid a trial. If they can charge you with something that can keep you out of prison, then you're likely to agree to that, right? And if not, you'll likely force them to trial, right?'

'This is all true, but I still don't hear any promises. I still don't see anything in writing.'

'Mr Veitch, we've already discussed how this country's justice system is not set up for doing deals with criminals. I promise to endorse a non-trial solution in your case, and put that forward to my boss, but I also promise that I will only do that if you supply information about another crime that helps us to catch another criminal.'

Veitch eyed up Tony for a full minute, before appearing to make a decision. He proceeded to explain a story about how he had been rumbled by Elspeth Armstrong in the course of setting up a con against the aggregates business nearly a decade earlier. Melville had been completely hoodwinked, but Mrs Armstrong was much more shrewd. However, her resolution had not been to involve the police, but to make the conman drop his approaches, and she would hold her silence as a banked favour for when she might need it.

Elspeth had telephoned on Sunday to cash in the favour: Frankie was to move a significant chunk of her husband's money to a numbered offshore account. He only had the numbers – Veitch did not even know which country the money was moving to. She insisted that it was very urgent, had to be done on Monday first thing, and it had to appear that Melville himself had moved the money.

Milburn inquired why she had wanted this done, but her story had not included the reason why. Frankie Veitch had only been told what to do, no background.

'Last question for now: do you ever go by some sort of nickname or *nom de guerre* – The Cleaner, perhaps?'

MM HUDSON

The exaggeratedly corpulent conman appeared surprised by such a strange question. He faltered, 'N-no, definitely not.'

Twenty-five

Monday, 2.33 p.m.

As Detective Sergeant Milburn exited the interview room, Diane Meredith trapped him in the narrow corridor.

'We need to go and interview Randall White again, Tony. Are you ready to come to Desanti's with me?'

This re-interview had been mooted in the murder team WhatsApp group, and DCI Hardwick had not only confirmed the action but had also identified Tony and his nemesis as the two to undertake it, saying that they should catch the man at work at the restaurant. The combination of familiar surroundings and the timing – after the lunch rush – was intended to tempt White into being over-confident.

White had been the one with the greatest opportunity to tamper with the haggis, and he'd also been close enough to make sure that his victim did indeed go up in flames. The intended target was presumed as Melville Armstrong, on the grounds that the black chef believed him responsible for blocking membership of the Friendship Society through racism. Motive, means and opportunity were all to be probed further in their follow-up interview.

Alberto De Santi looked the part. He was very Italian, his deeply tanned face wrinkled and with grey hair predominating the original black colour. He was clean-shaven and waved his hands around when speaking.

'Welcome, welcome, please come through and we will make you a coffee. We're all struggling to come to terms with Joel and Melville's deaths. My wife was in bed for twenty-four hours yesterday. We kept the restaurant closed, out of respect.'

Although the restaurant was empty, and they were in civilian clothing, the police detectives were ushered into a back

153

office adjacent to the large kitchen where they could not be seen from the customer area of the restaurant. Mrs De Santi, a shorter female clone of her husband, took an order for coffees, writing on a waitress notepad whilst insisting they would be on the house.

From the kitchen, Randall White's Geordie accent could be heard berating a pastry chef as they put together items for that evening's dessert offering. As the volume and level of swearing rose, Alberto became sufficiently uncomfortable that he excused himself.

'I will ask Randall to come in here.'

Once they were alone in the office, Meredith asked, 'Do you think he really is Italian? Or is that accent just copied from the movies?'

'Oh yeah, he's a well-known Durham institution.' Tony was pleased to be able to school Diane. 'He came over from Italy in the seventies as a teenager, to work in his uncle's restaurant. You know that Italian place up Claypath?' She nodded. 'He didn't have a word of English, or a work visa as the legend goes, and was set to work washing the pots every night of the week. After twenty years, he'd set up his own place. A pizza-pasta set-up like his uncle's. It's gone now, but after another twenty years with that one, he opened this place, aiming right for the top end of the markct, I expect this is the second or third most expensive restaurant in Durham. Enjoy your coffee!'

Mrs De Santi waltzed in just as Tony finished speaking, and she teased him: 'That's my line!'

Milburn was effusive in his thanks, hoping to send her away so that he could tell Diane the life history of the wife: similarly rags to riches. However, Signora De Santi was immediately replaced by Randall White. The tall man dominated the doorway, and his presence darkened the small office significantly. He sucked on his vape pen, and then held his hands together in front of himself. Milburn noted that he used his right hand to hold both the heated tobacco unit and the stump of his missing little finger. Together, as if the vape pen could stand in for his little finger.

ADC Diane Meredith made a point of waving away the vape steam that he blew in a careless cloud. Her movement increased from a small hand wave over the tiny coffee cup, into a grand sweeping gesture over her own head, although White seemed oblivious to her actions.

'Have you remembered anything further about Saturday night since you spoke at the hospital?' she demanded, then didn't let White even think about an answer before she leapt in with another question. This technique was intended to distract and confuse an interviewee's mind, so that they might give things away. 'What happened to your little finger? I mean, I can see it was a while ago, but I bet there's a story behind that.' She held up her own left little finger as a visual aid to support the question.

White looked down at his mutilated finger, saying, 'I work in a kitchen, with many very sharp knives.' He gave a chopping motion down with his right hand aiming at the left little finger.

'Ouch! That must have hurt like billy-o.'

Milburn sat silently, admiring his assistant's talent. Her tone, expressions and vocabulary all led people into her traps. He wondered how much of everything Diane had ever said to him had had any legitimacy.

She worked Randall White well. Within a few minutes, they knew how he had come to his choice of careers after years of helping his mother cater for his five siblings. From the way they spoke, Tony imagined that Meredith was an extra sister in that family. She took everything in and correctly speculated that his working hours made dating very difficult. Seamlessly, she had moved from the little sister that never was to the girlfriend that could be.

The chef believed, without any doubts at all, that he would be in charge of a giant catering outfit at some point in the near future. The only real question was what sort of outfit it might be. He ranged through everything from head of army rations development, through national top chef for a chain of pubs, to Hilton Hotels menu consultant. The only break that was needed, the only remaining obstacle to this meteoric rise, seemed to be membership of the Durham Friendship Society.

Their flirting rankled Milburn, and he interrupted to return to the police investigation. The other two begrudgingly stopped their own conversation, and Diane waved at Randall to answer. Friendly-flirty cop, bad cop, worked a charm.

The man was convinced that Armstrong had been the serial blackballer in the Friendship Society, and utterly hated the club's President. Joel Hedley was less of a directly mean person, but his close association with Melville meant that Randall White painted him with the same brush. The geologist was assumed to be racist, too. 'They all are.' By which it was clear that he meant all rich, white men. He was in flow: 'Two less white racists in this world is no loss if you ask me.'

'What about the haggis, though?' DS Milburn brought him back to his line of questioning. 'We need to detail its movements. Who did you see near it? Was anyone hanging around more than they should be? Somebody not doing their work properly?'

White laughed. 'Ha, they never graft properly, so that's no telling.'

'Right. Well, look, at the moment, you're the one who had the best opportunity to set up the haggis to explode in flames, plus you clearly didn't like Armstrong. Can you see how you could be suspect number one for the murders, unless we get some new information? Anything you might remember that could lead us to an alternative suspect could certainly help push you down that list.'

Suddenly, Desanti's head chef became serious and chastened. He looked Milburn in the eyes, and then turned his head to stare at the ceiling in thought. He wracked his brains as they all sat in silence.

'I really can't think of anything that felt off,' he admitted eventually. 'Nobody seemed shifty or did owt obviously out of whack to make me suspect them.'

156

Softly, Diane offered, 'OK, no problem. How about you just talk us through the events again from your perspective. Start with how and when the haggis arrived at the castle kitchens, and everything you saw and heard related to it. Maybe as outside observers we'll catch something that's odd.'

He nodded and began the story of his activities at the Burns Night Supper.

'It was always gonna be a tight-run thing. We finished up the lunch service here at the restaurant, and immediately went on to finish the prep for the Burns Night meal. We'd already done a lot, but there was loads more to get through before we ferried it all over to the castle. I was probably a bit harsh to this lot earlier.' White gesticulated towards the kitchen through the side wall of the office. 'They really pulled out all the stops to get us ready to drive the stuff over. The castle sent us one of the university vans to take it. They have a little fleet of them for driving food round from one college's kitchens to another one for their dining.'

'Really? I thought each college did it all in-house.' Milburn was so surprised at this idea that he wrote it in his notebook, even though it was irrelevant to the investigation.

'So did I,' Randall nodded. 'I had a chat with the driver on the way over and he reckons it's all organised centrally now. Big operation, that – probably five thousand students to feed every mealtime. I rode with all the food, and the rest of the staff came in a minibus the Friendship Society provided. Actually, it had "Armstrong Aggregates" on the side, although Mr De Santi said it was laid on by the Friends.'

Almost inaudibly, Tony commented, 'Interesting,' and made some more notes.

'We all unloaded the food trays there, and I made sure they were in the right order for cooking, reheating or just serving, depending on what it was. That was about five o'clock. The ceremonial haggis was delivered then, and I unboxed it and stuck it in the oven. It needed a couple of hours, and I'd already done

157

the rest of the ordinary ones. It was just that stupid ceremonial one that went in on its own.'

'Did you see the delivery driver?'

'Yeah, he was a big bruiser, that one. Mixed-race lad, shaved head.'

The detectives looked at each other, agreeing that driver would be Declan Tait, without needing to say anything out loud.

Tony probed further. 'And when he brought it in, was the box sealed?'

'Aye, was it ever! Loads of tape sealing it up. You know, the wide parcel tape, but clear, not the brown stuff. I mean, they'd sent it by courier from Scotland somewhere – I don't remember what the box said the company was that supplied it, but they really sealed it up. Had a picture of the Loch Ness monster in the logo.'

'Do you think that box is still around somewhere?'

White shrugged. 'It was probably put on the side, out of the way in the kitchen. Depends on whether they've been in to clear up yet. We were supposed to be responsible for clearing the place afterwards, but obviously that's all gone out of the window now.'

Meredith reassured him, 'It's still cordoned off as a crime scene, so if it was there, we'll have it.' She and Milburn nodded to each other to check out the haggis delivery box afterwards.

The suspect carried on talking, and Milburn continued to add to his page of notes called *The Timeline of the Haggis*.

'Just about on eight o'clock, Hedley and Armstrong met me in the kitchen to get ourselves all set for the little procession. They'd rented some Scottish bagpipes player too, and he led the three of us. Him, then Armstrong, then Hedley, then me carrying the haggis on a big square board. They paused suddenly in the doorway to make sure the crowd were all ready, and I bumped into Hedley's back. He was right uppity, thought I might have spilt some of the whisky on his jacket. I told him I hadn't. Didn't spill a drop – might have been better if I had.' He stopped abruptly, thinking he had misrepresented himself, and made a swift

158

correction. 'I mean, better that there might not have been enough of it for such a fireball, if they'd lost some on the way.'

Diane soothed again. 'Of course. Was that it then? Then you all paraded in and we've seen everything after that on the videos people took.'

'Aye, not much more to tell from our point of view, I don't reckon.'

DS Milburn stood up. 'Thanks for your time, Mr White. We'll head up to the castle now and see if we can find that box. We may need to speak to you some more, but that's enough for now at least.'

Twenty-six

Monday, 3.30 p.m.

By taking a route around HMP Durham, Tony Milburn brought the VW Golf along Old Elvet to find a parking space outside the Hotel Indigo, again opposite the Moranne Private Bank. Also opposite, and across Territorial Lane from the bank, stood the central administration building for the Army's reserve forces in the northeast.

The two men crossed the road, knocked and were shown upstairs to meet with Lieutenant Colonel Jack Griffiths, the man in charge of the local Army Reservists and Cadets. That day, the officer wore a tweed suit to work rather than any uniform. Milburn had been in his office once before, and again took a moment to look over the various paintings of modern combat scenes: twenty-first-century tanks and artillery cannons blasting shells into a distant grey sky, captured in old-fashioned oils and with a gilt frame around each one.

'Good afternoon, Colonel.'

'DS Milburn. I wondered when I'd get a visit. Really grim affair. I'll help in any way I can. What can I do?' He waved them both to sit down on a welcoming, deep sofa upholstered in brown suede.

'This is Acting Detective Constable Meredith,' Milburn introduced her, followed by: 'There are two things you can help us with, sir. Firstly, we'd like to go over the statement you gave to the uniform officer yesterday – what you remember of Saturday night, right from your arrival at the castle through to the events of the fire. And then after that, we're making inquiries about Mohammed Jackson, one of the waiters there. I believe you organised his employment as some sort of Army Veterans support thing. But the statement first. Meredith?'

It had never occurred to Tony that Jack Griffiths should be considered a suspect. Given *The Timeline of the Haggis*, as they had it thus far, the colonel would not have been able to gain access and arrange the methanol tampering – despite, no doubt, having the necessary military training for such an incendiary. However, the real reason was that Lieutenant Colonel Griffiths gave off such an aura of upstanding-member-of-the-community that Milburn simply didn't think of it.

Diane used a spiral-bound A5 notebook for her investigative records and had glued a printout of the colonel's witness statement onto one page. She annotated on the facing page, where she also rested her phone to record the conversation.

'Sir, you were in the dining room half an hour before the piping in of the haggis, is that correct?'

'Yes. Welcome drinks from seven-thirty, seated by eight o'clock was the schedule Joel had circulated. I'm a military man, so I was on time for a prompt start. G and T hour, as opposed to H-hour.' He smiled, but neither of the police officers understood the military joke. Griffiths assumed they were unamused due to the gravity of the situation, rather than because of their lack of knowledge of army terminology. 'Yes, quite. Sorry,' he said gruffly.

'So, Joel Hedley had organised the timings of the event?' Meredith resumed.

'I don't know if he organised them on his own, but he was our Honorary Secretary, so he was responsible for disseminating the programme details. The Society has a Burns Night Committee for all the planning and so on.'

Both the detectives made a written note of this fact. Details of who was on the committee and who had organised which elements of the event would be very useful information.

'You were seated about twenty yards from the platform where Armstrong and Hedley presented the haggis to the audience. How well could you see from there?' Diane asked.

161

'Very well, I would say,' the colonel replied. 'Randall White was there also, since as chef he gets to show off his work at Burns Night. Joel and Melville stood either side of the presentation table, and Joel recited the *Address to a Haggis*. He was very good. Did it from memory, and his Scots dialect was sound without hamming it up. The bagpiper stood on the far side, but just off the actual dais. So they made a sort of arc: Randall, Joel, the table with the haggis, Melville and then the piper. I don't know his name.'

Colonel Griffiths cleared his throat before carrying on.

'Joel got a little round of applause for his recitation of the poem, and then Melville raised the dagger up. He held it aloft for a long time, I remember, really milking the limelight. He was rather like that, I'm afraid. Melville always wanted to be centre of attention. He's quite the raconteur . . . *was* quite the raconteur, and I have little doubt that he stood for the presidency of the Friendship Society just to be number one on show at the various social events. My understanding is that his wife, Elspeth, and Joel did most of the actual work of the Society, whilst Melville rode along as the face of the organisation.'

ADC Meredith took a while to catch up with the writing in her notebook. Coming to a close, she was ready with her next question.

'Tell me about the fire itself.'

After stroking his moustache for a few seconds, Griffiths took in a deep breath and closed his eyes before speaking.

'I have seen that kind of thing before, of course, in combat, but it never prepares you for the horror. It happened when he cut the haggis. You know it's covered in flaming whisky as part of the ceremony? I saw Melville slash down on it with the knife, there was the briefest of fireballs, mostly blue flame and virtually no smoke, and then the two men were screaming and writhing. Things nearby, like the wall hanging and tablecloth caught fire, too, but it didn't spread too far. The men seemed to have been injured immediately, as they continued to howl and roll around for

162

maybe twenty seconds. And then they stopped, and there was an eerie silence. You get that on the battlefield sometimes, too. Then people started screaming and leaping up and shoving into each other. I tried to get up to run over and assist with first aid, but the tables and chairs were jammed so close together that I struggled to push my chair out enough to get out of it. Other people remained paralysed by shock; they stood immobile and gormless, getting in the way. Seen that in battle, too. By the time I did get over there, your man DI Barnes was at the bodies and told me to stay back. Said he needed to preserve the crime scene. The sprinklers had come on and extinguished the few areas of flame. Both Joel and Melville were lying stock still by then, so I assumed they were dead.'

For his first question in this conversation, Tony asked, 'Think back, sir. Imagine yourself at your seat in those early seconds. Scan around the room in your mind. Do you see anyone whose expression seems out of place? Perhaps they don't look dumbstruck, or they're not even watching. Or maybe you see someone leave suddenly. Anything like that come to mind?'

Carefully undertaking the visualisation of the room, Griffiths came up with many snippets of memory.

'Good God, man, you're right. Early on, Elspeth Armstrong's face did not seem concerned or even surprised. She had a sceptical look, as if she thought this was more of Melville's showing off. She was always very dismissive of his swanking about.'

Milburn and Meredith stayed silent to draw out more.

'And then there were two of the waiters who left. Randall White shouted at one youngster with blond hair to go and get a fire extinguisher. The lad headed away towards the kitchens, but I never saw him again. And Momo Jackson ran in with a fire extinguisher, but he didn't use it sensibly at all. Basically, he just waved it everywhere, as if he was trying to clear a path through the flames for his own exit. Thing is, there *were* no flames in the

163

main aisle; he was just spraying foam all over the place. And when he reached the far end, he disappeared out of that other door.'

'Ah yes, Momo.' Milburn made it sound as if the colonel had just reminded him of the other item to discuss. 'Is it right that you were involved in getting him that job as a waiter?'

'Absolutely it is.' Griffiths turned to fully look straight at the detective sergeant, brown eyes boring into Milburn's. He ran a hand over his short brown hair. 'I'm sure you're keenly aware of the plight of many of our veterans. The Army is not great at preparing soldiers for civvy street, although it is pretty good at damaging their mental health before it does release them back to normal life.' He made his fingers show air quotes as he said the word 'normal'.

'Momo is one of those suffering from PTSD, and he has been homeless all the time since he left us. In my experience, these men are perfectly capable if we give them just the slightest assistance. A bit of direction, orientation as to how life works when you don't have a quartermaster and a mess hall. Where possible I do this directly. I met Momo here in the Market Place a couple of months ago, walked him away from a fight – another street chap had called him a "Paki" – and did my best to help him without imposing my ideas of how a man should live. And he wanted to work, to earn his own food, and to be able eventually to rent his own place. He won't take the council housing on offer. He's insistent that he should make the money to pay for his own roof.

'Anyway, Saturday was the first big step along that road when I convinced Alberto to add him to the waiting staff – just for that event. If he proved worthy, then maybe in the long run a job at Desanti's might follow, but it's all about letting these guys prove their worth. Handouts don't rehabilitate them.'

Given that the DS was the one who had interviewed Momo, he took it upon himself to continue this line of inquiry without letting Diane ask anything. She chose to stay out of it, mostly because the Colonel seemed an unlikely suspect and so there was no need for the detectives to double team him with questions.

'I want to ask if there were any problems with him and this first job, but obviously I mean other than the fire. Did he seem to be successful, insofar as you and Mr De Santi could tell in the time he was working in a normal situation?'

'Oh yes, very much so.' There was vigorous nodding from Griffiths. 'The fellow showed himself to be competent, quick to catch on, and capable of anticipating problems and solutions – a positive boon. And that was all from Alberto, not me. I spoke to him and Mrs De Santi over a welcome drink at the start of the event. Their favourable reports were quite the opposite of the expectations from Melville and some of the Burns Night Committee when we discussed it a fortnight before.'

'How so?' Tony raised his eyebrows to emphasise his question.

'Some members of the Friendship Society are, um, shall we say . . . "old-fashioned". Armstrong made it plain that he did not trust Mohammed and was not keen on allowing us to take him on in the employment I was proposing. Luckily, this position annoyed Joel Hedley enough that he argued against him, berating his business partner in no uncertain terms. I have to say Alberto was less restrained – he accused our President straight out of being a racist. You can imagine how that went down. Anyway, after a ten-minute break, we reconvened, and the committee voted to allow Momo to work the event.'

The colonel paused.

'Armstrong huffed and puffed, but he knew the battle was lost. I don't think anyone wanted to create any more ruckus, so when he proposed that he would source the haggis himself, as he wanted it to be really special, no one demurred.'

At that moment, the police phones both beeped in unison, and Meredith held up the message for her boss to read. They both stood up, and Milburn apologised to Colonel Griffiths, explaining that they would have to leave immediately.

Twenty-seven

Monday, 3.49 p.m.

Milburn went blue lights and sirens up to Palace Green. Leaving the car outside the castle gates, he and Meredith ran through the courtyard and up the stairs to the Fellows' Meeting Room.

Genevieve Hedley was being restrained just inside the doorway to the scene of the crime by a police constable whom the DS did not recognise. Her short, reddish-brown hair was sticking up as if she had just got out of bed and hadn't brushed it. She wore a knee-length brown skirt and matching flat shoes with beige ankle socks.

The castle contained many unusual smells, but the one that Milburn easily identified was the smell of booze. He assumed the uniformed policeman had not been drinking.

Diane helped the constable to gently move Joel's widow away from the door, but kept a firm hold so that the distraught woman couldn't progress any further into the protected area. She was wriggling to try and escape their clutches, shouting, 'Get off me!'

'What on earth is going on, Constable?' Meredith asked slightly breathlessly. Her tone was conciliatory towards Genevieve, almost making it sound as if she thought the policeman was to blame.

'I was guarding the crime scene, and she just appeared at the top of the stairs here.' The officer waved his hand back, looking through the doorway, to indicate the old wooden staircase.

Mrs Hedley began weeping, and her sobs shook her whole body.

'This is the last place I saw Joel,' she said, slurring her words. 'I just wanted to be near him.'

166

DS Milburn decided it was time he took charge. 'OK, thanks for calling it in, Constable . . .?'

'Jared. Jared Coyne. I'm from Peterlee station.'

'Thanks for looking after this place, Jared, and for being on the ball enough to keep our crime scene secure. Carry on here, and we'll look after Mrs Hedley.' Tony gave Diane a nod, indicating that she should help the woman into the room and towards the place where her husband was set on fire.

The ADC linked arms with Genevieve so that they could go only where Meredith dictated. Milburn followed a few steps behind so as not to intimidate the woman. She was clearly drunk, and he wasn't sure how she would react to his presence.

At this point, Diane Meredith stepped back to let the widow grieve. She maintained alertness, though, ready to intervene should Mrs Hedley become taken with the idea of clambering on to the platform.

Blue and white tape still cordoned off this critical area of the crime scene. There was always a limit on timescales, and Tony wondered how long they would be able to hold off the castle and World Heritage Site authorities before having to hand this room back. He assumed that there was no further useful forensic evidence that could be found here, since if Dr Sedgley and her team hadn't collected it yet, no doubt it didn't exist. However, the protocols remained in place for any unusual – unexpected – turns in an investigation. For example, if evidence suddenly pointed to a suspect being connected to a Persian rug, they might have to ask forensics to go over the scene looking for a specific species of Middle Eastern dust mite. Whilst there had been no reason to collect dust initially, this new twist in an investigation would need the crime scene to be undisturbed. Otherwise, even the least competent defence lawyer would get the forensic evidence dismissed.

Tony's imagination ran away, filling his mind with images of Genevieve's dowdy skirt being infested with dust mites wearing tiny fezzes. Given the woman's propensity towards alcoholic drink, his imaginings reached a crescendo as the hat-wearing dust mites all clinked beer glasses together and took a big swig of ale.

'*Tony!*' Diane was struggling to assist Mrs Hedley, who was on the verge of collapse, to remain standing up. Dismissing the daydreams, Tony took her by the arm on the other side from Meredith, and the three of them wobbled over to one of the dining tables, still with its dinner settings in place.

'Hold up here for a sec,' he said. 'I'll get a chair.' He dragged one of the seats out, pulled it over to the women and helped Genevieve to slump down on it. He had positioned the chair in the middle of the wide aisle, so that she could not reach or touch anything else. It would be just his luck if that one chair had the crucial bit of forensics on it.

Diane fussed around the woman for a few minutes, making her feel comfortable and ensuring she wasn't about to fall over, or asleep.

Mrs Hedley kept repeating the phrase, 'I can't believe it.'

Penfold had sent a haiku an hour earlier, and Tony used the query his surfer friend had included in it as a good way to engage and distract the distressed woman, before engaging in more detailed questions about her other half's background, movements and possible enemies.

'Did Joel have any scars on his hands?'

'He had a perfect circle in the pad of his thumb. He managed to put a nail through it when the girls were tiny. They were fighting and he got distracted as he swung the hammer down.' Her brain took a turn into darkness. She wailed, 'Oh, were his hands so burnt you couldn't see the scar?' Loud sobbing followed, and Diane stepped in to soothe and calm Genevieve, giving her a packet of tissues to mop her streaming eyes.

After a while, when the sobbing had subsided, ADC Meredith eventually asked, 'Have you ever been up to the aggregates site? Did your husband ever show you around?'

'Oh yes, regularly.' Genevieve brightened up. 'I volunteer on many of the same committees and organisations as Elspeth, and we would often do work for those at the site offices, using the printer and photocopier and so on.'

'Ooh, really? That sounds interesting. What sort of organisations?' Milburn kept in the background, letting Diane work her people magic.

'Well . . .' The woman looked blearily around the cavernous room. 'We run the Dunelm branch of the WI.'

'You mean you and Mrs Armstrong, right?'

'Yes. Joel and Melville were the Chairman and President of the Friendship Society, but Elspeth and I helped out with almost everything for that. That's the one we really did together most often, up at the site.'

Meredith was nodding throughout everything Genevieve said, finally asking, 'So, when were you last up there?'

The woman stared around the room, her eyes lolling. It was unclear if she was genuinely trying to sift through her memories, or if she was being ironic about such a trivial question. She exhaled volubly through her lips.

'Oh, a week ago, I think it was. We had some final work to do on the seating plan for Burns Night. Had to keep some of what Elspeth calls "Undesirables" away from the "Better People".'

'I can well imagine,' Diane sympathised. 'How do "Undesirables" get to attend the dinner at all?'

This time, Genevieve's nervous laugh spluttered out at the start of her answer.

'Well, of course it's only really Melville who makes judgements like that. Most of us quite like everyone in the Society. But the Armstrongs never really approach anything with Friendship.' She emphasised the last word to make the connection with the name of the club.

'Oh, how do you mean? Are they not friendly people?'

Again, her high-pitched laugh came out before the words.

'No, not really. They just seem to be in it for themselves. And I don't just mean the Friendship Society: I mean everything. Elspeth is a bit selfish, but Melville was just horrible. Joel hated how he had swindled us out of owning part of the gravel pit. Of course, that man was too clever to do anything illegal, he just manipulated the business – and Joel – and ended up with everything. Joel was livid. Every time he's built the business even bigger, he's then lost his share. Three times! Talking about business ownership was about the only time he would ever swear.'

'Sounds like the Armstrongs were deservedly pretty unpopular, but I don't think it would be enough to kill for. Do you have any idea who might have the most to gain from the deaths of Joel and Mr Armstrong?'

Meredith's question must have triggered a vision of Mr Hedley in his wife's mind. She stared at the little stage he had died on and howled again.

'No one!' she cried out, tears streaming down her face. 'Nobody would gain anything from Joel's death. He was a gentle, kind man.' Speaking quietly now, she added, 'We don't even have much money. I suppose I'll inherit his half of whatever we have.'

Jumping back in, Milburn asked, 'How did Joel take your threat to divorce him?'

'I never meant that we really would divorce. The girls persuaded me to say it – told me it would shake him up a bit, get him to pay us all a bit more attention.' She stared at the haggis table and, after a moment, replied to the question. 'He responded in his usual Joel way, I suppose.'

A silence hung in the air, and the officers let it linger to push her to elaborate.

'At first, I was angry that he showed no feelings. God, it made me so angry.' She banged a fist on her thigh. 'I felt like he didn't care, and I should have done it years ago. I had a few drinks – sometimes I drink a glass too many – and I really shouted at him that next night. Poor Joel. He always was a quiet man. Cerebral, I suppose. He just took the information in for analysis later. When I shouted at him, he simply stood there and took it. Said nothing.'

Genevieve sniffed quietly and continued, 'And when he did talk to me, two days later, he didn't really say much at all about us, the girls and me. Everything was aimed at Melville. Joel said he understood my "issues", and that he couldn't believe Melville had managed to destroy us, in the process of stealing the company from us. That was how he phrased it: *stealing the company from us.*' She wiped the back of her hand across tear-stained eyes and then across the skirt at her hip.

'So that's the inheritance, what I'll gain from his death: not a single share of Armstrong Aggregates. All we have is a mortgage. And that bloody electric car—' She interrupted herself. 'No, even the car belongs to the company. Melville owns everything.'

'What about the Armstrongs,' Diane asked softly. 'Did they get on well with each other?'

'Ha!' This time Genevieve gave a genuinely amused laugh. 'Let's say they were a good partnership. Elspeth and Melville weren't exactly distant; I'd probably use the word "separate". They worked together well to advance themselves in everything in life, but they definitely didn't love each other.'

'Hmm.' Milburn's colleague made a show of mulling over things. 'If there's nothing to be gained by killing Joel, and you don't have any money, and I assume a private company geologist isn't going to have influence over anything that might cause somebody to want to remove him, then it must have been Melville who was the target. Who might gain from *his* death, do you think?'

Genevieve blurted out immediately, 'Elspeth, obviously,' then looked up at Diane as if to see if she had given the right answer. 'Well, I mean she must inherit everything, right? They don't have any children.'

171

There was a silence between the three of them, which dragged on. The penny finally dropped, and Joel's widow continued down the new path.

'Wait . . . of course! Why, that evil bully.'

This time Meredith had to clarify. 'Are you talking about Mr Armstrong?'

'No, no. Well, yes, he definitely was a big bully, but I meant Declan. Melville took him on at Armstrong Aggregates a few weeks ago.'

In Tony's notebook, he wrote a question to follow up on. He had understood that Declan's new job had been in place three or four months. He expected this suggestion of a few 'weeks' was the product of a wandering, alcoholic mind that never really paid attention to the calendar.

'That was just to keep him quiet,' Genevieve said spitefully, 'but it was minimum wage. He let Declan get away with doing very little, and let him use a works van, but it was no special job. I bet Declan can claim a pretty penny from the inheritance, though. And he's a real thug.' Her voice rose. 'Yes, I bet he did it! He was up at the site last time I was there, mouthing off at everyone and being, quite frankly, unprofessional. You can't shout at your boss that he ruined your mother. Oh my God, and *he* drove the haggis down here!' Her voice rose even more in volume and in pitch. 'Did he do something to it? Did he put an explosive in the haggis? I saw the fireball. He must have done it, he must be the one. Find Declan, he's dodgy as hell!'

Milburn started – he almost jumped in the air. He turned to face her directly.

'Say that again!'

'He's dodgy as hell,' she repeated, a bit scared by his sudden intensity. Her nervous laugh sounded especially shrill.

'No, the whole sentence.'

Diane stepped closer to Tony, leaning in, conspiratorially. She could tell something was afoot.

Mrs Hedley spoke quietly. 'Find Declan, he's dodgy as hell.'

Turning his head slightly, the DS whispered in Meredith's ear, 'Find Declan, he's dodgy. Findeclan, he's dodgy. Find her cleaner dead e . . .'

Milburn had never seen Diane caught out with surprise, but at this, her jaw fell open. 'Find Declan, he did it!' she gasped. 'Armstrong was naming his killer!'

Twenty-eight

Monday, 4.34 p.m.

Hartlepool's Seaton Carew beach was grey and gloomy. The wind off the North Sea chilled right to the bone. Milburn was pleased that it wasn't raining. He parked up on the promenade road and spotted Penfold below, halfway between the top of the beach and the water's edge.

As dusk closed in, Tony descended to the blowing sand, zipping his snowboarding jacket right to the top. He had never been snowboarding, but very much appreciated the steel-grey jacket Kathy had given him two Christmases previously. Hands stuffed in the deep pockets, one held his smartphone and the other battled the colder police radio for space in the warm.

A discarded surfboard lay on the sand beside the Kiwi, who stood gazing at the waves. His wet hair and granite chin gave the look of a catalogue model showing off the new season's best wetsuit. He appeared to simply sense Tony's arrival as he started speaking before the policeman had progressed enough to be within the man's peripheral vision.

'Don't ask. It's amazing what a difference just a couple of hours can make. Three o'clock this afternoon, the wind was absolutely calm, but the tide was wrong. I get down here forty minutes ago and the tide is perfect, but this wind is just closing it all out.'

'Isn't it just absolutely freezing?' Milburn didn't totally understand the surf talk but could tell that it was not a great day for riding the waves.

'No. I mean, sure the water's probably seven or eight degrees, but this works wonders.' He held out his arm and pinched the rubber covering his wrist. 'There's a little shiver when you first get water in it, but attacking the waves with decent arm-

strokes warms you up quickly. I must take you out there one day.'
He grinned. 'But I agree, we should probably make your first
foray into the swell on a lovely summer's day. Don't want to put
you off straight away.'

The tall New Zealander bent down to release his leg rope
velcro and picked up the board. He wrapped the rope around the
fin end and tucked it into itself. Stowing the board under his arm,
he set off barefoot up the beach. Milburn watched a long curl of
whitewater roll over itself with a crash and turned to follow up to
the sand-covered stone steps.

The gibbous moon struggled to light their short walk. The
firmament was not cloud-covered, but the coastal winter's night
seemed to drain the light away. Rather than shine, the moonlight
just seeped vaguely across the sullen sky.

Penfold's Victorian house had two large windows with a
Norman arch shape, and an oak front door in the same shape. He
peeled off the black rubber suit just inside the door and left it
puddling seawater on the floor by the doormat. Tony stepped over
it and into the kitchen to pour them both coffee, whilst the surfer
bounded up the spartan wooden staircase to put on dry clothes.
From his puffy jacket's inner pocket, Tony pulled out a tiny UHT
milk pot of the sort you might find in a hotel room. He grinned to
himself as he lavished it into his coffee mug and followed up with
a paper sachet of sugar. Milburn had finally remembered to bring
his own supplies.

When he returned, wearing baggy blue shorts and a lighter
blue *Surfers Against Sewage* T-shirt, Penfold tutted at the sight of
the little milk pot and ripped sugar sachet. He picked up his own
mug of thick black liquid – Milburn often referred to the coffee in
this house as 'Bitumen' – and led Tony down the cellar stairs.

On the way, Tony said, 'Forensics have found traces of a
thing called acrylamide on the ceremonial tablecloth. Mean
anything to you?'

'I was going to mention that. It's not only used by sand and
gravel pits, but it'd be a pretty big coincidence if you found it at

Durham Castle, so could highlight some potential suspect eliminations.'

The underground laboratory was dimly lit by a couple of desk lamps on the long work surface built against the old brick wall. At the far end of the large room, a couple of high windows – at ground level outside the house – added slightly to the illumination, but the twilight outside was rapidly turning to night.

Beneath these, seated on a high lab stool, Mantoro nursed a coffee beside a saucer of his favourite snack. The huge mane of dark hair shrouded his face as he tinkered on an aged laptop. Mantoro looked like the sort of odd loner who sits all day in the corner of a dingy bar.

As he pushed the saucer forward slightly, the South American drawled his standard refrain, 'Cashew nut, Tony?'

Milburn wandered to the end of the huge central worktable and picked up three or four between fingers and thumb. Thanking the man, he tipped his head back and dropped the lot in at once.

Pointing at the laptop screen, Mantoro looked up and informed him, 'That sword's up for sale on the dark web.' Tony was standing on the wrong side so could only see the lid of the machine.

'That old thing can access the dark web? I'm surprised it can even play *Snake*,' Tony replied, his mouth full.

Penfold interjected, 'Don't be fooled, Milburn. That shell is all about misdirection.' He pointed at the black plastic laptop. 'The insides of that thing were hand-built by Trident. It's probably got more computing power than NASA.'

'OK, I hear you.' Tony nodded, with a feeling of excitement at the clandestine activity. 'Wow, I bet NASA laptops are totally over-spec'ed.'

'I didn't mean a laptop, I meant the whole of NASA – but you're probably right, that is likely to be hyperbole. Anyway, tell us what you found, Mantoro.'

'Sure thing, boss.'

BURNS NIGHT BURNS

It was a struggle to listen to the findings, as Milburn was once again intrigued about the relationship between the other two. It never seemed as if Mantoro lived with Penfold, but the man was always at the Hartlepool house. He couldn't tell if the epithet 'boss' was just his American-English vernacular, or a genuine title.

He essentially understood from the snippets he took in that the stolen sword from Durham Castle had appeared on a site offering sales of various contraband goods. Milburn finally tuned in as Mantoro concluded, '. . . ten k in bitcoin.'

Penfold came back with, 'You mean ten thousand bitcoin or ten thousand pounds in bitcoin?'

'The second one.'

Penfold was leaning on the central worktable at the end opposite Mantoro. He had both forearms flat on the white plastic surface, with his coffee mug held between them.

Looking at Tony, he asked, 'Shall we set up a purchase?' After a moment's pause, his eyes flicked to the mysterious Mexican. 'I take it it's local?'

'Even says Durham – that's what triggered my filters to notify me.'

'Choice.' The Kiwi's eyes returned to the detective. 'So, want to meet the seller for a buy?'

'Absolutely.' Tony frowned. 'Where do you think would be a good location? We want to make sure they can't get away. And I'll need to be able to set it up with the fewest officers possible. I can imagine we'll have zero bodies available.'

They all thought for a minute. Penfold moved to the side counter near Milburn and flicked on a large computer screen. He typed quickly and pulled up a map of the City of Durham, with the river loop around the castle/cathedral peninsula centred vertically, as north-south would naturally place it. The New Zealander's finger was tracing along the course of the River Wear, and it stopped at Durham School's boathouse.

'There.'

Tony stepped over to see the proposed meeting place and nodded in approval.

'Good idea. That open terrace on the opposite bank from the Fulling Mill . . . I like it. There's a very narrow path both north and south but no other access routes. The bank above the riverside is too steep and densely wooded for any escape up there.' He looked even more closely at the map details. 'Nice little open space for a meet. And a ton of locations for hidden policemen to step out and block off the escape once contact has been made. That derelict house next to the boathouse could be useful too. I'm sure that's the old caretaker's house for Durham School. Do you think the seller will go for it?' He looked back and forth to the other two men.

Mantoro responded, 'In this sort of thing, seller usually dictates the meet. I'll give it a try, though. I'll go big on haggling – that's something law enforcement don't really do. They're always too keen to make the buy happen.'

'Mmm, and the riverbank path is pitch black at night. If you mention that to them, it may well help.'

'Uh huh.' Mantoro was typing incessantly and didn't look up.

Above the various scientific machines on the side counter, Penfold reached to pull down a folder from a high shelf and said, 'The key logs from Armstrong Aggregates make for interesting reading.'

'*What?* How did you get those?'

'You remember I had a very pleasant conversation with Hedley's PA? She gave me a copy of the last three sheets.'

'You sneaky git. I didn't spot you taking those from her.' DS Milburn was annoyed that Penfold had again gone off the reservation when it came to evidence gathering, but he was also amused by the man's audacity.

With a grin, the reply came back: 'Well, you had your own receptionist to sweet charm. Anyway, I wasn't sure at the time whether these would hold anything important.'

'But of course they did.' Tony knew Penfold's method. His friend never did anything that didn't turn out to be useful. He had no idea how that method could be so consistently productive, but he'd never seen it fail.

'Well, sort of.' Tanned fingers scratched the tanned chin. 'Unsurprisingly, the people using the key for the chemical store cabinet are Melville Armstrong, Joel Hedley, Declan Tait . . .' His tone left it hanging as if there was more to be revealed.

'And . . .?'

'Two other names you may or may not have come across in the course of the investigation – the blasting engineers at the quarry.' Penfold's fingers moved to the paper to point at the next two rows on the list.

Not recognising either, Milburn frowned, demanding, 'Blimey, how do you pronounce that?'

'I do not know. The PA told me he's a Filipino.'

As his fingers slid on down the list, Milburn halted, saying, 'I did not expect *that* one.'

'No, indeed. Do you think Elspeth Armstrong has any useful business being in the chemical store?'

'Well, she looked very businesslike when we were there – as if she was used to running the place.' The DS wobbled his brown hair and grey temples from side to side, musing in thought. 'So, I wouldn't put it as too suspicious, but I'll make a note to look into it.'

'She only signed the key out once, though. Nine days before the Burns Supper. If it was part of whatever work she did up there, wouldn't she be using the key more regularly?'

The house wi-fi was super-powered by Trident's hardware additions in the office over their heads, and Tony's phone had automatically connected to it, having been there many times. He sent himself an email with a brief reminder about quizzing Mrs Armstrong on her entry in the key log.

'Unfortunately . . .' Penfold's voice gave Milburn a feeling that a rug was about to be pulled from under his feet; he looked

179

up in anticipation. 'Unfortunately . . . the lovely young woman at Armstrong Aggregates told me that the key security is very lax. The regulars often took it out without signing the paper record. Worse than that, it's often returned after hours by simply posting it through the letterbox of the Reception Portakabin. Or during the day, it might be left on the Reception desk. I mean, they might as well leave the cabinet unlocked.'

Tony laughed. 'We've no reason to believe that they don't.'

'Ha, no, indeed, Milburn.' As their laughter died away, the room fell silent and was now quite dim. They stood motionless, each lost in their own thoughts.

'It's on.' The quiet was broken by Mantoro's voice. Despite the exciting news, he spoke deadpan. 'That little corner by the weir on the river that connects the Durham School caretaker's house across the river to the Fulling Mill. On that little terrace space at nine o'clock tonight. They'll turn up, give you the bitcoin details, you transfer the ten grand, then they'll show you where the sword is. They say, five minutes late, and they'll be gone. No bitcoin within five minutes and they'll be gone.'

Milburn nodded. 'I don't suppose they gave a name, did they?'

'That's about the only thing they did right,' Mantoro said. 'Everything else sounds very amateur. All those conditions I just read you, it's like they've scripted it from the movies.'

Penfold said, 'You be Keanu Reeves, and I'll be Patrick Swayze.'

Twenty-nine

Monday, 8.49 p.m.

Jeanette Compton walked with a squeaky-voiced police constable from Sunderland, along the banks of the River Wear towards Durham School boathouse. Jeanette worked at the County Police HQ as Chief Archivist, an arch librarian with a talent for investigating through paper and digital records like no one else Milburn had ever seen.

PC 'Squeak' and Miss Compton had been tasked with the undercover role of meeting the vendor of Durham Castle's missing sword. They were playing the roles of a go-between couple for black-market art dealers, and this was their final approach to the meet. Everyone else was in place, out of sight but ready.

She would play the knowledgeable expert, whilst the tall Sunderland cop would play the muscle. Before they left Durham City police station, in the back of an unmarked van with no windows, DCI Hardwick had instructed the constable to avoid speaking as much as possible. The pitch of his voice would undermine his bulky appearance as Jeanette's minder.

They had no idea who might be behind the theft and sale of this high-value antiquity. The police fully expected an organised criminal outfit, and this brought with it the potential threat of weaponry other than just the sword. Would they meet one lone thief, or an entire armed gang?

Hardwick had been extremely displeased with DS Milburn for involving Penfold, and, worse, Mantoro as well. People had heard the DCI shouting two floors down from his office. However, this would be a significant arrest and very good relationship building with both the university, which owned Durham Castle, and the World Heritage Site.

Tony had tried to plead that he had given Penfold information about the sword's disappearance to distract him from investigating the arson deaths. He tried to sell it to Hardwick as being so intriguing that it would keep Penfold's attention but had been stymied when the man had solved it so quickly. Not only was the chief inspector sceptical of this claim, but he pointed out that Penfold had not 'solved' anything; the sword had been put up for sale. Yes, there was a bit of dark web tech knowledge that had been required, but he couldn't really call it 'solving the case'.

They all hoped that it would turn out to be Thomas Malory's battle sword, but undercover stings like this were never a sure thing. Jeanette had a good knowledge of most treasures held by various organisations in the medieval city and had actually held the sword in question during a Heritage Open Day. As a police employee, she had been on the Test Purchase Operative training course: qualified, but with no experience.

The river that looped through Durham City was dammed by a weir all the way across, immediately below the west end of the cathedral, with an old water mill on the far riverbank. The headwaters above the weir were always calm, originally built to supply power to the now defunct mill. The moonlight on the still waters illuminated the riverbanks enough to avoid obstacles, but it was gloomy, scary. Hiding places abounded. Any shadow could turn out to be a violent thug. The waters below the weir flowed shallow that night. The dam effect meant that the pool above the mill, surrounding the boathouse, always sat with the same three yards depth. The dam wall was about sixty yards long, and a ten-yard stretch at the near end lay covered with broken trees, brought there in the river flood back before Christmas.

The police had gained access to a crumbling, derelict house on the western bankside, and Mantoro sat inside on a fishing stool with the creaky laptop on his knee. It was the only source of light in the large downstairs room. Five other people had also been holed up inside for two hours. Police Constable Bob Smith was stationed at the door, holding it shut against its own weight. DCI

Hardwick, DS Milburn, ADC Meredith and Penfold stood at the windows attempting to peek through any little gaps in the wooden boarding.

Silence was maintained amongst the occupants. Everyone wondered about the criminal contacts who should be arriving soon. Although they were prepared for a fight, the worst-case scenario worried them all. Durham was generally quiet and peaceful, but violence still came to town on occasion.

The house was whitewashed in a slightly pink, off-white paint. It glimmered in the moonlight. On the downriver side of it, a small, paved area with benches formed a viewing platform to look across at arguably the most iconic scene of Durham Cathedral. This terrace was the location slated for their clandestine nine o' clock meeting. Half of it was in dark shadow.

Milburn could barely see anything through the crack in the window boarding. He worried for Jeanette's safety. He knew she was committed to the job, but the possible danger was more than she should be subjected to. He nearly jumped out of his skin when Penfold touched his arm to silently gain his attention.

He breathed in Tony's ear, 'Found fingerprints on that geological hammer.'

Tony could not see how it was important in their investigation. Turning slightly, he whispered back, 'Whose?'

Before the Kiwi could answer, Mantoro's gruff voice echoed inside the cold stone cottage, despite his attempts to speak quietly.

'I've told them to expect my people in just a few minutes, and they've confirmed they will be here.' An anticipatory silence filled the room, soon broken again by the South American. 'Oh, hold on. Dang, who *is* this guy? OK, they've sent through a password system. When he says "Moscow Rules", we need to reply, "Deploy the SU-57s".'

Hardwick took a step closer to Mantoro and bent down to keep their voices as quiet as possible.

'Say that again. "Deploy the SU-57s"?'

'Yep, you got it. These things often go with some sort of strange codes system.'

'I know, but what kind of idiotic password is that?'

Hardwick's remit went beyond catching bad guys. He also had to balance the overtime budget and make sure all the right paperwork was signed off. It had been hard enough to pin down the superintendent in less than one hour to sign off as Authorising Officer for Jeanette to be allocated this undercover role. Although she was adequately qualified, she had little experience, but the super's biggest qualm was that she was Durham-based. It was not beyond the realms of possibility that if the crooks were local, she'd have passed them in the street sometime.

Undercover work usually required a change of locale. There was no easier way to scupper an operation than to have an agent bump into somebody they knew from their real life and have to try and ignore them or explain them away to a suspect.

Deploying SU-57s was, Hardwick assumed, some video game nonsense that he was not aware of. It made a mockery of the whole exercise and he questioned whether Penfold and his crony were going to cost them thousands of pounds in a failed operation. He could picture the regional senior CID officers' Easter conference, where he would have to explain the Moscow Rules approach to fiscal responsibility.

He relayed the passwords to Jeanette. At least one snigger came through on the comms earpieces. Listening in, Milburn was pretty sure it wasn't from Miss Compton. DCI Hardwick remained serious and reminded her that she must not do anything to encourage the contact to break the law. She should let them do all the talking and the most important thing was to confirm they had brought the sword itself: not a copy, not an empty cardboard tube, not a story about it being in the boot of a car somewhere. These buys often went wrong, because the vendors were scatty, nervous, drug users, mentally ill, all manner of reasons, but none that helped to reassure the taxpayer where the police budget was going.

The riverbanks were not lit at night, and in the deep wooded valley that surrounds Durham's central peninsula, the area was dark. The moon did a better job in the clearer skies away from the coast, but it remained weak. Outside, the two agents had gained their night vision and could see just about enough. In the house, the hidden group could only move about by touch, now that they were in operational no-lights mode.

Jeanette and Constable Squeak walked carefully down the path from Prebends Bridge towards the boathouse. Her mousy brown hair fell to collar length, and this had enabled the police to equip her with a radio earpiece that could be well hidden within the hairstyle. Her partner had no comms, as his head was close-shaved.

The DCI performed another radio check. However, the undercover pair were barely twenty yards from the rendezvous point and it was the appointed hour. Jeanette simply responded with 'Uh-huh,' and her 'minder' followed up with a conversation about other possible purchases they might make that week. Mantoro had suggested this as a way to legitimise themselves. If the seller thought they had overheard commercially sensitive information, they would be excited and distracted and would be more likely to miss the question of the meet being an undercover police operation.

The meeting place was empty. Jeanette sat down on a bench, whilst Squeak stood with his back to the wall of the house, imposing and ready, in the manner of an actual bodyguard. For more than ten minutes they remained in these positions in the freezing cold January night.

Tony could barely make out her features, but he could see Jeanette shivering. He shivered too. The silence and the darkness and the cold made everyone tense, but Tony was truly worried. This whole business could go wrong so easily, in so many different possible ways.

The dam pool rippled gently in the moonlight, and he could only imagine how cold the water must be. Hardwick's briefing had specifically said that nobody should enter the water. The risk assessment was clear: even if the sword was thrown into the river, nobody should go after it; there was a significant hazard of cold-water shock and drowning. Milburn shivered again. *What if somebody gets shoved in?* he wondered.

Hardwick was antsy and repeatedly asked the others if they thought it was late enough that they should call the whole thing off.

'They're not coming now,' he declared. 'Something's obviously got them spooked.'

Quietly, Mantoro reassured him, 'Chill out, man. These things never go like a military operation. They'll show.'

Thirty

Monday, 9 p.m.

In everyone's earpieces, they heard a voice: 'Good evening.'

Jeanette replied, as the man stepped from the shadows of some trees just off the paved rest area, 'Good evening. Can we help you?' She inclined her head slightly to indicate the big lad behind her, in case this was some sort of opportunist male approaching what they thought was a lone female in the dark.

'Moscow Rules.'

The mousy archivist went off-script. She was a clever undercover operative.

'We haven't got time to be kept waiting by the likes of you. Let's get this done and get out of here. I'm already not convinced this is legit.' She stood and waved a delicate hand up and down, indicating the stranger.

The moonlight showed an athletic young man wearing dark shorts, with purple sports socks and shin pads. His top half was a navy hoody, and he hefted a long thin rucksack on his back.

'Take it easy,' he said arrogantly. 'Our business will take just a couple of minutes and then we'll both be away into the night again – as long as we do have business together. I say again, Moscow Rules.'

Under his breath, Tony whispered, 'I know that voice.'

Meredith concurred, 'It's Carruthers. That student hockey numpty.'

DCI Hardwick warned quietly into the little radio microphone clipped to his collar, 'This is Delta Charlie Alpha: all stations prepare to move. As soon as he offers the sword and asks for money in exchange. Wait till we see the sword though. Boat launch, set off now.'

The police had brought in a rigid inflatable boat to assist with anything that might end up in the water. However, Durham was so small around the river loop that the launch would be spotted easily if it waited anywhere nearby. They had been stationed half a mile upstream, hiding under a tarpaulin at the city rowing club.

Action always relieved tension. Once things were happening, the unknown became known. When people came out of the shadows, they could be caught, they were much less of a danger. Tony's hands balled into fists as he prepared to bundle out of the building and take down the thief.

Another hundred yards downstream from the derelict house, two more uniformed officers hid in a rhododendron bush up the steep bank above the footpath. It had been a real scramble to station them up there, and Milburn hoped they'd be able to get down safely and in time to stop anyone who bolted away down the towpath.

'Prepare the revolution.'

The two hiding in the rhododendrons were on the approach to a bar called Revolution. Now that the suspect was on scene, Hardwick gave their cue to move down onto the path to intercept if he fled that way. They could not be seen in the dark at that distance from the meeting place. Milburn wondered if his boss recognised the irony in being so sceptical of Moscow Rules, when he himself came up with such absurd codes for the radio protocols.

Outside, Jeanette had relented and given the correct response. Harry Carruthers handed her a card with bitcoin transfer details printed on it. She pulled a tablet from a large bag slung over her shoulder and made the appearance of setting up the transfer. As she tapped away on the screen, without looking at the student, she said, 'I'll set this up ready, but I'm not going to type in my boss's password to complete the transfer until I've seen the merchandise. Is it here?'

'Money first.' His smartphone lit up his facial features, apparently monitoring a bitcoin wallet for arriving funds. 'When I see the ten grand has arrived then I'll take you to the sword.'

Jeanette lowered the tablet and held it in both hands in front of her waist.

'You're new at this, I can tell. So, I'm going to overlook all this ridiculous amateur stuff.'

In the building, Penfold spoke into Tony's ear. 'She's absolutely brilliant, isn't she.'

In the dark, Tony smiled to himself about the oft-denied attraction that Penfold clearly had for Miss Compton.

'My boss spends upwards of a million pounds a month on this sort of merchandise, and we have numerous other places to be and numerous other objets d'art to gain possession of,' Jeanette said harshly. 'Now you let me see the sword right now or we walk away.'

Harry Carruthers smiled carelessly, but his hands were shaking as he reached for his backpack. The hockey stick bag unzipped at the very top, and once he spread open that part of the bag, a metallic glint reflected the moonlight. He pulled a long piece of thin metal up and out, rezipping the bag before slinging it back over his shoulders. Only then did he step forward to present the centuries-old weapon.

Clearly nervous that these unknown buyers might run off with it, or worse, attack him with it, he would not relinquish the sword completely but gripped the handle tightly.

Constable Squeaky Voice shone a torch onto the three-feet-long blade for Jeanette to examine. She pushed her brown-framed glasses a little up the bridge of her nose. A couple of gentle touches on the hilt and the blade and she was convinced.

'That's a very fine piece you have there,' she said loud and clear.

That was the trigger phrase. She had pressed the button, and the police officers all came bundling out from the pink house and charged around it to the group of three on the terrace. With the noise of police issue boots and the emerging figures in the moonlight, the student thief recognised his situation. He waved the sword to fend off the officer with Jeanette Compton, and taking two steps back, threw it at the pair of them. The distraction worked as they both leapt back to avoid injury from the flying weapon.

However, four police officers were now heading down the small flight of stairs to the cathedral viewpoint. A briefly comical chase ensued, as the four ran after Carruthers around a pair of park benches. It only took one lap before Big Bob Smith separated from his colleagues and turned back to catch the fleeing lad. However, this was not the first time the hockey player had been tightly marked in front of goal. He dipped a shoulder in one direction, which put the weight of all the police officers on the wrong foot, as Carruthers then launched himself in the opposite direction. Flailing hands just failed to reach him. In the same instant, he put his own hands on the guard rail above the river and vaulted neatly over it.

The water surface was a yard below the path he had jumped from, and his entry was below the weir. He disappeared straight down into the water, right under the surface, before quickly surging back up with a yell. His heart would be going ten to the dozen, and Milburn could hear his teeth chattering. They made such a loud sound in the still night, Tony thought the suspect's teeth might break.

Once he stood, the liquid was only chest deep, and he waded to the base of the dam wall. Here, only a thin trickle of water passed over the concrete ridge at the base of the weir. The low water level made the little ridge a decent walkway.

The police launch appeared in the weir's impoundment, with two bright searchlights scanning the area. Milburn stood at the guard rail following the young man's progress across the river on the rocky ledge. The top of the dam wall created a perfect handrail and he clung on to it and moved slowly. The fit hockey captain could be heard sucking breath in and out, forcing his frozen lungs to operate. Milburn assumed adrenaline was driving him on. His colleagues lined up at the guard rail. All watched, but none tried to break with Hardwick's instructions about the cold water's risks.

Nobody had anticipated that a suspect could escape across the river. No officers had been stationed on the far side, and even though the police boat landed swiftly by the water mill, Carruthers escaped into the darkness of the trees on the peninsula riverbank. The two uniforms near Revolution ran up and over Framwellgate Bridge, whilst Meredith and Milburn ran back and over Prebends Bridge.

The bankside on the inside of the loop was wider and had a more complex path network than the narrow steep-sided one they had come from. The moon remained dull, so the only real lighting was from the boat's two searchlights. These were tight beams, and the way they scattered from tree trunks and bushes created a tenebrous web of shadowy contours.

Milburn and his colleagues spread out.

From the Framwellgate Bridge end, two paths headed upriver. One followed the waterside and the other went uphill along the base of the castle's thick stone walls. The two officers from near Revolution crept along these, one on each route.

Prebends Bridge end offered even more escape options. Meredith stationed herself at the archway gate entrance to the Bailey, the cobbled street that formed the entrance to the peninsula from this bridge. Blocking off the towpath further upriver towards Zoot nightclub, Harry Hardwick hoped to encounter his student namesake. That left Tony and Bob Smith to work their way through the woods around the Fulling Mill and two college boat clubs, joining the two officers who had disembarked from the launch.

Every step was fraught with nervous tension. Milburn moved gingerly through the undergrowth, his mind filled with the notion that Carruthers carried a quiver full of weapons. Police training insisted that one never make assumptions about a suspect, as errors in these suppositions could get you hurt. Whilst he seemed like a well brought up young man, leading his team as captain and struggling to gain an education over financial obstacles, Tony reminded himself that this did not guarantee he would avoid violence. He had never seen Sergeant Singh on the hockey field but knew the Sikh was very dangerous on the football pitch. He guessed that hockey must be a violent sport, and fully expected Harry Carruthers would be able to kill a man with a serious swing of his hockey stick.

The cathedral owned the riverbanks in central Durham, and deliberately left them to grow fairly wild in order to give the city a countryside feeling right in town. The undergrowth was a fantastic habitat, and every other bush rustled with some bird or small mammal. It was a heart-stopping search, with every yard leaving Tony drained as he recovered from scare after scare. His own little torch lit the way well, but never alighted on the navy hoody, or purple socks. Even the white legs were never spotted.

They searched the relatively small area for over an hour, but the lead was too great. Carruthers had disappeared into the night.

Thirty-one

Monday, 11.04 p.m.

The door to their four-bedroom detached house needed some oil on the lock. Tony and Kathy had moved in three years previously and the new build was just starting to need bits and pieces of maintenance.

Kathy met him in the hallway. He'd messaged her only once all day, and after their friction, and his early exit the previous night, she wanted some answers. Tony hung his coat up and followed her into the kitchen, rubbing a grey temple with his fist.

'Do you want a coffee?' She offered an olive branch.

'No thanks. I'm absolutely exhausted, so I'll need to be able to sleep. What would be wonderful, though, is one of those Go To Sleep camomile teas you have.' The tiredness he felt was exacerbated by a gnawing in his stomach. He was hungry, but this was more than that.

'How about I make you one of my Go To Sleep gin and tonics?'

He hated conflict with Kathy and wanted to reconcile their issue from the previous night quickly and easily. Going through a big discussion would re-open old wounds and most likely lead to further trouble rather than less. *Why can't she ever just take on board what I say and leave it at that?* he thought irritably.

'You know what?' he said. 'That sounds exactly what I need.'

The kettle gave its start-up noise like an accelerating plane. She switched it off again and went to the freezer for ice instead.

'Tell me about your day then. Seeing as I don't know anything about what you've been up to.'

He could tell that Kathy was opening the conversation with the intention to bury the hatchet, but she couldn't help herself –

everything was barbed. He had barely a second to start answering, or the delay in itself would come across as hiding something. Tony was desperate to get things onto a positive track, but he wasn't sure if the most successful tack would be to address her concerns about Diane Meredith head on, or talk through the activities of his day, to show that she barely featured in it. The second approach might come across as evasive.

After half a second, Tony took a chance and went straight in with, 'There's nothing going on with Diane. She's still a Crazy Cow, and I still want nothing to do with her. You know how good she is at manipulating things. She makes it impossible for H to avoid assigning us together. The crap staffing levels don't help, but she's always organising things so that we have to spend time together. But it's very much only police work. Nothing else.'

Kathy knocked the back of the ice tray and cubes scattered over the counter by the sink. Her hand darted out to try and gather them together. She dropped a couple in a nearly empty gin glass and put several more into a new one for him. She almost hurled the ice tray on the draining rack and corralled the remaining cubes into the sink.

Tony wondered to himself how much she had already had to drink. Picking up the bottle of Durham Gin, she sloshed approximate measures into the two large goblets. He opened the fridge and opened an oversize bottle of tonic, enough for both of them.

They clinked glasses with a silent nod – their own version of 'Cheers'. The sweet, chilled liquid quenched a thirst Tony hadn't realised was there, and he downed a second gulp immediately. The silence by now had lasted for over a minute, and Tony realised Kathy was holding her tongue, leaving him to continue with his excuses. As an interrogator, he knew that it is all too easy to fall into the silence trap and dig yourself a deeper hole. He pivoted, returning the spotlight to her.

'You do understand that there's nothing going on, don't you?'

194

The silence yawned. Tony was desperate to survive it.

After another big swig of her drink, Kathy banged down her glass. He flinched at the noise, fully expecting the glass to have shattered. Opening his eyes slowly, Tony found Kathy standing right in front of him. She stared straight into his eyes.

'What do you want me to say?' she demanded.

Again, Tony's mind reeled at how to answer. He had to make her understand the situation at work, ensure her imagination didn't go wild and ruin their relationship for no reason.

'Well? What are you expecting?' she needled him.

He put his drink down carefully, quietly, slow enough to have a second more to gather his thoughts. Then he took her hand and they moved together to the kitchen table and sat down opposite each other.

'Look, I know the job is probably harder on you than it is on me. When I'm out all day and night, at least I'm busy and focused so I don't really even notice the ridiculous hours. I can't imagine what must whirl through your mind when I don't come home, don't have time even to message you.' He had held on to her hand, but she now pulled it away.

'There's always time to message. You just have to want to.'

Tony watched as she pushed her loose blonde hair back over her shoulder and raised her head defiantly. This was body language he had seen before, proud and independent. He loved it. In this moment, though, he knew it meant he had to offer more.

Turning his hands over so they were palms up on the tabletop, he looked into her eyes and said, 'I'm sorry that I haven't managed to send many texts the last couple of days. It really is non-stop. There's only me and Madeline Aria and Meredith, with a few uniforms to do the plod work. There's a civvy and H running the manpower, but the actual investigation just means I've not had a second. I've not had enough time to even do the investigation properly.'

He bravely took hold of the elephant in the room by the tusks.

195

'Despite all this, I'm most worried about what you think is going on with Diane. I can't stand the woman, but we do have to work together. And I really need her 'cos she's a bloody good detective.'

'Of course she is,' Kathy sneered. 'She makes you need her, that's how she operates. Come on, Tony, you know the way she works – don't fall for it.'

'Please believe that I'm capable of dealing with her professionally. I'm done with anything more than that – she's a loon.'

'Psycow.' Kathy burst into giggles. She was tipsier than Tony had first thought, but he was pleased that her mood had landed positively. She was a split personality after drink, but more usually merry than mardy.

He responded with a relieved smile. The knot in his stomach eased off – not entirely, but he physically felt its relaxation. However, Tony knew the moment could slip away all too easily, and he put the glass to his lips again to forcefully stop himself speaking and putting his foot in it. The mood had lightened, but experience told him not to take this as the finish.

Kathy took the glass from his hand and tipped it to the ceiling, draining the remaining gin and tonic, with cubes of ice pressing her cheeks and nose trying to escape the vessel.

He smiled again. 'I can see you're not working tomorrow morning.'

'Nope,' she smiled. 'Two to ten p.m.' Durham University library was open enough hours that the librarians had to work varying times.

'Sounds like a shift with the police.'

'Ha, that'd give me a chance to keep an eye on you two.' Her bright eyes flicked to him.

Tony's nerves jangled and the worry landed back down on his shoulders.

'There's nothing going on,' he blurted out despairingly.

Kathy stood up, leaned over the table and put her hands on the sides of his face. She kissed him and remained in the awkward bent position with her forehead leaning against his.

'I get it.'

'Really?' He still wasn't reassured. 'You make me worry that you think I'm having an affair with her, and that's simply not happening. I've got a couple of recordings I could play you. I record every conversation I have with her, in case I need evidence again. I told you, I can't stand the woman.'

Their eyes were too close to focus on each other, but they tried to.

'I believe you.' Kathy pressed her lips against his, opened her mouth and Tony tasted the gin and tonic as her tongue pushed against his. They kissed passionately.

'That's all for now!' Her voice was lively, teasing, devilish. Kathy then moved around the table and took a step away. She held a hand back towards him. 'Come on, let's go to bed.'

Relief washed through Tony, and he immediately felt very tired. What he needed most of all in the world was a good kip.

As he raised a hand to take hers and rose from the seat, she replied, 'Don't think you're getting much sleep.' Her blue eyes flashed as she followed him up the stairs.

Thirty-two

Tuesday 31 January, 7 a.m.

'Good morning, Mr Tait.' Milburn breezed into the interview room and startled Declan, who sat up straight in his seat.

'What is this bullshit?' the young man growled.

'Please keep it pleasant, sir. The custody sergeant will be happy to let you use one of his cells to calm down in for a few hours if necessary.' Tony pulled a chair back on the opposite side of the table, but paused before sitting down to ensure Melville Armstrong's estranged son was going to co-operate.

The young man's fat fists pulsed open and closed on the tabletop. His skin, the colour of milk chocolate, contrasted against Milburn's winter pallor.

'Ah'm calm all reet,' Declan said belligerently. 'Ah just divvent knah why you dragged me out of bed and down here.'

'When I say calm, that includes keeping our discussion respectful and straightforward,' Milburn warned him. 'There's no need for any aggro. The quicker we get through some simple questions, the quicker we can get you out of here.'

'Those two coppers what brought me in said I was arrested for vehicular assault. What the hell is all this?'

Milburn put some files down on the table and sat down but did not pull the chair in yet.

'You deliberately drove at me and my associate up at Armstrong Aggregates yesterday. I could easily have been killed.' He opened the brown cardboard folder and pulled it closer, making a show of looking over some forms. He then turned the paperwork round, pointed at a line that read *vehicular assault* and said forcefully, 'Maybe I should amend this to attempted murder.' He stared straight at Declan.

The muscles in Tait's thick neck twitched, but the man restrained himself.

Returning Milburn's stare, he said, 'Ah splashed you by gannin' through a puddle. Nowt else. You weren't in danger, and you'll never prove owt else in court.'

'I agree.'

Declan was obviously taken by surprise at Milburn's response. His face showed confusion, and Tony was gleeful inside.

Externally, the policeman's expression gave nothing away, and he continued. 'I think we may be able to dismiss this whole thing, depending on how much help you can be with my investigations into Melville's death.'

The lines of uncertainty traced across the younger man's brow remained as he replied sulkily, 'Ah told you everything the other night. Ah had nowt to do with it.'

'Sure,' Milburn smiled easily, 'but there's a whole bunch of stuff that doesn't make sense to me, and I just want you to clear up some of that. It should help me work out what happened.'

'OK.'

'You don't need a lawyer, though, am I right?'

'No, Ah divvent need a lawyer. Ah told you, Ah've done nowt.'

'Brilliant.' The detective sergeant gave a thumbs-up sign. Whilst this appeared to be merely a body language confirmation, it was in fact a coded signal to Baz Bainbridge, on the custody sergeant's desk. Baz had been watching events on the camera screen, ready to assist Milburn if Declan got out of hand. This gesture confirmed that the interview was going to proceed: there was no apparent danger from the thug, and they didn't need to pause to call the duty solicitor.

'We've been having a look at the log sheets for signing in and out the key for the chemical store up at the aggregates site.'

'So what?' Declan rubbed a hand over his short-haired skull.

Milburn could not decide if the man was going to be aggressive throughout their conversation, simply as a matter of course – the normal, everyday approach to any conversation – or whether this line of questioning had hit something important.

'You told me you have to use the methanol from the store to treat the ponds for algae. From the sign-out sheets, it looks like it's all pretty loosely controlled up there. Can you tell me about anyone you know of up there who has also used the methanol for anything?'

Tait shifted in his chair, grunting, 'Ah'm not watchin' it all the time. Ah divvent just hang out by that big metal cabinet all bloody day.'

'Well, of course, but you do work there, so you may have seen something.'

'Aye. Sometimes Ah bumped into Mr Hedley getting bottles out of it. But he used everything. His rock tests used all the different chemicals.'

'Including methanol.'

'Yep.' In a demonstration of finality, Declan folded his thick arms over each other across his chest as best he could. They didn't fit properly, so he put his fingers under his armpits to hold the pose in place. It looked very uncomfortable.

Tony looked down, theatrically writing something on one of the forms, in order to give Declan a chance to put his hands back down without losing face.

'Anyone else?' he asked.

'Well, Melville went in there a few times, but I divvent knah what for.' Declan made a show of thinking. 'And Mrs Armstrong too.'

Tony scratched his chin for a few seconds. Much of this was a performance, but he was secretly concerned that this information seemed to validate a number of suspects. At the very least, Elspeth Armstrong could make for a legitimate alternative narrative of the crime, should a barrister need one in defence of

200

Declan Tait. He leant forward and wrote some more, this time in his policeman's notebook.

'OK, let's talk about something different.' He paused to let the man clear his mind. 'Tell me what you know about glass-blowing.'

'Eh?'

'Glass-blowing.'

'What you on about?'

Milburn mused on whether Declan was born a bit slow, had taken too many blows to the head in boxing training, or if perhaps steroid use was dulling his faculties.

'You know,' he explained, 'making vases and bottles and stuff with molten glass. Quite a common art form, people making pretty things for the house out of glass.'

In his mind, Tony was transported from the Brandon Boxing Club, and Declan getting punched repeatedly in the face, to a craft market in Barnard Castle community centre – one of Kathy's favourite weekend haunts. They owned several hand-crafted, coloured-glass Christmas ornaments. He pictured a generic artisan stall-owner, all silk scarf and patched dungarees, and wondered if those hanging Santas were actually blown glass, or some alternative crafting technique.

The whole concept was beyond Master Tait's experience. He still didn't get it.

'Fancy stuff made oot o' glass?'

'Yes.' Milburn nodded slowly. 'You blow through a long tube with a lump of liquid glass on the end – sort of half-liquid – and the glass fills with air, like a bubble, so it becomes a vase or similar.'

Declan's head slowly moved left and right, an indication that he did not understand. 'Wha'?'

The detective typed quickly into his phone and pulled up a random video of a man engaged in glass-blowing. The boxer stared in wonderment, and Milburn became convinced that he was genuinely clueless about this method of creating glassware.

'Right, let's forget about that.' Tony folded a page over in his notebook to start afresh. 'Let's talk instead about the haggis.'

There was no giveaway reaction on the round face. Tait shrugged. 'OK.'

'You drove it down to the castle from the aggregates site, right?'

'Yep. Ah told you that already.'

'I know, sorry. What I want to find out, though, is more detail about that. Where did you take it from exactly?'

'It was in the fridge in Armstrong's office. He wasn't there, but he'd shown me where it was the day before.'

'Melville Armstrong wasn't there, and he trusted you to go into his office and take it out?'

'Yes.' Tait sat up straight and put his palms down on the table. He stared at the back of his hands.

'Why wasn't he there?'

The interviewee's face lifted, and he looked at Milburn, scowling slightly in perplexity.

'Naebody was. It was Saturday. The office shuts at twelve, and Hedley and Armstrong hardly ever work Saturdays.' He corrected himself. 'Actually, Mr Hedley is in quite a bit on a Saturday, but he gans runnin', and does his experiments and stuff. He doesn't like to be disturbed when he's doing his experiments.'

Thinking of Penfold, down in his basement lab, Tony replied, 'I know how that goes.'

'Saturday's quiet. I don't usually stay after lunch. I go to the match most weekends.'

'But not on Saturday?'

'The game was away. I wanted to gan, but Armstrong insisted that the haggis had to be brought down on the day. He give me double pay, mind, and . . . well, I got expenses, so I agreed to work the day, and watched the match on TV at the boxing club. Taking his money, whilst supping a lager with the match. Sweet times.' He smiled beatifically at the memory.

'Wait – it was three o'clock kick-off, right? How did you get up to collect the haggis, and then drive back to Durham Castle after the match in time? You dropped it off at about five, didn't you?'

Interlacing his fat fingers, Tait looked down at them and mumbled, 'Nah. Ah picked it up before, like.'

A silent pause hung in the air. Milburn raised his forefinger then moved it back and forth to emphasise each step in the story.

'Let me just check that I understand this right. You picked up the haggis from the Armstrong Aggregates site in Northumberland at lunchtime, drove home and parked the van there whilst you went and watched the football match at the boxing club. And where was Jacqui during that time?'

'Me ma? What's she gotta do with it?'

'I'm thinking about the security of the haggis. If you left it in the van for two hours, outside your mother's house, might she have seen somebody going into the van to tamper with it? It was daytime, so she could easily have seen out of the front window. Was she at home? It'd be very useful for me to ask her about whether she saw anybody.'

'What do you mean, tamper with it?'

'The haggis is where the fire started. Somebody messed with it, and that's what set it on fire at the dinner. That's how Hedley and Armstrong were killed.' Tony had not wanted to give away quite so much information, but he was struggling with Tait's inability to follow a line of questioning.

'That wasn't me!' the young man said fiercely, the light of combat in his eye.

'I know.' Milburn paused to enable this confirmation to sink in. 'I know it wasn't you, but it was somebody, so together we need to work out who could have gotten to it to do that. Now, do you think your ma might have seen something? Was she home?'

'Aye. She made me a sandwich when I got back, but I had to eat it in the van as it was already time to go to the castle.'

203

'OK, maybe we'll get lucky. I'll catch up with her later today and see what she remembers. I assume you didn't see anyone breaking into the van?'

'Nah, and there's been no damage to it. It was definitely locked – Ah always mek sure o' that.'

Milburn nodded, showing agreement that it is good practice always to lock one's vehicle. Internally, he was sceptical that Declan would be so punctilious.

'I spoke to Jacqui before, but I don't think I made very good notes.' Tony flicked back and forth through a few pages of his notebook. His notes were perfect and complete. 'Did I remember right that Armstrong used to give her money, and had stopped that recently?'

'Aye, he's a mean old sod,' Declan said contemptuously. 'Gave me the job, but at the same time stopped me ma's money. He'd given her money every month since I was born. The bastard told me it was his wife what made him stop, but he's that tight, I bet it was his idea. Get me working for the money instead of giving it away.'

'How did your ma feel about that? I bet she was mad.'

'Aye, she was reet upset, but she'd never blame Melville,' the lad said grimly. 'She could nivvor see what a git he was. She blamed Mrs Armstrong. Said she's a stuck-up bitch, and a load of other stuff.'

'I know what she means. Wait here, Mr Tait.' And Detective Sergeant Milburn stood up and made his way to the interview room next door.

Thirty-three

Tuesday, 7.22 a.m.

Milburn entered Interview Room Two. The room was a replica of the one he had just left – small, square, with institutional grey walls, a white plastic table and four matching chairs.

ADC Meredith waved towards the recording device, and he responded to her cue, saying, 'Detective Sergeant Milburn entering the room.' Interviews were always recorded with video now, but the protocol to introduce oneself for the court, should the recording be aired at a trial, had continued.

Elspeth Armstrong almost shouted, 'What is this? Why am I here?' Her thin fingers worried at the hair tied back across her left temple. Evidently, the interview had not progressed very far.

The Armstrongs' long-time lawyer, Gareth Buckingham, was a man of similar proportions to the dead Melville. He spilled over the sides of the institutional plastic chair, and wiped his brow with a handkerchief that never left his sweaty paw.

'We've been here an hour, and there's been no indication of why my client has been brought here, or why you're holding her.' Buckingham tapped the sleeve of his jacket where a wristwatch would be.

'Oh, I'm sorry.' Milburn struggled to avoid the sarcasm in his voice overshadowing the question itself. 'Mrs Armstrong, did the arresting officer not tell you what you were being arrested *for*?'

'Yes, I did, sir.' Diane stepped in. 'Not only do they have the charge sheet in front of Mr Buckingham, but when I took Mrs Armstrong into custody, she answered "Yes" when I asked if she understood her right to silence and that she was being arrested for conspiracy to defraud.'

The lawyer waved her away with a chubby hand.

'Yes, yes, we know what the bureaucracy says. But we haven't been told why she's *really* here. What is all this actually about? How can we help you find and put away the killer of Joel Hedley and my very dear friend, Melville?'

Tony could feel that his sarcasm would reach heights previously unattained, if the fat man continued in this vein. He wished DCI Hardwick were here to furrow a more diplomatic rut.

But before Milburn could respond, Buckingham added, 'I was at the dinner on Saturday night, and I can't tell you how much I want to help catch the evil so-and-so.' He banged his fist on the table, like an accomplished thespian. 'So, please drop the whole suspect interview pretence and get to how we can assist the murder investigation.'

This brought the sarcasm the detective sergeant had so hope to avoid.

'You are a qualified lawyer, I assume?' he asked. No pause to let the man rise to this. 'In which case, I'm sure you're aware that assisting a known conman to move the assets of a dead man would easily fit the criteria for conspiracy to defraud. It would be more fitting of your position if you could advise your client that her best chance of avoiding prison is to plead guilty at the first opportunity.'

Mrs Armstrong turned to her solicitor, looking like Edvard Munch's *The Scream*, and accompanied the look with a shriek. Buckingham was clearly struggling as to what to address first – the impugning of his capabilities, or the distress of his accused friend and client.

Milburn knew he could not continue to be so combative, or they would achieve nothing. He stood to remove his navy-blue suit jacket and hung it on the back of his chair, simultaneously giving Diane a look. She nodded and stepped up to the plate.

'Perhaps we can take this all down a notch,' she said pleasantly. 'We'll definitely make better progress if we're all calm. We are making steady progress in the investigation of the deaths of Mr Hedley and Mr Armstrong, but that is not why we

206

brought you in, Mrs Armstrong. Yesterday, we caught a man called Frankie Veitch at the Moranne Bank here in Durham. He was impersonating Mr Armstrong and trying to move your late husband's money offshore.'

'That's *our* money.' Elspeth had turned to Meredith and hissed, '*My* money now.'

'Please.' The ADC lifted a hand. She paused, waiting for the woman to be quiet. 'The account Mr Veitch was attempting to access was solely in Mr Armstrong's name, and until the will is read, and probate set up and so on, the money cannot be moved. Veitch had many pieces of identification that belonged to Mr Armstrong, and he told us that *you*, Mrs Armstrong, had supplied those and put him up to the fraudulent attempt to move that money. The reason we are here today is to get to the bottom of all that.'

Milburn kept silent about the information Trident had supplied, that Melville had left no will.

Gareth Buckingham squeezed his bulk round to whisper into his client's ear. They had a murmured conversation.

In the end, Elspeth Armstrong stated defiantly, 'I don't know who this Veitch person is, and I've never met him.'

Milburn put the fingers of his right hand to the bridge of his nose, praying for patience.

'Please. This is not Frankie Veitch's first rodeo. The man's a career criminal. He has recordings of your meetings and phone conversations. This is your last chance to get ahead in the co-operation game, or we'll just send all the evidence to the CPS right now. It's pretty much an open and shut case looking at everything Mr Veitch has to give us.'

At this point, Meredith good-copped herself back into the conversation.

'Come now, Elspeth, save yourself the embarrassment of a media circus at trial. We can get you the best possible outcome if you talk to us, right now. All we want to know is why you were working with this Veitch character. He doesn't seem to be your sort of person at all. What happened exactly?'

Tears were bulging the woman's eyes, wetting her crow's feet ever so slightly.

'I just don't want those money-grabbing good-for-nothings to get hold of our hard-earned money.'

The ADC continued gently, 'What do you mean exactly? Did you help Veitch with the IDs he was using? Did you tell him the accounts to go after?'

The woman barely nodded, looking down at her clasped hands.

'Elspeth,' her solicitor intervened, 'you need to stop talking. Let's get them to lay out very clearly and carefully exactly what they're offering, and what the alternatives are. At the moment, these officers are just scaremongering. Let's not fall for it, please.'

The widow drew in a strengthening breath and lifted her chin to stare straight at Tony. 'As my lawyer said, Mr Milburn, there will be no more conversation until you clarify everything Gareth asks for.'

DS Milburn turned to the side and telephoned DCI Hardwick, hoping that the out-loud admission that they needed Mrs Armstrong's help would bring the couple on side. The conversation, deliberately held in front of the suspect and her solicitor, concluded with an offer.

Harry Hardwick, senior detective, well-known to both Buckingham and Mrs Armstrong, promised that he would commit to convincing the Crown Prosecution Service that it was not in the public interest to put her through a trial. He could not withhold evidence but held a lot of influence with the government's lawyers. The intention would be to minimise the trouble that Elspeth was in, to whatever degree that could be done. Hardwick's sway with these two was clearly enough to move things along, as they agreed that Elspeth would help to the fullest possible extent.

BURNS NIGHT BURNS

Tony Milburn began the new phase of the interview with, 'Right, let's start with how you know Frankie Veitch. I can't imagine you normally socialise with a common criminal.'

The detective sergeant navigated them through a conversation that confirmed what Veitch had previously claimed. Mrs Armstrong had intercepted him in the commission of a con against Melville and held this over him as a debt to be repaid when she found a need for his particular skill set. Several months earlier, she had discovered the monthly payments her husband made to his mistress, Jacqui Tait. Incensed, she had forced him to stop the payments. Melville, 'the cheeky sod', had complied but had also taken on his bastard son, Declan, as a dogsbody at the aggregates company, in order to continue supporting 'the grasping chavs'.

None of this came to Tony as much of a shock. However, there was something niggling at him, something that did not add up, but he couldn't quite drag from his brain the exact problem with her narrative. He turned to Meredith with a quizzical look.

She nodded and asked, 'You seem to have explained the reasoning behind your helping, or perhaps more accurately, instructing Mr Veitch, but I still have a slight confusion. Perhaps you can clear it up. Your money could be in jeopardy from Declan Tait, because Mr Armstrong has died, and his son would have legal claim on it.'

Elspeth and her lawyer both nodded along with the logic.

'However, our forensic team gathered Melville's wallet from his jacket, in the dining room at the castle. It was too burnt up to find any of his ID items like, say, his library card, and yet you were able to supply driving licence and other bank cards and so on to Frankie in order to impersonate your husband. It seems like stunning good fortune that you saw fit to safeguard these crucial ID items,' Diane said sweetly. 'Did you know in advance that they would otherwise get burnt up in a fire on Saturday night?'

Gareth Buckingham just about exploded with vicarious indignation at this question. Tony had to start fiddling with his

209

phone to keep himself from exploding too, with laughter at Diane's mocking tone. The distraction worked as he had a text message from Penfold.

No hand-blown glassware

in Durham Castle's cupboards

the Master confirms.

At University College, the college principal went by the term 'Master'. Milburn silently cursed the surfer, wondering, How the hell does he know the Master at Durham Castle?

Mrs Armstrong walked them through a claim that her husband maintained several different wallets, and the one for black-tie dinners never held any important items. She sounded convincing when she said that he habitually drank too much at these events to keep such items secure, and had long ago agreed to take only cash and business cards. She finished the explanation with what Tony considered a brilliant flourish.

'Oh, and of course, he always kept his library card in that black-tie night's wallet.'

Touché, madame, touché.

The proceedings were interrupted by a piercing sound. One of the evidence bags on the table – the props that Meredith and Milburn had been using in their interview process – started to vibrate, and the light from the phone screen shone through the whitened label portion on the front. It was Elspeth's phone, having been taken by the uniformed officers on Saturday night, along with those of everyone else at the dinner. Tony pulled the device from the bag. A notification across the screen began with an icon of a police car with flashing blue light. He held it up for the others to see.

BURNS NIGHT BURNS

Mrs Armstrong turned to her solicitor and said, 'That's the burglar alarm at the house.' Her face drained of colour. 'It alerts directly to my phone when there's a break-in.'

Thirty-four

Tuesday, 8.16 a.m.

'The alarm is coming from the house on South Street?' Milburn had already stood up at the interview-room table. This case continued to add layers of complexity at every turn. If there was a break-in happening at the Armstrongs' home, Milburn wanted to catch the intruder red-handed. This could be a follow-up to the murder of Melville.

'Ye-es,' Elspeth Armstrong faltered.

'Give me the keys and the alarm code and we'll go and catch them.' Diane held out her hands to the ghostly-looking woman, who produced the keys from her handbag and wrote the code on a torn-off piece of paper.

As per the nature of the profession, Elspeth's solicitor intervened.

'We are *not* giving the police free rein to go and ferret around the Armstrongs' home, when my client remains here in custody. With no warrant, do you really think you can do as you please in their house? It seems you believe we were born yesterday!'

'Gareth, please, I can't afford to lose anything more,' Elspeth said weakly. 'I probably didn't set it right on the alarm box. I normally set it on my phone, but the police had my phone. I suspect it's just a fault. Please, let them go and investigate.'

'No, really, Elspeth,' the lawyer was quick to say. 'This is not in your best interest.'

To indicate that they were wasting time and any opportunity to catch the burglar, Meredith simply tapped her watch.

Buckingham reconsidered. 'Oh, very well, but I'll come with you,' he told Milburn, 'then I can make sure that you are simply acting as good police officers should, and not looking around for things you have no business sticking your noses into.'

'Fine, let's go!' Milburn was already at the door, waving out Diane and the lumbering figure of the lawyer. 'The desk sergeant will come for you in a minute, Mrs Armstrong.'

The three hurried out to DS Milburn's car, and Diane drove fast along the streets around Durham's river loop towards South Street. The steep cobbled hill had cars parked all down the left-hand side. It was one way, so the remainder of the roadway was only wide enough for one vehicle. She screeched the car to a halt level with the front door, which they saw was wide open. Leaving the vehicle blocking the street, Milburn and Diane made straight for the entrance. Gareth Buckingham blustered from the back seat but was finding it hard to squeeze himself out of the car.

'Wait by the door,' Milburn shouted to the solicitor. Tony was two steps ahead of Meredith, who virtually shoved him over the threshold. Before doing anything else, she quickly input the security code that Elspeth had given her, to stop the hideous racket of the alarm, which had led to some people watching from behind their curtains. The entrance opened into a porchway, and the officers paused at the second door which led straight into a large reception room.

Despite it being early in the morning, the air felt stagnant, and the bright chill from outside seemed stuck, unable to enter the gloom, as if it also needed Meredith to shove it across the threshold. Furniture in a very traditional style aimed for a luxuriant feel, but it was muted, stifled by the stale atmosphere. Burgundies, browns, hints of gold and scarlet in the soft furnishings insisted that the room should be convivial and welcoming. Something in the air thwarted that intent.

As they took in their surroundings, a heavy wooden thud could be heard, as if an occupied coffin had fallen on the floor up above.

The two detectives looked at each other. Diane's brown eyes were wide. They both ran for the far door, the only other exit

213

from the front parlour, and made straight for the staircase. Almost immediately, another loud sound scraped their eardrums, this time as if the coffin were being dragged across bare floorboards. As their own clattering footsteps – four feet in stout leather shoes – banged up two and three steps at a time, the scraping stopped.

At the top of the staircase, Milburn hurtled breathlessly towards the only open door on that landing. Arriving in a large library-cum-office, he stopped, confronted by the figure of Randall White. The man was panicked, hands wiggling at his sides, and eyes searching for an escape route. Other than leaping through one of the leaded windows, he would have to charge through two Durham Constabulary officers to get away.

Milburn raised his left palm like a Stop indication when directing traffic. The man peered at them over a fancy wooden trunk. It was clear that he was torn between trying somehow to keep the trunk, and yet avoid being caught. The trunk had sounded extremely heavy when hitting the ground and being dragged along the floorboards. Tony felt confident they would lose neither the suspect nor this mysterious box.

Feeling Diane's presence in the doorway behind, DS Milburn took a step forward, his hand still held up.

'OK, Randall, I don't know what's happening here exactly, but we're going to need to go to the police station to sort it out. You understand that, right?' Unsure of the man's mental state, Tony made placatory hand gestures and took things slowly.

White made no reply, although his eyes continued to dart around the room, checking out each corner, the spaces by the bookshelves, underneath the two giant oak desks, and repeatedly past Tony towards the landing. Tall and athletic, the chef might well be able to give them some physical complications – if he chose to make the arrest difficult. White's foreshortened little finger on his left hand poked repeatedly into his thigh.

'Randall, talk to me. You're OK, are you?' The detective continued on a path of gentle understanding. 'Can we take you to the police station to discuss why you're in the Armstrongs' house?'

Finally, the man's eyes settled on Tony. He smiled, a big grin. Before anyone else could speak, Milburn's colleague side-stepped him and dived over the wooden trunk onto the floor, tackling White with her shoulder in his gut. He doubled over and went down winded. With lightning speed, she rolled him and cuffed him.

'Jesus, Meredith, what the hell?' Tony shouted angrily. 'You can't just go attacking people. He'd made no threat or even said anything. What are you thinking?'

'Get over yourself, Tony. I could see he was about to tear into you. Those wild, staring eyes – he's on something, or just plain mental.' She rose to her feet, turned her captive on his side, and pulled on an arm to give him the message to stand up.

'This is not OK, Diane: I had it under control. You need to learn to de-escalate things. I'll be reporting this, even if he doesn't.'

Randall White had recovered enough breath to splutter, 'I bloody will. "Wild, staring eyes" – how racist are you lot?'

'Shut up, you.' Diane pulled at his handcuffed arm. 'You're under arrest for assaulting a police officer. Right?' She looked pointedly at Milburn who remained silent. 'Plus breaking and entering. What is this you're after anyway?' She bent down and unclipped the latch holding the convex trunk lid closed.

Heavily varnished, and with stout, black iron hinges and handles, the chest had the crest of the Durham Friendship Society beautifully carved into the top. Inside, it held numerous folders and sheaves of loose papers. Detective Sergeant Milburn rifled through them at random, and discovered that the entire trunk-load appeared to be papers relating to the club for wannabe Freemasons. Along with an unusual soft hat – rather like a forest-green tam o'shanter – the non-folio objects in the box included a wooden plaque listing past Presidents with their years of office, and a yellow velvet bag of billiard balls. The two dozen spheres only came in white or black, twelve of each, and were heavy, as if they had a lead centre.

'What do you want with this stuff?' Tony held out some papers and the cloth hat towards the tall prisoner.

'I'm gonna get in, whatever they do.' White pointed a finger at the velvet bag. 'Without the black balls, those racist bastards can't stop me.'

Dropping the hat back into the trunk, Milburn said, 'I can't imagine that's how it would work, but OK.'

'And there's two empty spaces on the roster now.'

Tony winced at White's thought processes and radioed for a car to come and collect the prisoner and take him back to the station. Heavy breathing in the hallway outside the library gave away that Buckingham had finally made the ascent of the staircase.

'What is it?' he gasped. 'What's going on?'

'I told you to wait outside,' Tony snapped.

'Not on your nelly. Look—' The solicitor pointed at the papers in Tony's right hand. 'This is exactly the sort of illegal search I anticipated. Nothing you present in court will be admissible, *nothing*.'

'Whatever.' The DS hurled the papers back into the wooden box and led them all back out and down the stairs, where he input the security code that Elspeth had given him into the alarm and shut and locked the front door.

On their return to the nick's custody suite at a quarter past eleven, Milburn was embarrassed to discover that Elspeth Armstrong remained languishing in Interview Room Two. He had forgotten to radio Baz Bainbridge to take her back to a cell, and the solicitor let them know his feelings on the matter in no uncertain terms. Tony was ruffled. Many elements of this investigation were going awry.

However, his apologies to the newly widowed Mrs Armstrong did not continue very long, once her solicitor started

216

speaking. The man had remained standing up in order to impose his considerable bulk on proceedings.

'Thank goodness I went with them, Elspeth,' he said self-importantly. 'Exactly as I predicted, they were rummaging through some of Melville's papers. I put a stop to that immediately, of course, but we mustn't trust these lot.' He waved sausage fingers towards Detective Sergeant Milburn.

'Look, I can't take much more of this,' Elspeth pleaded. 'What was going on at the house? Was it a false alarm?'

'Hardly. That chef who brought in the haggis, he was there attempting to steal the Friendship Society casket.'

'I knew it was him – I *knew* it! Those people are all the same. I told Melville his sort are all violent. We should never have let him anywhere near the dinner.'

Milburn's distaste for the Armstrong woman turned into rage. He felt the pain of a thousand Randall Whites, held back by the entitlement of exploitative bullies like the recently deceased Melville Armstrong and his vile widow.

Tony and Kathy regularly lamented the difficulties in addressing the systemic privilege imbued on them through nothing more than the luck of birth. It was one of the reasons Tony had joined the police in the first place – to try to improve a broken system from within. To see a successful man like Randall White feel he had to burgle a wealthy white home to make progress in this world had brought Tony down to earth with a bump. Almost slamming the door of the interview room, he switched on the recording device. This would trigger a notification on Sergeant Bainbridge's console, and Meredith would be sent to join him as soon as Mr White was booked in.

'Could you sit down, please, Mr Buckingham, and we'll continue where we left off.'

'What?' the man roared. 'Are you seriously considering keeping my client any longer? You now have in custody the vicious brute who likely murdered my friend, Melville. I think it would be in everyone's best interest to allow this grieving widow to go home and try to rebuild her life, after everything that evil man has taken from her.' His bluster was accompanied by a movement of his hand, changing its direction to aim through the wall, a likely location of Chef White.

'Sit down!' Milburn's ire got the better of him.

The room silenced and Buckingham's arm dropped to his side. He stared at the detective.

'How dare you raise your voice at me. As I was just about to say, I think we had better get Harry Hardwick in here to put you back in your box and release my client with significant apologies.'

Dropping in the DCI's first name was a ploy that irritated Tony at the best of times. In this moment, he felt ready to punch the man. Fortunately, at that moment Diane entered the room and breezily introduced herself to the video camera. Her silky voice and light tone soothed Tony, and the enforced pause gave him just enough time to take a deep breath and rein back his temper. Casually, he pulled out his colleague's chair for her. Meredith gave him a questioning look but accepted the courtesy. Tony followed her in sitting down, and they both stared up at the florid Buckingham.

As Elspeth's lawyer prepared himself to launch into another tirade, DS Milburn took the wind out of his sails.

'I spoke to DCI Hardwick just now, whilst you were using the facilities. He was pleased that we had foiled the burglary, but emphasised that many questions remain about Mrs Armstrong's involvement with Frankie Veitch and the plot to fraudulently move money offshore.'

Sighing loudly, the solicitor finally sat down. The weight of the man flopping down into his seat caused Tony to wince in sympathy at the tribulations of the plastic chair. Gareth put a hand on Mrs Armstrong's arm.

'Just a little longer then, Elspeth. We'll humour these two and be away very soon. Is that OK?' His fawning and sudden concern for her caused Milburn to shake his head slowly in disgust.

The conversation turned back to the events inside the Moranne Private Bank, and Frankie Veitch's claims of being directed by the Widow Armstrong. Veitch had supplied some details of the information she had provided. These were denied by the solicitor, who did a good job of ensuring that his client said very little of her own concocting. For her part, Elspeth Armstrong sat looking grim, her lips compressed. As she had done before, she repeatedly stroked back the hair on the side of her head. The action was unnecessary as it had already been stringently tied in place. Additional clips and grips controlled every lock of her highlighted tresses.

The suspect only spoke when necessary, after Gareth had already detailed what she was stating, and thus only to confirm his answers, which were always vague at best. If this interview ever came to court, there would be at least three possible interpretations of every agreed sentence. In the end, the verbal fencing formed a somewhat skewed Mexican stand-off. It was two against one as Meredith and Milburn poked and parried Mr Buckingham for nearly an hour. He was a good lawyer, though, and understood the hidden agenda in all their questioning.

Elspeth alone was out of her depth. She could be as manipulative and conniving as the others, but since she was unfamiliar with the law or with court procedures, she very quickly fell into line, offering mere affirmations of the statements Gareth developed for her. The embittered widow avoided embellishment and proved a frustrating interview subject for Tony.

The only time Buckingham let his client roam free in the conversation was when she spoke of her knowledge of making glassware.

In an unexpected diversion, Tony asked, 'Tell me, Mrs Armstrong, what do you know of the art of glass-blowing?'

She glanced at her solicitor, who made a gesture indicating that the floor was hers to answer with whatever knowledge she had. The woman faltered briefly, a rabbit in the headlights look on her face. After a moment, however, her composure returned, and she answered his question with a question of her own.

'How did you know about that?' she challenged.

'What do you mean, Elspeth?' Diane stole in, velvet smooth, with her usual sense of timing. 'How did we know about what?'

'You already know, or you wouldn't have asked,' the woman burst out. 'Melville and I met in a glass-blowing club at university.'

ADC Meredith continued with her creamy tone. 'Oh, that sounds just lovely. How romantic.'

The woman looked tearful, but she was in control, and no tears escaped onto her cheeks.

'You'd have thought so, yes, but he drunkenly told me once that he only joined the club to pick up women. That was the phrase he used: "Pick up women." He was such a boorish lout. I can't believe I stayed with him so long.'

'How horrible. Why *did* you stay with him, if you don't mind me asking?' Gently, Diane probed.

Buckingham touched his client's hand, and she clammed up again, saying merely, 'He was my husband. I made a vow.'

The police officers both remained silent, not as part of any interview psychology, but attempting to think of where to take the interrogation next. Eventually, Tony spoke first.

'So just to clarify and confirm, would it be true to say that you have the ability to hand-blow, say, a glass vase?'

Elspeth looked at her solicitor, who nodded.

'Yes, I made half a dozen back then. I mean, it was thirty-five years ago, but I have done that before. Melville was annoyingly good at it. Seemed to pay no attention to the teacher, make very little effort, yet every one of his vases came out nicer than the best of mine. I think he's still got one of them on the windowsill in his office up at the aggregates site.'

'Are you claiming then that you have not created anything that way in the last few months?' Milburn asked, and waited.

'Of course not.' She looked at him more as if he was mad than as if she was taken aback with surprise. 'I don't have any suitable equipment.'

Meredith had no idea what the whole glass-blowing line of inquiry was about, but she was quick-witted and joined in with, 'What about your husband, though? Wouldn't the sort of equipment you need for that be the normal kind of stuff that an industrial quarry might have around the site?'

'Are you trying to make me feel awful?' Elspeth stared at Diane. 'Listen to what I'm saying: *he only joined the glass-blowing club to pick up women*! God, it makes me feel dirty just saying it. We were a partnership with little love for nearly twenty years, but I never hated him until the moment he told me that.'

Milburn came straight back with, 'When did he make that admission? Was it recently?'

Elspeth looked up at the white-painted ceiling for an instant, before returning to look straight into Tony's eyes.

'It was Good Friday last year. Another big dinner night for the Friendship Society every year. Of course he was drunk, and when we got home, he dropped a full whisky tumbler, a glass engraved with the coat-of-arms of Edinburgh University. I teased him that he could use his university glass-blowing skills to make a new one. And, well, in return I got a tirade of misogyny, which concluded with an almost proud announcement that his only trophy from that art club was me.'

'Gosh, how awful.' Meredith's sycophancy grated on Tony, but he seemed to be the only one who saw through it. 'What did you do?'

'I went to my mother's. Spent the weekend there thinking over how I'd wasted my life, before realising I hadn't wasted it, that in fact I had everything I wanted. Even though I was stuck with a boor of a husband, we were wealthy and well-regarded. I came back to South Street on Easter Monday to resurrect my life and since that day we've continued our working marriage – well, until Saturday night.' For a moment she looked shaken, but then

221

her voice became hard. 'And now I need to fight to keep what we built together against all those money-grabbers who want to take it for free. I've worked very hard for everything I have – I'm not going to let any Tom, Dick or Harry come along and steal it.'

Buckingham interrupted, 'Enough, Elspeth. Officers, this interview is over.'

'Yes, I think it is.' Milburn stood up. 'Mrs Armstrong, I'll get the custody sergeant to take you to a cell.' He walked out.

Thirty-five

Tuesday, 12.32 p.m.

The Daily Espresso was busy with office workers taking their lunch. Milburn was surprised that Penfold had managed to secure his favourite corner table. The asymmetry of the building put the spot that the Kiwi favoured in a narrowing corner. This meant that it was apart from most others by a little more than the normal spacing, and the level of illumination was dimmer than the others. In fact, the round table of cherry wood was intimate to the point of being clandestine.

As Tony walked over, Penfold's tanned face turned up to him with a bright smile.

'How go the fried friends?'

Milburn glanced around to see who might have heard this crassness, but busily chewing faces were glued to phone screens, oblivious to all other influences.

Clearly making to leave, Mantoro stood and offered up his chair. He patted Tony's shoulder and slipped a small clear plastic bag onto his saucer. It looked like an open, casual drugs hand-off, until the policeman scrutinised more closely and saw that the bag contained cashew nuts. Thanking him, Tony put down the brie and bacon panini he'd purchased, opened the bag and scattered some nuts onto his plate as well.

'Well, any glass artisans coming to the fore?' Penfold wanted to know.

The two men discussed the morning's interviews with Declan Tait and Elspeth Armstrong, as well as Randall White's ill-conceived plan to ensure enrolment in the Durham Friendship Society. The thing that most seemed to catch the New Zealander's attention was the question of whether a membership vote could be held if the black balls had indeed all gone missing. The ins and outs of the Society's constitutional rules interested him much more than any other news, even the fact of the Armstrongs' history with glass-blowing.

He muttered between sips of a large black Americano, 'And what if the voting bag was passed around and nobody noticed the absence of black balls for the first few votes. And would the vote still be valid if they later discovered the absence of black balls – because no one had wanted to use one, so it wasn't noticed during the vote?'

Wolfing down the food, Tony was happy to let his friend muse on such trivia. It was the first chance he'd had to eat since leaving home at six in the morning. Finally, he swallowed, then washed the last of the panini down with a swig of sugary latte.

'You seem distracted, Penfold. No great insight on the case? No, "So and so did it, and here's how and why"? I feel like you're getting slow in your old age.' Milburn was two years older than Penfold, so this tease was clear to both. The response, however, floored the detective.

'Well, I'd say we are just about in a position to get everybody together and explain exactly what went on. You'll have the odd arrest to make, but I guess you already know that.'

Milburn stared. 'Wait – you think you know who killed Hedley and Armstrong?'

'Not entirely,' Penfold said breezily. 'Just gotta confirm a couple of tests in the lab, and we also need to check out some things back up at the aggregates site. If you could convince Mrs Armstrong to let us into the site offices again, we should be able to close in on the solution to the murders.'

'Really?'

'Yeah, she'll be right.'

'What, who will?'

'Antipodean slang, sorry. "She'll be right" means "Everything will be fine". OK, you said you still have Declan and Randall and Mrs Armstrong all in custody, yes?'

With a nod, Milburn asked, 'Is it one of them?'

'Hold your horses! Remember, I've got two experiments still running at home. The results of these will confirm my hypotheses, and then we'll be ready to lay it all out.' From Penfold's cargo shorts thigh pocket squeaked a voice.

'Randall White and Declan Tait have both been released. White on bail, and Tait with nothing.'

'What is she saying?' Tony's face screwed up in confusion. The voice sounded like Penfold's sister, Trident. He imagined a tiny version of a cartoon manga girl stuck in the zipped side pocket of the beige shorts, scrabbling to get out.

The Kiwi answered condescendingly, 'I'm not sure how I could say it differently from what my sister just told us.'

'But how does she know any of that?' The detective sergeant checked his phone and saw two messages from DCI Hardwick confirming the releases.

'I'd better not tell you how easy it is to hack the HOLMES computer system,' Penfold said, followed by the voice of his sister, squeaking: 'It's bloody hard, big bro', but I'm a bloody good hacker.'

Penfold made no movement and just commanded, 'Shut up, Trident.'

'Your sister is in your pocket?' Milburn queried. 'How does that work then? Are you on the phone to her the whole time?'

'Ha, not at all. She hacks everything.' Penfold shrugged his powerful shoulders. 'It doesn't surprise me in the slightest that my phone holds no obstacles. I've always assumed she's listening in on my conversations.' He switched to addressing her directly again. 'First time you've decided to come out of the shadows.'

'In your pocket is hardly out of the shadows – it's horrible in here: salty and smelly.'

'Has she got a smelling app?' Tony asked naively.

'Ignore her, Milburn. She spins all the yarns.' His pocket sniggered and, through her laughs, Trident said goodbye. 'Peace out, suckers.'

Penfold turned from his cup to look at Tony, speaking more seriously: 'Even if she did hack the police systems, which I'm not saying she did, I haven't seen the evidence you have. My conclusions are based on my own investigations, plus the various things you did send my way.'

Detective Chief Inspector Hardwick would almost certainly have instituted disciplinary proceedings against Milburn, had he known that this surfer had seen the forensic reports, but Tony was confident that Penfold could balance the fine line between explaining his conclusions and revealing his sources. He had successfully done so many times before. More of a gamble was Tony's insistence to himself that, even if discovered, the constabulary's low staffing levels would force his boss to go down the verbal warning route, rather than anything more serious. His stomach roiled at the prospect of the conversation.

'OK,' he said, pulling himself together, 'but what did you conclude?'

'All in good time, my friend. As you know, I always need double blind confirmation, before I'll put my name to moving any hypothesis into conclusions territory.'

This did not help to placate the stomach churning that had Milburn gripping the tabletop. He could not decide if some of it was due to having eaten his lunch too fast, or excitement that the case was nearing a solution, but he knew the majority of his discomfort stemmed from having involved Penfold in the investigation. Hardwick had been crystal clear that, despite personnel shortages, they would *not* be taking the Kiwi on as an external consultant. It was the one thing Hardwick and Penfold agreed upon.

'I'm taking a punt that what you work out is going to be correct,' Tony said. 'However, even if it is, I need to be able to insert evidence in a way that we are allowed to then use it in court.'

'Rest assured, my friend, one way or another, that will not be a problem in this case. You have my word.'

They sat silently for a couple of minutes, drinking their coffees and musing on the wood grain of the table.

'Do you want me to make us an appointment at Armstrong Aggregates?' Tony offered. 'I'm sure I could get Elspeth Armstrong to give us permission. She's in a precarious position right now.'

'Yes. Great idea.' Penfold nodded enthusiastically. 'And make sure you bring her along to unlock doors and so forth.'

'That's not quite what I meant.' Tony's voice faded away as he realised that he had backed himself into a corner. Mrs Armstrong, and her lawyer, would probably insist on going with them anyway. 'I don't think I can get her out of the station on my own, though. A prisoner transport will need at least two police officers.'

Penfold squinted slightly, mulling over this.

'Take Meredith.'

'Are you nuts? You know very well that the last thing I need to do is give Meredith a Sword of Damocles to hang over my head.'

'Trust me.' Tony's friend indicated that they should leave. The detective followed, heading for the café exit.

Before they got there, Penfold turned and said, 'I can tell you who *didn't* start the fire.' Without another word, he then stepped out into the cold afternoon, with only a T-shirt and shorts against the winter wind.

'Forget it. Tell me who didn't start it, when you tell me who did.' Milburn held both hands up in defeat as he watched the figure stroll away from him.

227

Thirty-six

Tuesday, 1.15 p.m.

Walking up the cobbles of Silver Street into Durham's Market Place, Tony worried about how he could organise the prisoner outing that Penfold had requested. He imagined Diane's face as he drove them all in a police-liveried Transit van and suddenly swerved away to head towards the A1 motorway and up to Northumberland. Even if they drove with flashing blue lights and sirens wailing, the journey to Armstrong Aggregates would take nearly an hour – assuming that the traffic around the Metrocentre would play the game at 4 p.m. on a Tuesday. Grey clouds scudded overhead, threatening rain, which would lengthen the journey further.

In reality, they would all have to go in Milburn's VW Golf. No van would be available in the motor pool, and he didn't want to announce the trip more widely than was absolutely necessary. He hadn't even considered how Andrew Singh, as the custody sergeant coming on for the late shift, might be convinced that DS Milburn had good cause to take the suspects out for an evening in the national park countryside.

Fact-finding trips out with suspects were possible, but usually the arrangements were made much further in advance. As he'd predicted, Elspeth's lawyer would insist on going along too, he had little doubt. That might, in fact, help – lending the scheme a bit more legitimacy. Tony questioned his faith in Penfold, but finally hit upon the solution. He himself would have to come up with some suitable question that he needed to have answered so that the trip stood up on its own, regardless of Penfold's investigation up at the site. His mind whirled through the items that Armstrong and Hedley might have kept in their offices, and to which Elspeth could give him access. They might just hold some significant breakthrough possibilities.

The statue of the Marquis of Londonderry astride his horse dominated the view as Tony walked into Market Place. In fact, the horse's rear end was the principal aspect from Silver Street, but he knew the statue well and it barely registered in his mind. Tony felt very tired. After one night with no sleep, and the previous one with very little, his exhaustion was coming home to roost. Then he suddenly jerked into full alertness.

On the steps below the horse's tail, Momo Jackson stood talking to another homeless man. DS Milburn stopped walking, moved to the side and watched the interaction. He recognised the second man, since he knew most of the street folk in the city, but wasn't aware of his name. Both men wore tatty old combat jackets in green and brown camouflage patterning.

Despite Tony's precautions, Momo had spotted him lurking. He glanced at Milburn for a second and then turned and fled. Tony hadn't thought he needed to speak to Mr Jackson, until the man took to running away. Instinctively, Tony gave chase, but the aching in his knees limited his pace. The short legs of the Indian ex-soldier gave a turn of speed that took his pursuer by surprise. Without handcuffs at his back, Momo ran properly, and even with his old service backpack on, he steadily increased the distance between them.

Luckily for Milburn, Jackson chose to head past Greggs the bakers and across Old Elvet Bridge. The bottleneck of lunchtime pedestrians included gaggle upon gaggle of students in puffer jackets, hoodies, scarves and, bizarrely, shorts. The crowds made fast progress impossible. Tony had to shove a few of the young people aside but caught his quarry by a giant planter on the middle of the medieval bridge.

Pushing the man against the stone parapet wall, the detective demanded, 'What are you running for?'

'I told you before, on the street you always run from the police.'

'And I told *you* before, that the police are reasonable people if you behave reasonably.'

They were both panting and took a few moments to get their breath back. Momo recovered first.

'Look, I'm sorry I ran off, but I can't afford to spend time in a cell this afternoon. I've got another job on, and I need to go and meet the colonel right now.'

'What sort of job?'

'I don't know exactly. He's arranged for me to serve teas and coffees at somebody's private do today, a paid gig. I've got to be ready at Colonel Griffiths' office, to be picked up at fifteen hundred hours.'

Looking down the bridge towards the Royal County Hotel, Tony could not quite see the large white building where Griffiths worked. If he stepped back ten metres to the other parapet, he might be able make out the black barrels of the small cannons that sat outside the old military building. Milburn did step back, but only a metre.

'Well, keep out of trouble,' he said lamely. As an afterthought, he more positively suggested, 'And good luck with the job. I hope it turns into something long term.' They stood looking at each other. 'Off you go then.' Tony felt he sounded like a teacher telling a naughty child that their disciplining was finished, and they could leave. He cringed inwardly.

Momo turned to walk back up the bridge the way they had come.

The detective called after him, 'Wait, I thought you were going to meet Griffiths at his office?'

Tapping the green cuff of his old jacket, Momo replied, 'It's not time yet and I need to change my clothes.' He jerked a thumb over his shoulder to indicate that the rucksack contained a more presentable outfit for work.

With several steps, Milburn closed the small gap that had initially opened up between them. His voice was muted, discreet.

'I don't know if you have a plan, but I reckon the toilets in the Prince Bishops shopping centre would be a good place to change.'

Momo smiled. 'There's lots of places. I'll be OK.'

Tony caught himself by surprise. He stuck his hand out for the man to shake, and said, 'Go well, Momo.'

As they walked in opposite directions away from each other, he wondered what had come over him. The friendly sentiment made for good police relations, but he had never used the phrase 'Go well' in his entire life. He smiled, shaking his head at himself, and plodded on towards the station.

At the top of the stairs from the front office, Milburn could see across the open-plan CID office. He noticed that the small security window on the door of his office held a yellow Post-It note stuck to the outside. The office was busy. Meredith and Aria were conversing whilst pointing at something on Aria's computer screen, while the civilian administrator for the murder team was also focused on her own screen.

Tony walked over and pulled the note from the door. As he did so, he could see through the small pane of glass that the voicemail message light was blinking on his desk phone. The Post-It read *My office now*. No punctuation, no identification. No need for Harry Hardwick to sign the note, Tony knew the handwriting well. Nobody other than the DCI could give such a command anyway.

As he headed up the next flight of stairs to Hardwick's office, Milburn flicked through his phone messages, to find that the boss had repeated his summons in both WhatsApp and voicemail. He had little doubt that the red blinking light on his desk would hold another version of it. Feeling apprehensive, he knocked and entered immediately as was their usual practice. Hardwick waved to the chair, mobile phone at his ear. He held it away and looked at the screen, before tapping it and placing the phone down on the desk in front of him.

'Communication, Tony. It's all about communication. I don't know how to tell you in more different ways and get it into your head for once and for all: *you need to keep me and the others in your loop.* We don't have enough team members as it is, so we all need to know everything that's going on.'

It wasn't entirely clear which element of the investigation the boss was referring to, but Milburn had not relayed any news to him that day at all, so he accepted the rebuke.

'Sorry, H. The trouble is that with too few people I've always got the next thing to get straight on to. Meredith was in this morning's interviews, has she not updated HOLMES with all that?'

'Of course she has. *She* understands teamwork.'

Tony widened his eyes pointedly. Hardwick understood his sergeant's silent argument.

'And of course, Gareth Buckingham had plenty to tell me about the arrest of Randall White. I know we're offering Mrs Armstrong generous terms with the CPS, but don't mess it up so that we've got nothing on her that could stand up in court.'

'No, I get that.' Milburn nodded. 'As far as I'm concerned, we did everything there by the book. I don't trust Diane, but she should corroborate it. That lawyer, by the way, is a whole lot of talk.' He chuckled. 'Aren't they all.'

'Yes, don't worry, I can handle Buckingham. But I know you, Tony. Don't go off the reservation and blow it. I trust Penfold has been left in Hartlepool the whole time?'

'Oh, yes. I'm sure he's at home right now. If he's not in the sea.'

'Good.' Harry nodded. 'Now, I spoke to Meredith and watched the highlights of your interviews this morning, and I've released Tait. We've got nothing to hold him for. That whole assault with a van thing is bullshit, and you know it.'

'What?' Milburn was annoyed. 'Why do you always do this! I know we haven't got anything really strong yet, but Declan's no good, he's dangerous.'

232

'What do you mean? Do you have evidence of a crime he's committed?'

'You mean apart from being named as the killer, by his victim, on the victim's deathbed?'

'Evidence, Tony. I heard that tale about "find the cleaner" – oh, that obviously means "find Declan, he did it". And I don't buy it. If Armstrong knew Declan was going to set this all up, he wouldn't have cut the haggis at all.'

'No, of course not, but once it had happened, Armstrong realised that Declan had transported the haggis, so it must be him. Worked it out in his hospital bed and told the only person he could.' Nagging at the back of Tony's skull was the memory of the interview from that morning, where Declan Tait had unwittingly convinced Tony that he had no knowledge of glass-blowing and therefore could not be the killer.

Hardwick helped Tony out of his hole. 'Do we have any evidence?'

'No.' Said with exasperation.

'That's settled then. Randall White, I have also released. We charged him with breaking and entering and bailed him. I don't think there's much more to that case. He's plainly obsessed with the Friendship Society as his meal ticket, so to speak.' Hardwick paused to relish his pun, but Tony remained stony-faced. 'The attempted burglary was small fry.' Another pause for humour, which Tony again refused to rise to. 'Anyway, we've got nothing more on him, at least not according to HOLMES, so don't start telling me you've got a dossier on him but just haven't gotten around to inputting it into the system yet.'

'No, you're probably right.' Milburn shrugged. 'I mean, he has motive and opportunity, but we haven't quite got him with the means yet.'

'Which is where forensics will give you hard evidence anyway. Motive and opportunity are always just circumstantial.'

'Yeah.' Tony didn't sound convinced. 'Anything else, sir? Or shall I get on with trying to find our arson murderer?'

The DCI gestured DS Milburn away, but not before reminding him, 'Communication, Tony. We're all in the murder team WhatsApp group, so stick information in there so everyone knows what's happening. That'll save time being wasted by duplication of efforts, and give us much better chances to follow up good leads. WhatsApp immediately, and HOLMES whenever you or Meredith get the chance. WhatsApp is for us, HOLMES is for court.'

As he left the room, Tony thought, I wonder if Trident can hack the murder team WhatsApp chat as well.

Thirty-seven

Tuesday, 2.29 p.m.

In his office overlooking Old Elvet, Lieutenant Colonel Jack Griffiths accepted Momo's returning teacup and put all the crockery back on the tray for his secretary to tidy up later. The two men then walked down the wide staircase together, passing the ubiquitous photograph of the royal Commander-in-Chief.

Outside the entrance, a tangerine-coloured 1972 Volkswagen Beetle sat waiting at the kerb. In the driver's seat, Penfold leaned over and opened the front passenger door. Griffiths and Jackson shook hands and Momo got into the car. The colonel stood and watched as Penfold drove them away, with an engine noise like a loud lawnmower.

Driving north for an hour gave Penfold the chance to chat with Momo about life in the army, comparisons of growing up in Birmingham, England and New Zealand, and the job that Momo was to do that afternoon. Penfold explained that they would be in a large office, but that there would be as many as a dozen people attending, and he had engaged the ex-soldier as a waiter to make and distribute refreshments for the guests.

En route, they swung by a big Sainsbury's to pick up all the teabags, coffee, sugar, milk and biscuits that such a group might request. At Momo's suggestion, they added some juices and sparkling water to the shopping. Penfold chose a collection of extra mugs and glasses as well, along with a couple of tea towels, working on the assumption that there might not be enough available for the whole group.

'What about washing up?' Jackson asked. 'Is all the gear for that already there?'

'Good question. I'm going to guess that facilities will be adequate for the clean-up before and afterwards, so we'll gamble and not buy any. After all, we're bringing all these gifts, so I think we'll be OK to use up some of their dishwashing liquid.'

As they continued along smaller lanes in the Northumberland countryside, the grey clouds produced the rain that had threatened all afternoon. The Beetle's wipers were utterly inadequate for the job, but Penfold drove on through the shower, oblivious.

DS Milburn turned off the rain-soaked tarmac of a Northumberland byway onto the muddy gravel track that formed the entrance drive to Armstrong Aggregates. His more modern Volkswagen had better windscreen wipers than its more than fifty years older grandparent, but he still couldn't see very well. At five o'clock on a dark Tuesday evening in January, the quarry had already closed for the day and was unlit. Negotiating the slippery surface proved difficult enough, so Tony felt grateful that he did not have to avoid oncoming gravel trucks as he crawled along the unmarked road.

From behind his head, Elspeth Armstrong continually gave directions as to where the track curved and which big potholes would threaten the car's suspension. He responded graciously throughout but felt that her back seat driving was more intended to gain some sort of social dominance.

Elspeth and her lawyer, Gareth Buckingham, had agreed to undertake the 'fact-finding trip' to her dead husband's business, but both had complained throughout the journey that Milburn had given them no clue as to exactly what facts they might be looking for. The detective sergeant repeatedly told them to wait and see. He assured Buckingham that it would all be in his client's best interests, but the man was not quiet about how sceptical he was.

Acting DC Meredith could offer Tony little support, as he had not given her much information either. He had had to obfuscate so much because Penfold had not explained to him what was going on. Milburn couldn't very well tell them that the

236

civilian, non-investigator Penfold would reveal all when they arrived.

After a lot of thought, Tony had finally come up with a valid reason for the trip. He hit upon the idea of comparing the chemical store log sheets with the actual amounts of liquid left in each bottle. Penfold's presence could be explained as the scientific consultant who could ensure accurate measurements and understand the meaning of the notes on the recording sheets. Moreover, it was not a thing the forensics team would have thought to measure, and he was pretty sure they hadn't visited the aggregates site yet anyway.

He knew the pretext was weak, but convinced himself it would be enough to justify the jaunt – at least afterwards, when asking for forgiveness rather than permission. Sergeant Singh had been business-like, not really concerned with the investigative details, but more with ensuring Milburn signed the right forms in the right places.

From the car, they hurried towards the Reception doorway, trying to avoid puddles. The two officers had solid police shoes, whilst Gareth Buckingham wore fancy brogues and Mrs Armstrong's smart loafers were ruined by the ten feet of mud she had to cross. She rummaged in her handbag as she led the climb up the stairs, looking for her office keyring.

However, before they were halfway up the staircase to Melville's penthouse Portakabin, the ground-level door adjacent to the admin office swung outwards. The foursome stopped at the noise of the door banging right back against the wall, and they saw Penfold standing on the threshold waving them back down. Nobody argued – they turned and hurried down into the welcoming dry of Joel Hedley's office laboratory.

As they piled in through the doorway, Penfold accidentally 'bumped' into Tony, whose jacket felt heavy afterwards, on the left side. Putting his hand in the deep raincoat pocket, Milburn felt a plastic bag with a large solid lump in it. He left it in the pocket and could not catch Penfold's eye, as the man had his back to them all, closing the door again. The peace was short-lived, since as soon as Penfold had shut out the elements, Elspeth was up in arms.

'How did you get in?' she challenged him. 'The lights are off next door, and everyone has gone home. They didn't leave the door unlocked, did they?'

Penfold cut a slightly strange figure, in a light rain jacket in dusty pink worn over shorts and black rubber sandals.

'Please Mrs Armstrong, don't blame your hard-working staff. They agreed that it would be best for us to make everyone some refreshments before you arrived. Here are the keys they lent me.' Onto the large map table, he dropped a pair of keys attached by a thin wire ring to a yellow rectangle of plastic.

She grabbed them up and read the tag, snapping, 'Why did Joel have the chemical store key on his office keyring?'

'Ah yes, don't worry, I only used them to get in here. I haven't been out to that store. Not today, in this weather.'

She stared at him, and Gareth interjected, 'Detective Milburn, why are we here?'

DS Milburn plucked the keyring from Elspeth's bony fingers and began to mutter about how it was just what they needed.

Penfold interrupted, 'Please be patient. The others will be here shortly, and we'll get some clarity on a variety of issues. In the meantime, please do take a seat and Mr Jackson will serve you with refreshments.' He waved towards the big table. The table with the maps attached had been a conference table originally, and it had ten chairs around it. They were all tucked neatly underneath and appeared not to have been used for some time. The two office chairs on wheels at the computer desk and the microscope desk looked as if they were the only two items of furniture that Hedley had utilised recently.

At the far end of the room, Mohammed Jackson stood beside the mini-kitchenette sink unit, with a collection of the new, freshly washed mugs and glasses awaiting drinks to fill them. He looked smart in white shirt and black trousers.

'Ladies and gentlemen, we have tea or coffee and a variety of juices or sparkling water. Can I get anyone a drink?'

Penfold smiled and pulled himself out a chair. Milburn followed suit, after which each of the others slowly took a seat.

To break the awkward silence that followed, Penfold made a gesture towards Momo, who reached out a hand and clicked the full kettle on to boil. The sounds of the element heating and the rain against the thin walls could placate Buckingham for only a few seconds, though.

'Who exactly are we waiting for? And why are we even here? I think we've had quite enough of the cloak and dagger stuff now.' The lawyer didn't know who he should direct his annoyance towards, and with Penfold and Milburn on opposite sides of the table, he kept turning his head back and forth between them.

Diane Meredith leaned back in her chair, and clasped her hands behind her head, the silky brown hair soft in her palms. She stared at her boss with a feline smile.

Milburn was anxious in case he had placed too much trust in Penfold, with too little information. He dangled the keys and announced that they would be visiting the chemical store later, and asked Mr Buckingham to wait until they'd all warmed up with a hot drink, as the store was outside. His imploring look towards the New Zealander brought no response, since Penfold's attention was focused out of the window.

The sound of another vehicle engine made the rotund solicitor struggle out of his seat and stand to see what was going on.

He quickly sat down again, muttering to Elspeth, 'Just one of the works vans.'

This prompted her to stand up and demand, 'What the heck is that idiot doing here? In winter, the place closes at four, the stupid fool.'

It was Declan Tait. He parked his van up beside the black police Golf and dashed to the door labelled Reception.

Thirty-eight

Tuesday, 5.25 p.m.

Heaving away at the admin building's Reception door, Declan Tait's sheer physical strength shook the whole place, making the entire stack of Portakabins wobble. With the rain still thrashing, it felt like a huge storm, rather than a little rain and a big oaf who'd been locked out. DS Milburn jumped up, opened the door of the geology office and stuck his head out.

'We're in here, come on!' It was just loud enough to catch Tait's attention. The detective already felt cold from the wetness in his shirt. The added rain and breeze outside brought up goosebumps, but he knew that mostly this was due to his uncertainty about the whole situation. The gloom outside, half an hour after sunset, added to his disquiet.

Declan wandered inside, seemingly oblivious to the rain and cold, and Milburn clicked the door shut. Tait peered out from under a grey hood, which he pulled down to see the whole room better.

'Please – join us.' Penfold's hand indicated the seat at the end of the table.

Elspeth Armstrong visibly recoiled at the presence of her husband's illegitimate son, as he landed down only two seats away from her.

'The working day is finished,' she hissed. 'What are you doing here?'

With his big fists resting on the edge of Northumberland – at least the paper version of it taped down in front of him, Declan looked askance at her.

'You messaged me, woman. Ah know Ah'm a bit late but we're all here for the will, right?'

'I did no such thing!' Mrs Armstrong almost exploded. 'What are you talking about, you imbecile?'

A placating gesture on her forearm, accompanied by a patronising *shhh* noise from Gareth Buckingham did nothing to calm Elspeth down. Brusquely, she shook him off and pointed to the door.

'Get that creature away from me!' she shouted.

Meanwhile, Declan was rifling around in the pocket of his tracksuit trousers, seeking something. He finally pulled the whole pocket inside out and dumped his phone on the Hexham area of the map in front of him.

'Look, Ah'll show it to you.'

Everyone waited for Declan find the message. Ignoring Mrs Armstrong, the young man held the phone across the table for Diane Meredith to see. DS Milburn stepped back from the door to look at it over her shoulder.

The message did indeed ask him to meet at Armstrong Aggregates at five o'clock and was signed off *Elspeth Armstrong*. It did not mention Melville's will directly but made a much less clear suggestion that the writer would *sort you out financially once and for all*. Tait's phone listed the number that had sent the message, but there was no name. The sender was not in his contacts list.

Meredith said, 'Show her,' and Declan passed the phone over to Elspeth.

The widow surveyed the screen doubtfully and sniffed, 'Well, that's not my number. Anyone could have sent that.'

The solicitor took the phone from her hand and laid it next to his own, which was in the North Sea on the large geological map. He tapped his own mobile a few times, and then twisted in his seat to look at his client.

'That *is* your number, Elspeth. What are you playing at?'

She grabbed Tait's phone back up from the table and looked, unseeing, at the screen. 'But . . . I *didn't* send it. Truly I didn't!'

Ferreting around in her handbag Elspeth then produced her own slick smartphone. Held in an expensive, protective cover of matt black, it completely absorbed light, giving the impression of a hole in existence. Milburn was mesmerised by its appearance. He imagined falling into the black case, shrinking, to be swallowed up by it, as if in some science-fiction movie.

In a bit of a flap, Elspeth poked her forefinger at the screen, and Tony gazed into the nothingness she held. She carried on protesting repeatedly, which meant that he grudgingly did not dismiss her claims entirely. She then jabbed the black phone close to Buckingham's nose, almost shouting that the message to Tait was not in her message records. Her pasty white face had become flustered and pink with indignation.

'Right, let me intervene here.' It was Penfold. 'Confession time. I do apologise for the subterfuge, but it was actually me who sent Declan that message. I have assistants for whom spoofing a phone is child's play, and we used that capability to encourage Mr Tait to join us here this afternoon.'

Gareth Buckingham exploded, even before his client had a chance to be outraged.

'*What?* What is this?' He turned from Penfold to look across to Detective Sergeant Milburn, but the latter was equally surprised and confused.

Penfold came to Tony's aid as he took the spotlight again.

'Look, as I said, I apologise for the unorthodox approach, but we needed to get everybody here, and some might have refused to join the party if they knew the whole guest-list. Please, we are still waiting on a few late arrivals, so could we all take a drink and biscuits, so my colleague doesn't feel like a spare part in the corner there. I promise this meeting will not take much longer, and I also promise that it is definitely in everyone's interest to be here.'

Before Armstrong or her lawyer, or indeed Declan Tait, could protest any further, Penfold swiftly set the ball rolling by turning to address Momo.

'Could you make me a black coffee, please? And I'll definitely have one of those chocolate Hobnobs. I know how Milburn likes his coffee.' He screwed up his face in theatrical distaste. 'Make his white with sugar, please. Hobnob, Milburn?' Even before Tony could respond, Penfold had asked Meredith, 'And what about you, miss? I bet you love a chocolate biscuit. Coffee or tea with it?'

'Tea, please. White, no sugar.' Diane was sufficiently dragged along by the pace of Penfold's delivery that she didn't question anything he had said.

Momo passed a plate of biscuits to Penfold who placed it in the middle of the table, in the gap between the two maps. He took one himself, and before biting into the Hobnob, he offered Declan a drink. The boxer asked for tea the same as Diane's. Elspeth and Gareth seethed but requested a herbal tea and a white coffee.

Down below, an Uber slipped into place beside Declan's van. The electric car had arrived silently, whilst the rain continued noisily on the windows. Standing by the computer desk at the business end of Joel Hedley's office, the movement of the taxi caught Milburn's eye, and he opened the door to welcome Jacqui Tait inside quickly, out of the weather. Her hand immediately went to her chest.

'Thank God you're all right.' She was addressing her son and moved the hand from her heart to his face.

'What you on about, Ma?'

'I got your message, and I came straight up here. What's going on?' Jacqui scanned around the room, mostly focusing on the police officers.

'What message?'

'Your message about being in trouble.' She turned back to look her son in the face. 'I came straight away.'

'Ah nivvor text you no message.' Then the penny dropped, and Declan jumped to his feet, raising a threatening fist at Penfold. Fortunately, his mother and the eight-foot table were in the way, in a cramped room. He could not easily reach the culprit, so he

243

had to make do with merely appearing hostile. 'You been pretending to be me, is that it?'

Penfold's body language remained open and calm. He put his hands together in a prayer gesture again.

'Please, Declan. I am sorry. As I said a moment ago, this was the only way I could think of to get everyone in the same room at the same time. If you would sit down, all will become clear. And you *will* benefit from what will transpire here today.' Separating his hands, Penfold went on, 'Now, Jacqui, what would you like to drink? Coffee or tea, or juice? And please help yourself to biscuits.'

Momo sprang into action, bringing Declan's cup of tea over to ADC Meredith to pass down the table. Diane leant across, smiled at Declan, and placed the cup in front of him. The young man focused on the moving teacup, then looked down at the breasts bulging against the tight material of Diane's rain jacket. She leaned back again, and he took a drink of his tea, his eyes not moving from her chest.

In similar fashion, Mrs Armstrong's eyes had not left Jacqui Tait since she entered the building.

'We won't be staying in the same room at the same time for long,' she said tightly. 'That woman is not welcome on the premises of my company.' She pointed a long white finger at Jacqui and commanded Milburn: 'I insist that the police escort this trespasser off my property immediately.'

Again, Penfold attempted to keep the peace.

'Mrs Armstrong, I understand your frustration and anger. It is unfortunate that we need to have this meeting, but this is all about who killed your husband, and I'm sure you will want everyone to be a witness to what we are about to reveal. If you would indulge me just a little longer, all will become clear.'

The implication that Jacqui was the killer did the trick. Elspeth put her hands together in her lap and sat back a little.

Tony stepped over and offered Mrs Tait the chair next to Diane, beside her son, and away across the table from Elspeth.

244

The empty chair beside Mrs Armstrong also kept a breathing space between her and Declan.

Momo Jackson took the opportunity to slip forward with the other drinks and place them as close to people as he could reach. The solicitor's bulk blocked off the aisle on the side of the table by the experiments table, and the conference table was sufficiently close to the wall on the other side that Penfold, Diane and Jacqui's chair backs were up against it.

As they settled to sipping their drinks and choosing a biscuit or two, the roar of a diesel Land Rover engine overpowered the rhythmic patter of rain.

Thirty-nine

Tuesday, 5.44 p.m.

The Land Rover Defender pulled to a halt close to the Portakabins. Back in his role as doorman, DS Milburn timed opening the door exactly, and welcomed Genevieve Hedley inside. She turned back to her two daughters, chivvying them in out of the rain. The three had mostly avoided getting wet, and their Barbour jackets gave the appearance of a shooting party waiting for the weather to clear before heading out onto the moors.

Milburn ushered them around so that Genevieve could sit beside Elspeth, putting a buffer between her and Declan Tait. Beth and Eloise had to squeeze into a tight space behind their mother, standing against the wall between the business desk and the experimental table.

Hedley's office had quickly filled with damp people, and the small blower heater under the table struggled to prevent the windows from steaming up. With that many bodies, it wasn't overly cold, but Tony needed to close the door against the elements. He did so and then reached up over the business desk to open the little aperture at the top of the front wall window.

Gareth Buckingham sneered, 'What clever ruse did you use, Milburn, to mislead poor Genevieve into attending this ridiculous powwow?'

'Whatever do you mean, Mr Buckingham?' she responded. As a member of the Friendship Society, she knew him well. 'The girls brought me for an important meeting about Joel's death.' She addressed Tony. 'Has there been any progress, Detective Sergeant?'

'Actually,' Penfold announced, 'it was me who asked Beth and Eloise to bring you here, Mrs Hedley. There have been some new developments, which I will explain to everyone shortly.' He waved a large hand towards the younger Hedley women crammed together behind their mother. 'We felt it would be healthy for your grieving process for us all to get everything out in the open and clear up where the investigation has taken us.'

Worried that he himself had no idea where the investigation had taken them, Milburn rocked uneasily from foot to foot.

The Kiwi failed to mention that he had led the daughters to believe that attending this meeting might help their mother to stop drinking. He obfuscated further by diverting everyone's attention to what the Hedleys might like to drink. Beth and Eloise both ordered tea, and Genevieve was discreet enough not to ask for a glass of wine when none had been offered. For a few minutes at least, Penfold would succeed in keeping her on the wagon.

Momo refilled the kettle and delivered a second plate of biscuits to the top end of the table. This was duly passed along, but Declan Tait was the only person to take one.

'Have we missed anything?' Genevieve asked brightly. 'Everyone seems to be here already. Sorry we were a bit late, but we had to clear up some things at home before we could leave, and that took a bit longer than it might have done.' She spoke coherently, but Milburn sensed she was not totally sober. An hour in the car had probably helped a lot.

She looked around the room again, saying, 'I think I know everyone here except this gentleman,' she indicated Momo Jackson, 'and you.' She pointed across her husband's maps at Meredith. 'I'm sorry, what is your name?'

Softly, the police officer replied, 'We have met, Mrs Hedley, on Saturday night, but I was in police uniform then. It's not surprising that you don't recognise me. I'm Detective Constable Diane Meredith.' Her sentences were brief and simple. 'I'm one of the detectives investigating Joel's death. I'm so sorry for your loss.'

She failed to mention the previous afternoon's incident at Durham Castle, when Mrs Hedley had tried to get inside the protected crime scene and had argued with the constable on duty.

247

More than likely, her level of intoxication during that incident meant that she could not remember much about it. Meredith looked above her head at Beth and Eloise. Despite having come to the castle on that occasion to collect their mother from Diane, the daughters remained stony-faced. No doubt the two had long since learnt to gloss over much of what went on.

Milburn chafed inwardly at Meredith's failure to use the title *Acting* Detective Constable, but he was not about to undermine the kindness she had shown the widow.

Nobody had a chance to introduce Momo, because at that moment, Elspeth Armstrong burst forth. Hissing very much like the sound of the kettle heating, she spat her words across the space at Jacqui Tait.

'You don't belong here, homewrecker. You don't belong anywhere. Look at you.' The contempt in her eyes left no one in any doubt about her feelings. 'I'm under duress to let you stay just now, but when this is over you are out, lady. Out for good. You'll never get your nails into anything more from Melville. His death means we'll finally be rid of you.'

Although petite, Jacqui Tait sat firmly in her chair, square on to Elspeth and not intimidated.

'I never had to take anything from Melville. He couldn't wait to get away from you and into my arms. All the time, all over the place, he wanted *me*. He laughed at the thought of sex with you. We even screwed on his desk upstairs. Regularly. Why do you think he wanted that shower installed up there?' She pointed a finger vertically up towards the Portakabin above. 'He never got his hands dirty out in the quarry. It's 'cos of all the things we got up to in his office.'

The room was silent, stunned.

Having seen photographs of the portly, red-faced anachronism that had been Melville Armstrong, Miss Tait's words gave Milburn a sick feeling in his stomach. The images also moved him on to remembering the blackened, naked body on

248

Andrew Gerard's mortuary table. The nauseous feeling intensified.

Expecting things to kick off after this exchange, he stepped away from the door again, positioned ready to grab hold of Declan or Jacqui as necessary. He hoped that Genevieve was blocking the space enough that Elspeth would not attempt anything physical. He was wrong.

With an incoherent scream, Elspeth launched herself over the map of Northumberland and clutched Jacqui's curly bunches of hair. She made to smash the woman's face down on the table, but for such a small person, Jacqui was strong. She grabbed Elspeth's wrists in a grip of iron and held firm so her attacker was stuck and could make little movement. The two were locked in a stalemate.

Buckingham eventually took hold of his client's shoulders, and Declan did the same with his mother. ADC Meredith pried the widow's thin fingers from Jacqui's thick hair. Once released, both women were dragged back into their chairs and held there.

'That's quite enough of that,' Meredith told them both. 'I don't want to hear any more between you two.' She pulled handcuffs from the pocket of her raincoat. 'I'll happily restrain anyone who needs it, and outside too if necessary. Got it?'

The women maintained a staring contest, and Diane had to repeat herself.

'Have we got that clear? No more. Neither of you talks to the other at all. *Right?*' She pointed at each woman in turn, until they nodded a grudging assent.

It was fortunate that Milburn had stepped away from the door, as it flew open at that moment and a bedraggled man in a purple jacket was propelled in at speed through it. Behind him, Mantoro stepped over the threshold just enough to pull the door closed behind himself. His normally giant hair had succumbed to the rain and hung limp and dark over his shoulders.

Harry Carruthers picked himself up from the floor, water dripping from his hair and coat.

'Ah now, Milburn,' Penfold told him. 'Here's another one from the scene of the fire, but we don't need to keep this one in here with us.'

'What the hell?' Despite his surprise at the appearance of the student hockey player and sword thief, Tony took a handful of Carruthers' jacket in his hand.

Penfold continued smoothly, 'Thank you, Mantoro, a job well done.'

Tony looked across to the surfer in confusion. 'What's Carruthers doing here?'

'This guy thought he might make a quick buck,' Mantoro said scornfully. 'Got himself pegged as a dealer in antiquities. A mug and his freedom are soon parted, aren't they, buddy?' Carruthers said nothing.

'Sorry, I'm totally lost. Can you explain, please. We've got the sword back at the evidence room.' As Milburn spoke, the South American stroked his bushy black moustache. The rest of those present watched in bewilderment.

'Sure thing, pal.' Mantoro grinned. 'I sent this dude a message on his dark web channel from the other night. Told him I'd seen his message selling the sword and that I needed to offload something valuable super-fast.' He leaned back against the door behind him, relishing the telling of Carruthers' downfall. 'Pretended I worked here, and I'd dug up a box of silver coins, probably a Viking hoard. Made it sound like I didn't know what I was doing but knew they were worth something. Like I thought he must know exactly what he's doing if he had that stolen sword to sell. Said I needed to find a buyer for it fast.' Mantoro mimed casting and winding back in a fishing reel. 'He fell hook, line and sinker – came straight up to meet me, what a moron. I picked a remote corner of the quarry out there to meet and then dragged him back here.'

Milburn chuckled. Without letting go of Harry's coat, he reached over the table to receive the handcuffs from Diane with his other hand.

'Not such a clever student after all, are you?' Meredith relished the hockey player's foolishness. 'I can't believe anyone would fall for that twice.'

Mantoro responded, 'Oh, I wouldn't be so sure. A brain fogged with dollar signs will convince you anything can be true. Even if it's too good to be.'

Diane suggested, 'Especially if you're so arrogant you think you're untouchable. No escape this time, Mr Carruthers. I'm going to enjoy booking you in to the custody suite. Maybe I'll go round to your digs and ask your housemates for some of your things, telling them you're stuck in jail.' She was enjoying needling him, and Tony imagined a cat playing with a mouse it had caught. The student looked forlorn, crestfallen.

'Mantoro, perhaps you could take Mr Carruthers out and lock him in the car, please,' Penfold requested. 'As I said, we don't need any unnecessary extras in here. Is that OK, Milburn?'

'Actually, no. Harry Carruthers, you are under arrest for the theft of high-value antiquities. You do not have to say anything, but it may harm your defence if you do not mention, when questioned, something which you later rely on in court. Anything you do say may be given in evidence.' Milburn looked over to the New Zealander. 'I'm afraid this one will have to stay in here with us, in proper police custody. Mantoro won't cut it there. Can we sit him down in that spare chair?'

Squeezing the handcuffed prisoner behind Jacqui and Diane took some doing, but once seated, the student had no chance for an escape. He'd have to climb over Meredith, or the table, or Penfold, in order to make any progress. With Milburn also guarding the only door, the cramped room would make a serviceable jail cell for the moment.

'And then round the back for the other thing,' Penfold called to Mantoro, as his friend exited out into the wind and rain again.

Closing the door behind the man, the detective sergeant turned back to the room and asked Penfold, 'All present and correct then?'

'Not quite. There's one more to come, and he should be here any minute.' Penfold waved his smartphone in the air.

Forty

Tuesday, 6.29 p.m.

An awkward silence filled the stuffy room as those gathered there waited for one more to arrive. Elspeth Armstrong and Jacqui Tait continued to give each other daggers, whilst Genevieve Hedley's eyes flitted over the map on the table in front of her. Carruthers was not offered a drink.

Penfold's phone vibrated, and he looked briefly at a message. He typed a reply, and Tony saw a phone light up in the darkness out by the Land Rover. Mantoro's face was illuminated, but he was clearly hiding. Within seconds, the phone light went out, and the stocky man shot off across the gravel space at a speed that startled Milburn.

The light emitting from the Portakabin window through old Venetian blinds made stripes of light and dark fall across a swathe of blackness, over the cars and all the way to the chain-link fence and the trees behind. Mantoro had been gone only moments when Tony spotted him re-emerging into the light, frog-marching another man towards the buildings. In the dark, stormy night, the new prisoner remained unidentified. He stood more than a foot taller than Mantoro and wore black tracksuit trousers and a black hoody. Soaking wet, the hood was raised and clung to his head, keeping the face in shadow.

The man wriggled and squirmed, but Mantoro held him in a vice-like grip and gave him the occasional kick in the calves to keep them on course for the gathering in Joel Hedley's office. To mount the few steps up to the landing outside, they both disappeared from Milburn's view, but they were close enough that he felt it was the time to open the door.

Where Harry Carruthers had been thrown through the entrance to the floor, Randall White was shoved straight into DS

Milburn's grip. He pivoted neatly and deposited the chef into the wheeled office chair at the computer desk by the window. With a swiftness of movement that impressed himself, Tony pulled his own handcuffs from his right-hand coat pocket and clamped the man's wrist to the chair handle. At that moment he remembered the weighted bag Penfold had hidden in his left pocket earlier. He stuck a hand in there to check it was still safely in place.

The entire action of Mantoro bringing him in and Milburn securing him had taken just a few seconds. Randall White's eyes were screwed up against the sudden bright light, and he still hadn't worked out what had happened. After rattling against the handcuff, White slowly pulled down his hood and eyed up the various people all staring at him.

'What the hell is this?' he asked hoarsely. 'Where's Mr De Santi?'

Penfold answered. He had remained standing at the head of the conference table. 'I'm sorry, Randall, Mr De Santi won't be joining us.'

'Why not? We arranged to meet here! What's going on?'

'I'm afraid that all that stuff about finding papers for the Durham Friendship Society here . . . and looking through them together to see how to fix your membership – that was all me. It was a bit of a trick to get you to come and join us here.'

It took Randall a moment to understand his predicament. After that he raged in the chair, pulling at the handcuff and thrashing about wildly. When he tried to stand, Milburn pushed down on the high seat back to keep the wheels on the floor. Luckily, White wasn't really attempting an escape, simply expressing his frustration at having been duped, and caught. His free arm could easily have landed a punch on the detective sergeant had he attempted it.

'Easy there, Randall,' Tony said quietly. 'Remember you're on police bail – let's not do anything to make matters worse.'

Seeing that the situation was under control, Mantoro said, 'I'll be just out here if you need me,' and closed the door.

Tony stepped back to his post inside the exit and confirmed with Chef White that he was going to play ball.

'If you sit quietly and listen to what goes on here, I will be in a position to release you back onto your bail when we're finished. Do we need further restraints, or will you participate as necessary?' He had realised halfway through this speech that he didn't know if what Penfold was to reveal would mean that Randall White might need to return to Durham in a Black Maria, but he would be happy to go back on his word if that turned out to be the case.

Looking up at Milburn with fire in his dark eyes, White raised his voice: 'You'll be in a position to release me? You've got no reason to cuff me at all. This is racism, pure and simple. I've had nothing but institutional racism from you lot since Saturday night.' He parroted: ' "He's black so he must be guilty".'

Elspeth Armstrong butted in with, 'You *are* guilty. You broke in and desecrated my home. I hope they throw away the key, you—'

'Stop it!' ADC Meredith took the reins. 'I've already warned you to be quiet, Mrs Armstrong. Not just towards Miss Tait either. You don't speak at all unless we tell you to.' She moved her slim hand to indicate herself and Milburn. Sceptical of Penfold, she deliberately left him out of the positions of authority, despite the fact that he was clearly running the whole show. 'If you can't control yourself, I'll put you in handcuffs too.'

No further insults came from Mrs Armstrong, but her hateful looks were now aimed at Meredith.

'Can we get you something to drink, Mr White?' Penfold asked politely. 'We have tea and coffee if the chill has gotten to you, or a variety of soft drinks. You will see that there are biscuits near you there too. I'm sure Declan will pass them over to you.' Penfold waved towards the shaven-headed boxer, sitting idly.

The realisation that he had been invoked sparked Declan into life, and he robotically picked up the small plate of biscuits and turned to the newcomer to offer a snack. Equally dazed by this turn of events, Randall White robotically picked up a Hobnob and took a bite.

Before the chef could spit out the crumbs and call out the whole situation again, Penfold pressed him for a drink order. 'Tea or coffee?'

'Tea with milk.'

'Very good. Momo, do the honours, will you.'

The waiter for the afternoon made an executive decision. He sensed that nobody was in the mood for waiting much longer, so he did not boil the kettle again. It remained hot from the Hedleys' order, so he poured water into the cup and used a spoon to worry the teabag into making it strong enough. The place had become too full for Momo to personally deliver the drink, and a human chain system did the job instead.

The assemblage was finally to Penfold's satisfaction, and he squeezed back past Momo to stand again at the head of the table, framed by the black rectangle of window glass that covered most of the far end of the Portakabin.

In daylight, Joel Hedley had had a fantastic view of green Northumberland countryside. From the scientific desk behind Penfold, Joel had been able to sit and stare at fields and forests. Many of his long-distance running routes criss-crossed the scenery on display. At the big table, Mrs Hedley's finger followed pencil lines across the area map. Only she had realised that they traced out the running trails her late husband had so loved.

In planting foot after foot over the terrain, Joel had physically felt the geology beneath. He had developed an innate sense of where they should send the diggers, but he had gained little financially from this subtle sixth sense. Where Hedley had run over the earth and learnt how to exploit it, Melville Armstrong had run over the geologist, similarly knowing instinctively how to exploit him.

256

BURNS NIGHT BURNS

Only Milburn spotted the tear that fell from Genevieve Hedley's cheek onto the bottom corner of the faded paper sellotaped to the table.

Forty-one

Tuesday, 7 p.m.

A natural orator, Penfold had attracted attention by his movement to the central position at the top of the table. Here he paused and waited for those present to stop any chatting, to put down their drinks and focus their entire concentration on him until there was complete silence. A sense of hushed expectation hung over the crowded room.

'Ladies and gentlemen, let me repeat my apologies to any of you to whom I told a white lie or two to arrange for your presence here this evening. It is sad that we have met here in order to discuss the untimely deaths of Melville Armstrong and Joel Hedley. Mrs Hedley, perhaps I could call on you first to tell us all about your husband, please.'

'Oh, er, well.' Flustered by being put on the spot unexpectedly, Genevieve stumbled through some platitudes that anyone might expect. 'Joel was a nice man, a kind man. He loved nature and rocks. And running. We were married for forty years and have two wonderful daughters.' She half-turned to indicate Beth and Eloise, standing behind, shrunk into the tight space by the wall.

'Thank you. A nice introduction. Could you now tell us about his time in the aggregates business – about his partnerships with Melville?' Penfold carefully emphasised the plural of the word 'partnership'.

Mrs Hedley shrank visibly. She tried to turn her head to look at Elspeth Armstrong, whose pupils were boring into Genevieve.

'Um, well.' She pointed at the maps as a distraction. 'You can see here how much he knew about the geology of this area. The two men had been in this business together since shortly after

258

university.' She attempted to distract further. 'You know we were all at university in Edinburgh at the same time?' Her right hand was waving in a circle, not quite indicating Elspeth and not quite avoiding her.

Penfold pressed, 'And was he happy with the way they worked together, the way the spoils were shared out? I mean, he was the brains behind the operation.'

Elspeth bristled but was silenced by a look from Meredith.

Genevieve licked her lips. She needed a shot of whisky, or at least a glass of wine, but all she had was some cold tea, which she swigged like a sailor at a rum bottle. The silence finally cajoled her into continuing.

'Not really.' She stared at the wall behind Diane, ready to crack if anybody caught her eye. 'Melville cheated my husband out of his share of the business, over and over again. I wanted to shake Joel and tell him to stick up for himself, to get what was rightfully his. Joel had found all the right spots for the quarries, but each time there was some new business problem or change that meant he had to sign everything over to Melville.' Her voice strengthened. 'It was a load of rubbish. All the tales of international price drops and squeezes on the company finances were lies Melville told to get his own way.'

Jacqui Tait raised her hand to cover her mouth, eyes wide. She had always liked Joel and had had no idea that her lover kept cheating the naive geologist.

Mrs Hedley carried on, buoyed by what she had already said, relieved by the chance to let out their bottled frustrations at the selfish, manipulative Armstrongs.

'The trouble was, my Joel was not the kind of man to go courting conflict. He could never bring himself to challenge Melville. Instead, he became more and more angry at home.' She turned around to Beth and Eloise. 'That's right, isn't it, girls? You saw how much it was eating away at him.' They nodded mutely.

'In the last few weeks, his anger had really stepped up. He ranted about how Melville was living the high life, making a fortune from the profits of the companies, whilst he only ever made a regular salary.'

From the end of the room, Penfold asked more specifically, 'And you told us that Joel had a scar on his thumb, right? A perfect circle you said, yes?'

Genevieve looked at the Kiwi, perplexed. She nodded.

'One thing I didn't ask you about, though: I know that Mr and Mrs Armstrong were in a club at university where they did glass-blowing together. Did Joel do that ever? Glass-blowing, vases or similar?'

Gareth Buckingham had not been the centre of attention for a considerable time and interrupted.

'What is this, the parish arts and crafts class?' he asked rudely. 'That Melville and Elspeth took glass-blowing classes as undergraduates is absolutely irrelevant forty years later. Have you got some information about his murder or not?'

'If you please, Mr Buckingham, this is utterly relevant.' Penfold fixed him with a gaze, then turned back to Mrs Hedley.

'Is there any history of Joel glass-blowing?' Penfold reached behind Joel's big microscope machine and lifted up a small round glass vase carrying a dozen snowdrop stems, the small white flowers hanging their heads.

'Oh, I had no idea he still had that!' Genevieve's face lit up. 'Yes, Joel made that when I was pregnant with Eloise. He said the concentration of carefully turning the pipe and controlling the breath worked wonders to take his mind off the worry when I was ready to go into labour at any moment.'

'Ah still divvent knah what you're on about. Blowin' on glass?' Declan looked around the room to try and get some clarification, or perhaps agreement, from somebody else.

Penfold smiled. 'It's a way of making things from glass.' He put the vase on the table. 'And that's important because the haggis contained a glass vessel filled with methanol. Not open like this one, though – it was completely sealed. It was a difficult piece of workmanship, to blow it to the right size and shape, and then fill it with the accelerant, and then seal over the hole so it was hermetic.'

Buckingham said pompously, 'What do you mean, a glass vessel? Are you saying there was a bottle secreted inside the haggis with extra fuel in it that caused the fire?'

'Essentially, yes – not a bottle but a very carefully blown glass ovoid that exactly fitted the shape of the haggis. With methanol as the accelerant, the fire would burn hot enough to kill when the haggis was sliced open and the contents of the glass container were released. The scene would be confusing to onlookers. It's not surprising that nobody rushed forward to help the men, to try and put them out – because nobody could see the flames. You wouldn't know they were still on fire, because methanol burns with almost invisible flames. Allow me to demonstrate.'

He turned and powered up the screen attached to the microscope, pressed the menu button on the side and set his phone to display on the screen. With no introduction, Penfold played the video showing the downdraught chamber explosion in his Hartlepool basement lab.

The group sat dumbstruck.

'That demonstration was one I put together to illustrate the concept. You see, we have forensic evidence – a piece of hand-blown glass from the crime scene with traces of methanol on it – which proves this was the killer's methodology.'

Penfold paused for dramatic effect. 'The question is: *who might have wanted to kill either – or both – men*?'

The audience were not afforded any time to respond, as he pressed on almost as soon as the question had been posed.

'Jacqui.'

All eyes turned to the mistress. Even before she had a chance to protest her innocence, Penfold explained her motive.

'You had for many years suffered from Melville Armstrong's boorish ways and his selfishness in keeping you and his son in poverty, as a means of control. The occasional fancy dinner or hotel night away could never have excused twenty years of being forbidden to work, since his pitiful contributions were less than you could have earned. He denied you the chance to have a job you enjoyed, where you could have made friends and had a regular income and self-esteem – and worse still, just a few months ago he stopped the money supply completely. That must have cut you to the bone and through the heart.' Penfold concluded: 'You gave your best years to him, and Melville just threw you away.'

'No, I . . . I loved him. I couldn't hurt him.'

Penfold moved on quickly. 'Your son is called Declan Tait. Armstrong wouldn't even let you use his name! His only son, effectively excommunicated from the Armstrong family and its fortune. Even you could see that the job he gave Declan here was a Mickey Mouse affair, Jacqui. And Declan, discounting your anger at his treatment of your mother and his refusal to acknowledge you as his son, the simple motive here is that you could now be in line to inherit plenty.'

The young man shifted in his seat, muttering, 'Ah'm glad he's dead, but Ah didn't kill him.'

Penfold was far from finished.

'Then there's Randall White. After rising rapidly through the lower career stages of catering, Mr White, your progress stalled, and you became obsessed with the idea that you deserved to continue that meteoric rise.'

'Screw you, copper. You can't stand to see a successful black man get on in the world, can you.'

Milburn bridled at White's suggestion that Penfold was a policeman but kept schtum. Uproar could well ensue from challenging that.

'I think your anger was more strongly, and more accurately, directed at Mr Armstrong,' Penfold went on. 'A clear racist, it is certainly likely that he did indeed hold your career back, whether that brake on your progress was deserved or not. You wanted to

262

join the Durham Friendship Society and suspected Armstrong of blackballing you due to your race.'

'We are not racist!' Elspeth Armstrong shouted. Her claim was contrary to the belief of most in the room. All ignored her.

'Well, Mr White, you have demonstrated how far your obsession might take you by breaking into a dead man's house to try and burgle your way into his members only club. So, we have a third suspect who could have been driven to commit murder.'

Barely a pause for breath, and Penfold proceeded with the next suspect.

'Let's have a look at number four.' He turned towards Genevieve. 'Mrs Hedley, you told us how wonderful your husband was, but you made no mention of your recent commitment to divorce Joel.'

Sudden intakes of breath from all three Hedley women gave away their understanding that this could provide significant weight to a prosecutor's explanation of motive.

'Indeed,' Penfold continued inexorably, 'a divorce would only garner you half the family wealth, limited as it might be through Armstrong's greed, but now, well, you inherit it all. Another strong financial motive backed up by the impending divorce indicating a clearly loveless marriage.' He paused and made a calming gesture towards the poor woman. 'That's too strong. I'm sorry, I know the divorce threat was just a bluff. I'm merely highlighting that, as much as anyone in this room, you have money to gain from your husband's death, and thus a motive for murder.

'Let's move on to a far more likely murderess. The poor, grieving Widow Armstrong. The cold, calculating Widow Armstrong.'

The older woman said nothing, clearly afraid of Meredith's threat.

'The simple financial motive applies to you as well, Mrs Armstrong. Twenty years as the wife who knows of her husband's philandering could prove infuriating, I have no doubt, but in my judgement of your character, I'd plump for a more clinical, straightforward greed.'

'Mr Buckingham,' Penfold intoned, 'you will be pleased to hear that I do not have any notion that you might have been involved in this crime. Which leaves the Hedley daughters. An inseparable pair, who have seen their mother ground down by their father's aloofness and lack of interest in family matters. With little connection to a man who preferred to spend hours running through the countryside rather than bouncing them on his knee, one could easily imagine Beth and Eloise developing an unhealthy detestation of poor Joel. The man who effectively caused their mother's alcoholism will forever put a bitter taste in their mouths.'

This solicited more gasps from the Hedleys, and Beth raised her hand to her lips in disbelief at the secrets being bandied about.

'But murder their own father? I don't think so.'

'Thus, we have established that each of you had sufficient cause to potentially be driven to commit this crime.'

'What about him?' Elspeth Armstrong pointed an accusatory finger at Mohammed Jackson, standing in the corner leaning against the kitchenette sink.

Fear washed over Momo's face, and he stood to attention. 'I – I . . .'

'He was there, in the banqueting hall,' Elspeth said nastily, 'and he ran off as soon as the fire started. What's more, he's ex-military, disturbed in the head and probably knows all about explosives, I expect.'

Penfold joined in sarcastically, 'And he's not white, not "one of us", so he must be guilty.'

A long quiet descended on the room, broken only by a mutter from Randall White. 'Bitch.'

Gareth Buckingham took up his client's baton.

'It's easy to call names, Mr Penfold, but Elspeth's points are all valid if we are to objectively find the killer. What about this man? Do you deny he had all the requisite skills and the opportunity to tamper with the haggis? As to motive, the derangement of PTSD can make someone capable of anything. What's more, we are aware that Melville had attempted to block this man from working at the dinner, for exactly these reasons. That could well have angered Jackson enough to commit murder – it doesn't take much.'

The master of ceremonies addressed this new query.

'No stone unturned is the cornerstone of good investigative work, you're right. There are several reasons I discount Mr Jackson as a suspect. Firstly, he did not arrive at the castle in time to do anything untoward to the haggis, which was already in the oven when he did report for work. Secondly, whilst he may have encountered chemical combustibles in combat, he does not have the skills to make the necessary glass container.'

Elspeth scowled, and Penfold paid no heed to her.

'So, which of you did have the capability to create the methanol vessel, and the chance to insert it into the special haggis that Melville had procured?'

From the science table under the end window, beside the big microscope, Penfold picked up a clear plastic evidence bag.

'You may be able to see in here.' He pointed at a piece of glass pressing outwards at the bottom of the bag. 'This shard was taken from the crime scene. It is the classic composition of an amateur blown glass. Durham Castle have confirmed that all of their glassware is regular, factory-made stuff. The functions cause too many breakages to use anything more expensive, as handmade glasses would be.' He pointed back at the TV screen which was paused in a freeze frame at the end of his explosive demonstration video. 'On this piece, we found traces of methanol, the accelerant used in the fire, but it also carried a fingerprint.'

He paused for effect. The assembly was gripped. This news blew everything else out of the water.

Tony knew he could not interrupt the proceedings, and he cursed Penfold inwardly. The man should have shared this evidence with him beforehand. He couldn't even imagine Harry Hardwick's response to Penfold's retaining this crucial information. He found himself shaking with rage and had to grip hold of the door handle behind his back.

With a flourish, another evidence bag was pulled from the table behind Penfold, and he held it aloft. The ordinary royal blue toothbrush inside the bag remained difficult to see as the clear plastic was marred with white printing and black marker writing on the outside.

'The same fingerprint is on this toothbrush,' Penfold stated. Both bags were placed on the table, and all eyes were on Penfold.

'And the same fingerprint was also on a third object. Detective Sergeant Milburn has that item.'

All heads turned the length of the room to look at Tony. Showing a confidence he did not feel, he withdrew the larger evidence bag from his coat pocket and threw it onto the table. It spun and slid across the maps, coming to a stop in the middle of the table, beside a plate of biscuits. Inside the bag, a long, thick handle covered in blue rubber gave way to a heavy, metal T-bar end, one branch of which curved to a sharp, silvery point.

This time everyone gasped and turned to stare, except Randall White. His view was blocked by Declan and Genevieve. No better visibility came from trying to wheel his chair slightly to the side.

Frustrated, he called out, 'What is it?'

The rest were looking at Mrs Hedley, in front of him, so Randall stared at her too.

Penfold calmly answered, 'This is Joel Hedley's geological hammer. The fingerprint on all three is of a thumb with a perfect circle scarring it. The toothbrush DNA will confirm the fingerprint description we had from Genevieve, and the link is then made to the glass shard. Joel Hedley perpetrated this crime.'

The overweight solicitor was first to ask the question in many people's minds.

'Why on earth would he kill himself too?'

Having witnessed the experimental rerun in Penfold's basement, and watched video footage of the fire many times, DS Milburn knew the answer.

'By accident,' he stated.

'What?' Genevieve Hedley had tears in her eyes again.

Penfold concurred, 'Yes indeed, it was due to a miscalculation.'

Tony felt it was time to take charge of explaining the case.

'The methanol was under extreme pressure from the glass vessel being in the oven for so long. At the first touch of the knife the glass collapsed but, unanticipated by Mr Hedley, the squirting methanol shot out *on both sides* of the blade. Half of it took out Mr Armstrong as intended, but half spewed back at Hedley himself.'

Mrs Hedley held her face in her hands and sobbed. Beneath her crying, muted pleas to her dead husband could clearly be made out.

'Oh Joel, Joel darling, why couldn't you talk to me?' she wept. 'Why? We could have avoided all this. I'd still have you, and our daughters would still have their father. We could have taken Armstrong to court, or just gone away from here. We could have started again, worked together to make a new future. We could have been happy again.' And then she sobbed as if her heart was broken and nothing would ever mend it.

Forty-two

Wednesday 1 February, 11.10 a.m.

Kathy plonked down a tray of coffees and pastries on the dark wood table. She dropped into the third chair and left the men to move everything into place and remove the tray to the nearest empty table. Tony had invited her to join them at The Daily Espresso, but she had then been sent to the counter to place the order. Since she was more often than not working at weekends, this Wednesday morning coffee out with her beau excited Kathy. Hearing the saga of the arson and murder from Penfold promised to make this meeting even more tantalising.

'Thank you, Kathy, most generous.' Penfold nodded to reinforce his thanks and sipped from the hot Americano.

'Well, spill the beans about all this,' she threatened, 'or I'll make you pay me back!'

Tony checked around for listening ears, but the coffee shop was quiet, and they would not be overheard in their intimate corner. He gave Penfold the floor, but with a brief to explain only the scientific and forensic details. Tony wanted to be the one to inform her of all the charges that had been decided on, that morning.

After ten minutes, Penfold had exhausted Kathy's wonderment at his talents, and he signed off the story for Milburn to complete, declaring, 'In the end, a significant number of crimes cleared up, eh, Milburn?'

Tony nodded and put down a half-eaten croissant.

'Yup. Joel Hedley's one of the few who'll be getting no jail time for all this. Elspeth Armstrong and Frankie Veitch are both likely to go down for some part of their banking fraud plan. Frankie will be playing the system all he can, but he's got such a long record that I doubt they'll let him off completely.

Annoyingly, Mrs Armstrong's trial will put a ton of money into Gareth Buckingham's grubby mitts.'

Penfold reasoned, 'It's the world we live in.'

'At least that insufferable student is almost certain to go down – the sword was such high value, it's a big crime.'

'That's a shame,' Kathy said. 'I mean, I know he did it and deserves to be punished, but it's a pity that material envy can push otherwise decent people to try and take the easy route. I feel sad for the poor boy. It is an awful world we live in.'

'You're such an idealist,' Tony teased, and she punched him gently under the table.

Penfold mused out loud, 'Randall White essentially suffered the same societal pressures. He's another one driven down the wrong path by the pressures we ourselves have built up.'

'Yeah, actually, he might avoid a custodial sentence,' Milburn put in. 'First-time offender, good career prospects, I expect the CPS will go for some minimal suspended sentence.'

Continuing with the more positive outcomes, Tony followed this with, 'It's good to hear that you've convinced Momo to take that flat the council offered, Penfold. With Colonel Griffiths finding work for him, hopefully I'll never have to chase him across Market Place again.'

'Where's your best buddy, Diane Meredith?' Kathy was now the one teasing. 'You should send *her* to chase the dregs around town.'

Despite knowing that she was poking fun, Tony felt a twinge in his stomach. Having to work with the Crazy Cow never sat right with him, and he had made that plain to her and to the DCI. However, when they were tasked jointly, all Kathy ever saw was them having to spend time together, often just the two of them, and often late into the night. He well understood how she might get the wrong idea, and that worried him.

'H has her nailed to her desk. I got the massive bollocking, but she got pretty much the same for letting me go along with

Penfold's shenanigans and not putting a stop to it at the earliest opportunity.'

'How come you didn't get traffic detail?'

Tony shrugged. 'Solving so many big, complicated cases in one go is major kudos for the force. Especially when we're running on empty, staffing-wise. H can't deny that, and I'm happy to let him have the TV airtime about it.' He turned directly to Penfold. 'I wish you'd just sign up to be a proper, authorised civilian investigator. Give the money to charity or something, but it'd make all our lives much easier.'

The head of fair hair shook gently, and Penfold stuffed his hands in his shorts' pockets.

'Except mine. Following procedure would severely restrict the investigative leaps I can make, knowing that the ideas that come from my subconscious are right, but I haven't yet got the evidence to make the leap. Sorry, Milburn, but it's not gonna happen.'

Kathy eased them away from what she knew was an ongoing bone of contention.

'What about the mistress, Jacqui Tait? What'll happen to her?'

'I don't know. Not much, I guess,' Tony said. 'She never did anything wrong, but she's got no claim on any of Melville's money. I suppose she'll now be able to get the job she's never had – if anyone will hire a woman with no experience who's passed the midpoint of her working life.'

'If she was ex-army, Griffiths might help out.'

Milburn joked, 'Ha, maybe we should introduce them. I'd say she's probably endured more by putting up with Armstrong than any career soldier!'

They all laughed, and Penfold followed up with, 'And with that son of hers too. She's spent her life between a blob and a hard brain.' More laughter.

'Wait!' Kathy put a hand on one arm of each man. 'What about Melville's last breath naming Declan?' Her face turned left and right looking at each one in turn.

'Who knows. Maybe he just assumed it was Declan. Maybe the toerag had threatened him. Or maybe that's not even what he was trying to say. The forensic evidence is open and shut. Joel's fingerprint nails it. We'll probably never know what "her cleaner" was all about.'

'Nails it.' The Kiwi chuckled. 'Very good, Milburn.'

Tony just rolled his eyes.

Kathy asked, 'Will the son inherit any of the aggregates business then?'

Her boyfriend answered, 'Almost certainly. I wouldn't expect it'll be too long before Declan ends up in prison too, though. He'll do something illegal one day soon, I've no doubt. Especially if he's suddenly got a load of money. It's Genevieve I really feel sorry for. Her whole world has fallen apart.'

'Yes, Hedley's poor wife.' Kathy used both hands to push her blonde hair back behind her shoulders. 'Sounds like they didn't have a brilliant marriage, but how do you live with that, your husband a murderer who accidentally kills himself in the same act.'

Penfold nodded. 'Joel had neglected his wife and daughters for years, and ignored their needs, so all three of the women were trapped in a horrible kind of half-life filled with empty wine bottles. In the meantime, he ran around the Northumbrian countryside, nursing his rage against Armstrong before planting that hand-blown vessel in the Burns Night Supper haggis, the glass vessel containing not only the deadly methanol, but also his boiling hatred for the man.'

'If only he had stuck up for himself from the beginning against the bully Armstrong, this story would have had a different ending,' DS Milburn added gravely. He stirred more sugar into his coffee. 'The worm finally turned, but it was too late. As in your haiku, revenge is a dish "best served cold". Joel failed to

271

remember that, and he, too, was consumed by fire along with his enemy and sent to an early grave.'

Penfold nodded. 'Indeed. Hardly poetic justice, but he was, quite literally, hoisted by his own petard.'

Find more books from this author at

mileshudson.com